STRAPPED

DOWN

*To everyone who supported
STRAPPED, this one is for you!*

*I hope you continue to enjoy this
wild adventure.*

PROLOGUE

Stroke. Stroke. Stroke. Stroke. Breathe. Taylor chants the words over and over again in his thoughts as his body carves through the cool water of his pool. Swimming has served as a great distraction for him as long as he could remember, but this time it only works for a few minutes. He rests his forearms on the edge of the pool as he wonders what he should do next. *I should let her go.* He has known this from the beginning. He should never have pursued Shyla when she scampered out of the coffee shop on that fateful day. He should never have offered her that ride, or the job, or all of the gifts.

He has always had control; in fact, that was the only thing Taylor had been certain of, his ability to control every aspect of his life. But this woman, who looks like an innocent doll, has somehow managed to turn all of the meticulously planned order of his life into chaos. And yet, he cannot stay away. There is a pull, something beyond either of their comprehensions that continues to bring them back to each other.

I thought I was broken. Ever since Taylor could remember he has never felt warmth or affection towards anyone in his life. He often wondered if he was defective. After a while he came to terms with the fact that he would never have those moments of passion; those moments of pure emotion that he occasionally observed in other people. He often mocked those who were newly in love. *A form of insanity*, he told himself. And now, to his disgust, he cannot will logic or rationality over his feelings for Shyla. When he is sitting in a meeting or being driven in his Bentley, his mind often wanders to thoughts of her and he has to hide his grin. He tries to stifle his emotions in hopes that she will walk away and save herself from a terrible fate, but just the slightest hint of sadness in her eyes melts his facade. He feels that he must guard her, protect her in a way that he has never felt towards his subs. Yes, he took care of some of his subs, but this is more than that, this is not just about control. *I am in love. Fuck.* There is nothing he can do to stop it. He is now one of those hysterical, irrational, pathetic people he once looked down upon.

Taylor pulls himself out of the pool and wraps a towel over his wet body as he heads back into his house. He let her walk away after the incident because there was nothing left for them to say to each other. The experience they shared said it all, and it was now up to Shyla if she wanted to stay. Beneath all the lazy Sundays, extravagant gifts, and cute texts: this is who he really is. The right thing for them to do was part ways and let the flames cool. But really, he let her walk away because he knows she'll come back. She'll come back because she feels it too. And while it was ugly, while it was demented and pathological, it was also real. And if—when—she returns, he knows he can have all of her. She'll put up a fight (that's one of his favorite things about her, she makes him work for it), but she won't run away for good. He grabs his phone and sends her a message.

Taylor:

I meant what I said to you in the darkroom.

He knows the rational thing to do is to tell her to leave, save herself before it is too late, but Taylor's love is greedy. Taylor's love is selfish. His love doesn't want to see her with someone else. His love does not want her to live a life without him. His love will consume Shyla whole until there is nothing left. There is no other way; there is no happy medium.

Taylor stares impatiently at his phone. Maybe this is the time she comes to her senses after all. He paces in his bedroom, resisting the urge to call her. This has to be her decision. This will only work if it is her call. He tries to think about anything else, but all his thoughts come back to her. The way her soft flesh turned red under the crop like a sweet apple. The way she winced and bit her lip to stifle the screams and instead let out a faint yelp. He didn't want to be aroused, but there was nothing he could do to stop it. Taylor thought he could have lived a vanilla life with her. He was happy to do so, but then she asked. She asked to try the lifestyle and now that he has seen her tied and gagged and begging for mercy, he can never erase that. *He wants it all. He can finally have it all. There is no going back. There is no one else, but Shyla.*

The phone rings. *It's her.* He knew she would call because despite their many differences, in many ways they are the same. He lets it ring once, then twice, to remind her this is what she wants. Taylor accepts the call.

"Shyla?" His voice is a whisper.

There is a thud. Then silence. Finally, the faint voice of a man in the distance: *"You have no idea who you're dealing with."*

7

CHAPTER ONE

I grab the knot on my towel and slide away from Eric, slipping off the bed and onto the floor, hitting the wardrobe behind me.

"I'm not gonna hurt you." Eric's voice is muddled under his swollen upper lip.

"Please leave," I am so frightened and confused, it's all I can muster.

"I just want to talk."

"Please leave. If you don't leave, I'll scream. I swear it."

"No one will hear you; you know that. Taylor has a taste for isolation. I don't want to subdue you, but if you scream, you will leave me no other choice."

"What do you want?"

"I'm not the type of person Taylor is making me out to be."

"And you prove this by breaking into my apartment?"

"I had no other choice. You don't know my brother. He is a master manipulator. We're just pawns to him."

"No, you don't know your brother and you know nothing about our relationship." Inside I tremble; my boldness is only a mask to cover my terror.

Eric laughs, then grabs his jaw, wincing in pain. "Do you see what he did to me? Is this your sweet Taylor?"

"I wasn't there to make a judgement." His injuries seem to be far greater than what I expected from the punch Taylor inflicted after the car chase.

Eric sighs and pauses to think of a way to appeal to me. "Shyla, really be honest with yourself. Are you the same person you were when you first met him?"

"Yes," I say through clenched teeth, but it's a lie.

"You know you don't mean that. You know you're slowly changing, to be the person who can fix him, but you can't…you may think the person you are becoming is by choice, but nothing around Taylor happens by choice."

"You don't know me. Just because you may be spying on me, or whatever it is you're doing, you don't know me."

"I know more about you then you think," His tone is not threatening; it's assured, almost seductive. Eric slowly motions towards me as I debate whether to attempt to flee or to stay put, but he has me cornered. I know attempting to escape will only end in failure and potentially anger Eric. He stands above me and offers me his hand. My eyes dart to it, then his eyes, then his hand again. *Where he is going with this?* I hesitantly take it and he helps me up. We stand face to face, my back pressed against the wardrobe, his body just an inch away from mine. My entire body vibrates with nervous energy. He leans in so that we are eye to eye. My chest touches his with each inhale and while I am breathing deeply, I cannot seem to find air. "I know you like me despite what you tell yourself. That's why you talked to me at the bar." He pauses to wait for a response.

"I talked to you because I was being polite." I try to sound confident, but my vocal chords quiver.

"I don't think you have a problem being impolite."

"That was before I knew anything about who you are."

"Was it?" He leans in closer, his voice calmer than ever.

"I don't understand what you're trying to accomplish here."

"After that day at the bar, I understood why my brother had taken a liking to you. And I think you liked me too, and I need you to think back to that day at the bar and realize that I am that same guy and you can trust me."

"But you're not and I barely knew you even then."

"But I am…" his lips graze mine and I freeze. I still can't gauge if I should be defiant, or if I should play along. I remain still. "You can't tell me that if you weren't already with Taylor when we met at the bar —"

"No."

"Yes." And he kisses me so softly, his lips gently tugging on mine as he pulls away. I'm not sure if I kiss back, and only after I open my eyes do I realize I had closed them in acceptance. The kiss is dangerously sweet and familiar. I catch my breath -- these Holdens have a way with the ladies, but he is not Taylor. He does not seek permission; he does not ask me what I want; he does not want me to want it. He simply takes, he takes without permission and I cannot let him for a second think he has consent to touch me ever again. I shove him away.

"You and I are nothing. Nothing. What do you want from me?"

He backs away and looks me over, shaking his head. "Look at you: cuts, bruises…a busted lip. The picture of mental health. You honestly don't see what's wrong with this picture? How am I the dangerous one?"

"How dare you pretend to be concerned about my mental health? You, of all people! Taylor has been honest with me from the very beginning. You're the one who has played a twisted game of hide and seek."

"Have you stopped a moment to think about the fact that your precious Taylor might be fucking with you? He's done it to me my entire life. He drove me out of my home, away from our family...and now he's doing it again! If he felt at all threatened by my presence, he would do anything to keep you close to him."

"That's ridiculous. You act as if you being exiled from your home had nothing to do with your actions. You have been scheming ever since you arrived! You're not even supposed to be here. Taylor said you left town. If he knew you were here..."

"But, no, he let you leave, didn't he? What does that say about him?"

"Stop trying to analyze me."

"You should do a little background research on his all of his old girlfriends. I bet you'll see there is stuff you don't know about your saint Taylor."

"I know about his past," I say defiantly. Immediately, I almost wished I hadn't confessed that as Eric would think me a fool for staying with Taylor.

"Do you know about Emily?"

"Emily Brown?" Eric's face registers surprise, as if he expected this to be a bombshell.

"Yes. He told you about her?"

"Ye...yes." It makes me wonder if there is something I don't know, but if I ask, it will appear that he is somehow winning me over. Before Eric can say anything else, the sounds of a muffled voice grab my attention. Instinctively, my eyes dart to it, and so do Eric's.

"Shit!" Eric grabs the phone and sees it's Taylor on the other line. He throws the phone across the room, and it fractures against the wall. He looks around nervously and runs over to one of my bedroom windows and peers out past the curtain. "Fuck. I have to go." He points at me. "You need to look into Emily Brown. Do you understand?"

I nod, relieved that he is finally leaving. He runs out of the front door, leaving it ajar. As soon as I am certain he is gone, I grab the phone, which is cracked but still working.

"Taylor?"

"Shy, are you okay? What the hell is going on?"

"No...no. I'm fine. I wasn't sure if you would pick up."

"What was all that commotion? I couldn't make out what was going on."

"It was Eric." Tears begin to pour out of me.

"What!"

"He broke in somehow. He's gone now. You scared him off. I'm okay. He didn't touch me." I know no good would come of telling Taylor about the kiss.

"I'm already on my way. Lock your doors. Do not open to anyone. I have a key."

The elevator can only be accessed using a key, and then I check on the stairwell exit, which is ajar. It was locked, but Eric must have found a way to jimmy it. I sit on my bed, shaking from the aftereffects of the nerves, and stare at my phone anxiously awaiting Taylor's arrival. He makes me feel safe even though one might suppose that after last night, "safe" should be the last thing I feel around him. I don't know why, but in that moment, even though I was wailing in pain, I felt the most secure in my place with him than ever before. Maybe it's because he was finally being honest.

It is almost 10 minutes before the elevator door opens. Taylor bursts through, shouting my name. I call out to him from the bedroom and he rushes over to embrace me. I melt in his arms, shaking uncontrollably. The events of the past 24 hours finally begin to settle in.

"You're safe now," he murmurs. He opens his mouth to ask me a question but then his eyes catch one of my forearms. I had forgotten about the cuts in the midst of the chaos. He grabs my wrist and pulls my arm towards him to get a better look. "Shy, what is this? Did he…?"

"No! He didn't touch me. He pretty much stood over there the entire time."

"That wasn't me? Was it?"

"No. It wasn't," I say hesitantly.

Taylor's facial expression morphs from a state of confusion to one of realization. "Did you-"

I look down in shame. How can I explain this to him? All this time he thought he was the only damaged one.

"Yes. I'm sorry."

He guides my face up by my chin. "What are you doing to yourself? You're cutting?"

"I'm sorry."

Taylor runs his hands through his hair and shakes his head in dismay. "Shyla…is this because of me?" He asks as if he is afraid to hear the answer.

"No, this is not your fault. I used to do this a long time ago. It's just a relapse…It's because of the other thing."

"Eric?"

"I just feel like I am hurting you. It's not you, I swear. I used to do it in high school…" Really, it's not any one thing, it's everything all at once.

"What? No! Don't blame yourself. This is all Eric. I know this. Even yesterday, I knew it. I was just jealous and angry and I needed to work it out. Why did you do it in high school?"

"I don't know. It just made me feel when I couldn't or distracted me when I was stressed or depressed. I don't know. Those were tough years for me."

14

"I know exactly what you mean."

"I am better now. I swear."

Taylor nods, but his eyes tell me that he is thinking much more than a simple nod can reveal.

"What are we going to do about him?" I ask. We can't go on like this much longer.

"He should have been gone, I had him escorted to the airport yesterday evening. I'll have to find out what the hell happened with Harrison. This is inexcusable."

"Don't blame Harrison."

"You are so protective of him."

"I trust him. Eric looked like he was in bad shape. He said it was you."

"Shyla, I don't care if you think less of me. He deserves much worse than what he got."

"I never said I did. It's just that I am in the dark about what happened…"

"Let me take care of the dirty work."

"I don't like not knowing, Taylor." Taylor maintains eye contact, but remains silent and I know this is his kind way of telling me to shut the fuck up about it. "So what do we do now? Do we call the police?"

"We can call the police, but…" Taylor hesitates.

"What?"

"You're covered in cuts and bruises. They'll ask where it's all from. They'll also ask why you think he was here. Are you okay with revealing that?" What he is really trying to ask me is if I am okay with revealing all of that about *him*.

I shake my head. I already made the decision that I would not share that hotel room story with anyone ever. "I'm not, but there has to be something we can do."

"He's a fucking coward, sneaking around like a weasel."

"I just want this all to stop."

"Me too, and it will, I promise. He's not slipping through the cracks this time. Let's get you dressed while we think about this." I begin to stand up, but he gently presses his hand on my shoulder to keep me seated. "I'll take care of it."

Taylor walks over to one of my dressers where I keep my pajamas and pulls out a three-quarter sleeve, heather blue henley nightshirt. He scrunches it up and asks me to remove my towel. I do, and he slides the neck opening over my head, then guides each arm into the appropriate sleeve. He brushes stands of wet hair away from my face.

"Your lip?"

"That was me too, with you though."

"I'm sorry, I didn't realize you bruised so easily. You're like a peach. The crop usually leaves red marks that fade."

"That's what my mom used to say when I was a kid. I would just be covered in mysterious bruises all the time."

"I can be gentler."

"It's on me. I didn't tell you to stop."

"Let me grab some hydrogen peroxide, I'll be back."

While Taylor is in the bathroom, my wheels turn. There has to be a way to solve all of this: to make Eric pay for what he did to me while not revealing any details about my secret life with Taylor. Taylor returns with some cotton balls and a bottle of hydrogen peroxide. He gently swabs the cuts, paying very close attention to each one. It's hard to reconcile that this was the same man choking me the night before. He opens his mouth as if to say something, but then he hesitates and stops.

"What is it?" I ask.

"Nothing."

"Tell me."

"It was a fleeting thought. I can't put you through more than what you have already experienced."

"Taylor, I wish you would stop underestimating me. I think I have a say in how we handle Eric and I want all of the options."

Taylor stops swabbing my cuts and takes a deep breath. "I was thinking we could get him on the hook for all of this. Make him pay for everything. He's been so careful, but I think he has finally slipped enough that we can get him."

"I'm not sure what you mean."

"We can say he did all of this." Taylor motions to my body with the hand holding the cotton ball.

"You mean frame him?" I ask in disbelief. *Do people do that in real life?*

"Yes…but, never mind. Lying is difficult for most people. You're not like me, and I don't expect you to be able to pull something like that off." I feel a little offended by his underestimation.

"What would we say, that he did all of this? The cuts and bruises?"

"Shyla, do you have any idea how hard it is to lie to the police convincingly?"

"I mean, I know it's hard, but I want to get him so bad, Taylor. I want to make him pay for everything. For what he did to me, to us."

"Me too, more than you know, but undertaking something like this is a big deal. There cannot be any holes in our story. Your wounds, for example; they're not typical of an attack. We would have to have a story that is consistent with these types of wounds. If you say he sexually assaulted you, well then did he make you bathe? Did he wear a condom? They will go over these details many times with you. Are you prepared to handle that? Are you prepared to lie at this level?"

"Are you?" Taylor gives me a look of disbelief. Of course he can, Taylor does whatever he wants. "And if we don't do this, what is our other option?" I ask.

"Shy, I have tried other avenues. He is not easily intimidated and he's a smart son of a bitch."

"So there aren't other options?"

"The other options would be outside of the law. Well, all of our options are actually."

"You wouldn't -"

"He's crossed a line. I can do only so many favors for my father."

"Taylor, if you do anything serious to him, then you go to jail and I am not going to let you go down that path."

"He's asking for it. And I am smart enough not to get caught."

"I can't believe we are even talking about that as a possibility. I won't let you put yourself at risk to protect me, or even yourself." I know what has to be done. I have to protect us from Eric, and more importantly, protect Taylor from himself. If the injuries on Eric are an indication of Taylor holding back for his father, I am afraid to imagine what Taylor would do with abandon. Even if he was never caught, he would be pulled further into the darkness. I cannot lose Taylor. "So, how would we pull this off?" I ask.

Taylor looks at me and cocks his eyebrow. "Are you sure? Have you really - "

"Yes. We don't have much time. The longer we wait, the more suspicious we appear. How do we pin this on Eric?"

"Shyla, if this were just me, I would have no reservations, but you have been under a lot of stress and this is only going to add to that. This is not some movie; there are serious consequences. I don't mean legally, I mean the weight of living with a lie forever."

18

"I am already living with the consequences. I think I have continually proved that you have underestimated my ability to deal with all kinds of things."

"Just understand that there are huge implications for both of us if we fuck this up, so you need to nail the story."

"Taylor, I want to protect us and I want Eric gone. I am so sick of him and his sick, twisted bullshit. I don't want you to put yourself in a position to go after him. There is no way they can prove he didn't do this to me. It would be my word against his! It's just stretching the truth about what happened. He broke the law, he violated me. I'm just giving the legal system the opportunity to get him this time." Taylor thinks in silence for a while. I give my final plea. "I know you can take care of yourself Taylor, but I just want this to be done. If the police start looking for him, then you and I can just go on with our lives." I caress Taylor's cheek. "We deserve to be happy. You deserve to be happy."

Taylor smirks his crooked, devilish grin. "You're amazing. Is it fucked up that I kind of find this conniving side of you really hot right now?"

"Yes, but I like fucked up," I reply.

Taylor takes my wrist and slowly kisses each cut one by one.

"You're making me really horny Shy."

"Likewise...This is bad," I remind him. How can we even be entertaining the idea of sex right now in the midst of all this? His coolness under pressure is contagious; so is his libido.

He runs his hand up the nightshirt, squeezing my behind. "I know," he says as he leans in and kisses my neck. Then it flashes unexpectedly: the image of the man covered in black leather hovering over me. I shudder and Taylor stops.

"What is it? Are you okay?"

"Yes. Yes, I'm fine. Sorry."

"Oh…I, uh…I'm sorry." His face sinks, remembering his brother's trespass.

"No, it's okay," I reassure him.

"We really shouldn't right now." He's right, but I want to erase Eric, I want to purge him from my body. And the only way I know how is by replacing him with Taylor.

"You're right, if they examine me, it wouldn't look very good." We sit up and I pull down the nightshirt. "So what's the story?"

Taylor stands up and scans the room. "You cannot say he attacked you in a conventional manner. We can make this work because you can tell them he has been following you, that he has some sort of obsession with you. This will not be the case of some stranger coming in and throwing you around. It has to be more sinister, more calculated…"

"That makes sense. Eric is careful, he is methodical. We know this."

"Your cuts, your bruises are not from defending yourself against an attack. They come from consensual acts, albeit rough acts, so we have to have a story that supports that physical evidence."

"How?"

Taylor walks over to me and looks at my wrists, which are lightly bruised from the handcuffs he used last night. "You are going to say he cuffed you to your bed at knifepoint, turned you on your stomach, and whipped you with his belt buckle." I take a deep breath. Taylor is right -- even though this didn't happen, it will be difficult to retell. Taylor pulls down the neckline of my nightshirt to reveal bruising around my neck. "He then turned you back onto your back, and assaulted you, using a condom, while choking you. He cut you too, before intercourse. As far as your lip, just say that happened the way it actually did. This is not some random attack, this is a man who is obsessed with you and did not want to harm your beautiful face."

"This is sick, Taylor."

"Shyla, remember what he did to you. He is just as depraved as we are making him out to be. He just didn't get caught the first time around. Who is to say what he would have done to you in the hotel room if you had discovered it was him and not me?"

I nod. He's right. Sometimes in order to get rid of scum, you must grovel in filth.

Taylor paces around the room, walking through the scene like a sleuth would in a crime film. "Then, he uncuffs you and forces you to bathe, just in case. He leaves you alone in the bedroom for a few seconds, where you find your phone, call me and the rest happens as it did. The lack of forensic evidence is in line with his experience in security. However, I am sure they will find something of his in here, at least enough to place him in the scene."

Taylor makes me rehearse the story over and over again until he is sure I have every important detail down. "Now Shy, it is important that you stick to this.Do not change or add anything. If they ask you a question that throws you off, only repeat back what you have already said or just say you can't remember. Do not add layers to the story, it will be impossible to keep track. Just stay consistent and simple."

"Okay."

"One other thing…how bloody were those cuts when you first made them?"

"Uh, I don't know, I mean they're shallow, but there was a small stream of blood. I do it in the tub."
Confessing that very private ritual makes me feel uneasy, but Taylor is unfazed. He knows all about the darker side of humanity.

"They are going to wonder about blood on the sheets, or lack thereof, but there is no way I am having you spill anymore blood today. Just tell them that the cuts were slowly made and did not draw much blood. Stick to that no matter what they say."

"No, we shouldn't leave any holes."

"You're not doing it again. No."

"Taylor, we can't have any holes in the story. Just this once."

"No." Taylor looks stern, immoveable, so I stop. He is not thinking logically, he doesn't want me to draw blood because he *loves me*, not because it's the smart thing to do.

"So, when do we call?"

"Whenever you're ready, but you should rehearse the story a few more times."

"Can I have a second? Alone? I just need to focus in."

Taylor looks surprised, but then nods. "Sure, I'll be in the kitchen. Do you want something?"

"Tea would be great."

Taylor, steps out of the room. When he clears the hallway, I slip into the bathroom, grabbing the razor blade I used earlier. I reenter the bedroom and lock the door behind me. I walk over to the head of the bed and lift the razor to my forearm. My hands are unusually shaky since I am not used to rushing this. It's usually a painfully slow and drawn out ritual. One slice is carved, a little deeper than the others to ensure blood drips. I squeeze the cut, dripping as much blood as I can. Then I wrinkle the blankets, smearing the blood so it doesn't look so perfect. Taylor knocks on the door.

"You okay in there?"

"Yeah."

"I have your tea."

"Give me a sec."

"What's going on?"

"Uh, nothing." I scramble to the hydrogen peroxide on the counter, desperately trying to clean my arms, but blood continues to run.

"What are you up to in there?" I don't answer. "Shyla…Shyla? Are you—? Are you fucking doing what I think you're doing? Goddammit! Open this door or I'll fucking knock it down."

In my panicked haste to clean my arm the bottle of peroxide tips over. "Shit!" I pick up the bottle and look for something to wipe the mess on the counter. My favorite red shirt lays on a chair. *No way in hell am I going to ruin that with peroxide.*

"Shyla, I am counting down from three. Three-two-"

I whip the door open. "Taylor just relax. I need a towel from the linen closet."

"What the fuck?"

"I spilled peroxide, please just grab it." My arm is still dripping blood, albeit slowly. Taylor was gone for five minutes and I have already managed to create a mess so quickly. Taylor returns with the towel and I direct him to the spill, which he soaks up. He turns back to me, grabs my arm and sees the fresh cut. "Fuck! You just promised me not fifteen minutes ago that you would never cut yourself again!"

"It wasn't like that. This was business. We needed the evidence and now we have it. You weren't thinking logically, you were trying to protect me. It had to be done."

Taylor sighs, and sits on the edge of the bed. He knows I am right. "We need a vacation, and not to New York, to fucking Mars or something."

The surprising levity of his statement makes me chuckle. Then Taylor starts to laugh, which in turn makes me laugh harder. In seconds, we are laughing hysterically, tears streaming down our cheeks. This might be the hardest I have ever seen Taylor laugh. The tragic ridiculousness of this entire fiasco is not lost on us. The laughter is cathartic, in a much different manner from my cutting earlier in the evening. When we are finally able to breathe again, I sit next to Taylor.

"Give me the razor. We have to clean it and put it back where you would normally hold it. We'll just be honest about the peroxide, your clumsy ass spilled it when we were cleaning your wounds," Taylor says.

"Okay. I've got this. We are going to nail him." I say, trying to psych myself up.

"You are a little devil. A hot little devil."

"Only if someone messes with you." Taylor's gorgeous crooked smirk makes an appearance. "Okay, well should I call?" I ask.

"No, I'll do it."

"Okay."

Taylor grabs his cell phone and walks out to the living room. Seconds later I hear him in the distance.

"Hello. We need the police."

CHAPTER TWO

In minutes, the apartment crawls with police. The first officers do a brief initial round of questioning, but soon after they tell me I must go to the hospital for a rape kit. An ambulance waits for me, but Taylor offers to have Harrison take me instead. I am happy to take him up on the offer as the ambulance will only serve to heighten my nerves.

I put on some yoga pants, but keep on my nightshirt. Taylor hands me a chunky cardigan from the wardrobe. I couldn't care less how presentable I look, in fact, the more disheveled, the better I assume.

When we slide into the back of the SUV Harrison and I make eye contact through the rear view mirror, his are softened, unable to hide his concern. Harrison is the only other person who has even the remotest idea of how rough of a night I have had. Being in Taylor's arms with Harrison at the wheel in the confines of the dark SUV make me feel like I am the safest person in the world.

"Ms.Ball, I am glad you are okay." He is a man of a few words, and that simple sentence, in an unusually warm tone, fills my heart.

"Thank you, Harrison. We should get together soon and finally plant some flowers."

Harrison nods and smiles.

Taylor looks at me and cocks his eyebrow and I mischievously grin. I am forming my own relationship with Harrison outside of my universe with Taylor.

When we arrive, Taylor is asked to wait alone while I am taken into an examination room and asked to put on a hospital gown. Sitting on the table with my ass hanging out, I realize I much prefer the gown Taylor gave me in Russia. This "gown" hardly feels luxurious.

Shortly after, a very young doctor enters the room and introduces herself. She calmly explains the exam she is about to perform without any excitement or emotion in her voice. It is oddly comforting not to be spoken to like a victim. I explain to her that I was forced to bathe and that there will likely be little she can recover. She takes note and performs the exam. On the ceiling above the exam table is a poster of a stony brook. I let it take my mind elsewhere, imagining Taylor and I hiking towards it, then Taylor guiding me across it, catching me as I slip. But then, in the distant woods, hidden by old trees, I see Eric coming for us. This cannot be our lives, he will always be lurking unless I can pull this off. The exam is over much faster than I had anticipated, and once she is done, she informs me someone will be entering the room to photograph the injuries on my body.

A female officer enters with a large camera in hand as the doctor leaves. Like the doctor, she briefly summarizes what she will be doing and then quickly gets started.

"Can you show me your forearms, like this?"

I do, and she snaps a shot.

"Can you tilt your chin up?" She snaps.

"Miss, can you turn around and reveal your buttocks?"

I nod and lift up the hospital gown to reveal red marks along my butt and hamstring. The woman in

26

front of me is completely professional, not letting any emotion peer through, but I am sure she sees me as a victim. What would she think if she knew that all of these marks, these bruises and cuts, were things I consented to? Would she see me as a deviant instead? I don't consider myself to be either one, but if I am neither, then what am I?

"We're finished," the officer tells me after what feels like one hundred snapshots. She gives me the option to get dressed again before the detectives enter to speak to me and I oblige. A few minutes later, there is a soft knock on the door.

A tan, short, balding man, who looks like he never met a double cheeseburger he didn't consume, enters the room.

"Ms. Ball?" He leans in. "I'm Detective Acosta." I stand up. "No please, have a seat, I just want to go over what happened tonight."

"Of course."

"It has been an especially busy night so I don't have another detective with me. However, if you would prefer the presence of a woman, I can bring in an officer to sit with us."

Keep it simple. "No, thank you, but it's okay. I am fine speaking alone with you."

"I understand this is very difficult, but the more details you can provide, the more likely we will be able to solve this. I am going to record this, so we don't have to make you relive this with the same questions over and over."

"I understand. Anything I can do to help catch him." For some reason, I had expected to have Taylor at my side during questioning. I had not planned for this scenario. "Did you speak to my boyfriend, Taylor?"

"Yes, we took a statement from him while you were being examined. Why do you ask?"

"Well I uh, I was just hoping to have him here."

"Of course, it's all up to you, but as I mentioned every detail is important, and I will need you to be able to speak freely about what happened."

"Oh yes. You're right, there are things I am not sure I want him hearing. At least not yet." I don't want to stir the pot any further, so I nod in acceptance.

"Okay. We'll, let's just begin with what happened, start to finish."

I rehearse the story like a pro: Taylor and I had a disagreement, so I came home late into the night. I was unaware that Eric was already in my home until he approached me, blade in hand. He cuffed me and assaulted me, beating and cutting me. Afterward, he forced me to bathe. He then left the room for a few moments. I barely managed to dial Taylor. Just before Eric returned, I tossed the phone hoping Taylor would hear us and call the police. When Eric realized the phone was on, he ran, fearing the police were already on their way. I don't need to conjure up tears, they flow freely on their own. There are plenty of real reasons to cry. I have never considered myself an expert liar, but my motivation to protect Taylor is strong and I deliver the story so well I almost believe it myself.

"Do you know why Eric left the room, giving you time to call?"

"I think he was trying to wipe things down like the doorknobs, but I'm not sure since I couldn't see and was too preoccupied with trying to call Taylor. I only had a few seconds and I was terrified of what he had planned for me when he returned. Thankfully, Taylor's call seemed to throw everything off for him."

"Yes, that was very brave of you. You may have saved yourself from a much worse fate. Can you tell me why you called Taylor instead of 911?" I hold my breath for a millisecond; the question feels mildly accusatory.

"I guess because I am so used to calling him. I guess I trust him the most. Eric is his brother, he understood the history and I thought if I didn't make it, he might be able to shed some light...I don't know, it was just instinctual." Uttering that thought aloud, that Eric might kill me, raises goosebumps on my forearms. All this time, I never truly feared Eric. At least, not in the way that made me wonder if he was capable of killing me. After I found out that he was the man in the suit, it wasn't fear I experienced, but ambivalence and later, anger. Even when Taylor told me about the hit Eric put out on him, I just couldn't reconcile the Eric I met with the Eric who Taylor described. For all of Taylor's warnings that Eric wants to hurt me, last night, he never touched me except to help me off the ground...and to kiss me.

"So Ms. Ball, tell me about your relationship with Eric."

"My relationship?"

"I mean before this happened, you said he was following you?"

"Yes, he would show up at random places, trying to talk to me about Taylor. They don't get along and it freaked me out, but I never thought he would resort to this." I purposely leave out the phone calls, as that would open up more layers, which Taylor advised against.

"Did you report this to the police?"

"Well, no. It didn't seem like I had much to hold against him. It was my word against his. Like I mentioned, I thought he was misguided, but not this depraved."

"Why don't Eric and Taylor get along?"

This was not a question we had rehearsed an answer to. Just as Taylor instructed, I keep it simple. "A very serious case of sibling rivalry. As far as I know, they just can't stand each other. Never could. Mainly it's because Taylor inherited the family business and Eric did not."

The detective jots some notes on a pad. I try and take a peek, but the handwriting is illegible.

"Did Eric tell you anything about where he might be headed?"

"No, he left so abruptly."

"And did he mention why he was doing this? Revenge towards Taylor?"

"No. He did say he thought we had a connection. That he knew me better than I thought. Maybe it was a mixture of both, revenge towards Taylor and an obsession with me."

"Is there anything else? Anything else he told you that could provide some clues as to his whereabouts or motivations?" *Emily Brown.* I had completely forgotten how adamant Eric was that I look into her. This will lead back to Taylor though, so I keep that out of my account. *Keep it simple.*

"No. I have told you everything I can recall. If anything else comes up, you will be the first to know."

Acosta's cell phone rings and he raises a finger to excuse himself as he takes the call. There are a few yeses and nods and then he hangs up.

"Good news. We were able to get our hands on the surveillance footage from your building. It shows Mr. Holden entering and exiting the building according to your timeline." It takes me a second to realize he is referring to Eric and not Taylor; just that moment of confusion makes my heart speed up. Lying this big has put me so on edge, it even makes me nervous about the truth. Acosta closes his notepad, shoves it inside his jacket pocket, picks up the recorder and rises from his stool. "Alright Miss Ball, we have an APB out on Eric Holden. As soon as I have any updates, I will let you know. Here is my card. If you remember anything, any new details, please call me. Forensics is still at your house trying to collect evidence so it would be best if you stayed with someone who you are comfortable with. Do you need to reach family?"

No, no way can anyone know about this but Taylor and me. "I'll go home with Taylor. Thank you."

"I understand this might be difficult, but I may have to come to you with more questions. You have been very helpful, but often it helps to come in when you are more refreshed and go over your account again."

I very much do not look forward to recounting the story again, but this is what I signed up for, so I take the card, nod and thank him.

Detective Acosta turns to leave and I say the first sincere thing to him since he has walked into the room.

"Detective?"

"Yes."

"Please get him."

He reveals a faint, sympathetic grin with the faintest of sighs. "I'll do my best, Miss Ball."

When I step out, I see Taylor sitting in the waiting area, his head in his hands. I hadn't noticed before that he was still in his pajamas: sandy sweatpants and gray hoodie he seems to have thrown over his bare upper body. It's so unlike him to not be dressed to the nines out in public. Hunched over like that, he looks so shrunken, nothing like the tall statuesque man I am so used to admiring. He senses me watching and looks up with a smile, but his eyes look so heavy.

"How'd it go?"

"It was okay. They were all very nice. I am so tired though. I just want to go home."

"Me too. I hate hospitals, so many damn people and bad memories." Now I realize the heaviness in his eyes is not from lying to the police or the looming threat of his brother. I often forget about his anxiety, but it is the one thing that truly weighs on him.

"Bad memories?"

"I just hated it as a kid." He's holding something back as usual, but all my mental energy has been used with Detective Acosta.

In a rare glimmer of fortune, it's Saturday and neither one of us have work obligations. When we get back to the house we lie in bed for awhile due to a brief second wind that keeps us from sleeping.

So what did you think about Detective Acosta?" I ask Taylor.

"I think he's shrewd. Sorry, I wasn't on my A-game…fucking hospitals. God, I wish I didn't hate that so much. I just hope he didn't misinterpret my anxiety as something related to the case."

"Hey, as a concerned boyfriend, you have every right to be shook up. I think they would understand that."

"I know, I just got a vibe from him…He gave me his card, he said he might have more questions. I'll invite him to my home office if he wants to talk more. My territory."

"I hope we did the right thing." I don't want to make him think I am not all in, but ever since I spoke to Acosta, I have had a knot in my stomach. Taylor's right, I'm not like him. Despite feeling that my actions are justified, it still feels so wrong to frame Eric like this.

"We are giving the law a way to right these wrongs for you. He thinks he has the upper hand, but not any longer. Remember, you wanted to do this."

"I know," I remind him. "You're right. I'll be strong. I promise. But, what if this becomes messy? He knows things about us."

"I'm not concerned about that. His credibility is nil. I have ways of keeping my past in the past. If anyone spoke a word, they would be so tied up in litigation and legal fees they would never see the light of day again. And I always have far more on them than they do on me. Plus, I am a major contributor to Mayor Roth. This will ensure the detectives go easy on us. Eric had this coming. In the meantime, I want you to stay here until they catch him and I don't want to hear a single complaint from you about that."

"You won't. I want to stay here with you."

He looks at me in silence for a few seconds and then glides his finger over my forearm. "Don't do this anymore. We can do whatever you want, but please, don't do this to yourself."

"I wish I hadn't. I feel so stupid, so juvenile. There's just been so much to deal with. More than I ever imagined I could handle"

"I'm not trying to belittle you, you're strong. What you have dealt with these past couple of days would have broken anyone. I just don't want you to feel so lost that you need to resort to this. When you need to feel something physical to work through things, that's my specialty. You keep telling me I need to open up to you. It goes both ways." Taylor pulls out his medication from the nightstand and takes a few pills.

"You're going to sleep until Monday."

"I know, but I can't risk it. You don't need any more bullshit piled on top of you today."

"It seems as though it's working."

"I think so, but I think what's working most is having you in my life. Today was a high stress day though, and it brings out the worst in me."

"I understand. Hey, Eric said something weird. He asked me about Emily Brown."

"Really? What about her?"

33

"Well, just before he left, he implied that there is something I should know about her. Is there something I don't know about?"

"I've told you everything about her, I swear. I haven't seen her since she left."

"I just felt like he was trying to drop a bombshell or something."

"I think he's just messing with your head. If you want me to find out how she is doing, I can do that. I won't get in touch with her personally, but I can have my attorney find out about her. I have nothing to hide about her and if it puts you at ease…"

"That would make me feel better. It's not that I don't trust you…I just…maybe there's something we both don't know." I decide to let Taylor take the reins on this and leave MacAllister to his work on C.O.S. I doubt Taylor would risk lying to me about her, it would be too easy for me to find out.

"You're right…" Taylor's voice trails off, followed by a heavy silence. There is still so much to talk about, so much left unspoken: the threatening texts I have yet to mention to Taylor, the news about his mother. I continue to pile up a list of secrets from Taylor despite my intentions to be open. But when is it the right time to tell your protective boyfriend, whose brother has violated you, that you had warning signs, but you chose to keep them to yourself? How do you tell him that you trust him, while at the same time hire a private investigator to research his family history? How do you break the news to him that his mother, whom he has long accepted as dead, may still be alive?

And then there's last night. I've never been the spiritual type, but we were two bare souls: open, raw, and exposed. I haven't even had the time I needed to process what happened, but here I am, back in his bed. Despite it all, it feels like home. And for some inexplicable reason, I want to connect with him like that again.

Taylor breaks the silence. "About last night…"

"Yes?"

"Do you want to talk about it? The events that happened afterward brought you here, but I need to know if you would be here if Eric had never showed up."

I take a moment to think, even though I already know the true answer. "I would be. I knew I would be when I walked out the door. I just thought we needed some time to let the air out, to settle. I've never experienced anything like that in my life." I look away because I am almost ashamed to admit it. "It was so painful, but so…intense. I just wanted to help you take the pain away."

"I thought if you saw that side of me, you'd be terrified."

"I don't blame you, but the thing is you showed me that no matter how angry you are, no matter how hurt, you would never do anything I didn't want to do. I understand the need to manifest the emotional world into the physical. *I get it.*"

He glances at my arm. "I guess you do."

"I want to see the real you. All sides of you. We all have our ugly sides."

"Are you sure?"

"I have never been more sure. I want you to do with me whatever you want. I want to make you feel complete."

"You want everything?" He asks.

"I do. I want to learn everything. I want to be your everything."

He leans in and guides my face so that I look into his eyes. "You need to know this: I will protect you. I will provide for you. I will give you all the physical pleasure you could ever imagine in ways you didn't even know were possible. You're mine, and when someone tries to hurt or take what is mine, I get vicious. It's like taking a bone from a dog. I will fucking bite, I will rip flesh off of bone." Chills run along my arms and back. He is reciting a vow to me. He is making a promise, one I am terrified he will keep. I nod, but have no words; he is not asking for my opinion, he is telling me the way things are now.

We lay in silence, my head on his chest; I listen to his heart, counting each beat. Finally, my eyelids begin to feel heavy. I try to fight the sleep, to stay in the stillness here with Taylor before we have to face all the chaos of the world again.

"Taylor," I murmur in a sleepy voice with my eyes half closed, "Who did that to Eric? Who beat him up so bad? Was it you? Harrison?"

There is no answer. I open my eyes to find Taylor asleep, his peaceful exterior hiding the storm brewing inside.

CHAPTER THREE

I wake up in a cold sweat, my heart pounding so hard I can barely catch my breath. I sit up and look at the clock: it's three thirteen in the morning. Normally, Taylor would wake up at the slightest flinch, but his medication has put him in a deep sleep. After staring into the darkness for 15 minutes, I rise to get a glass of water, maybe find something to read in Taylor's library. I now know the restlessness that wakes Taylor late into the night; I guess this is the price I must pay to be with him. I throw on my chunky cardigan and slip out of the bedroom quietly. The house is so still and its vastness in the dark is like a terrifying black hole. The light switches are impossible to find amidst all this wall space, but finally, I find one for the kitchen. As I drink an ice cold glass of lemon water, I spot the faintest spot of marinara sauce on the wall, evidence of the rage Taylor experienced. *I must find the cleaning supplies. I must erase this.*

I wander to the sliding glass doors that lead to the back of his property, hoping to find what I seek. The cool breeze lifts my hair off of my shoulders and I inhale its purity deep into my lungs. In the garden, the various colors of foliage are barely visible in the light of the full moon. There is a bed made from rose petals, hundreds, maybe thousands of them that I had never seen before. Then two large, warm hands, such a contrast to the chilly late night air, rest on my shoulders. I jump and almost vocalize, but the person behind me simply leans towards my ear and whispers "shhhh."

The hands slowly slide down my front side onto my breasts, gently caressing the nipples through my satin camisole. He knows just how to do it, and I cock my lower back to signal he is on the right path. One hand covers my breast, while the other slowly glides down past the edge of the slick camisole into my panties. He massages my lips with his fingers in a circular motion, stimulating the clitoris beneath. I lean back to accept and feel his hard cock against the small of my back. It throbs, with each pulse, begging me to pleasure it. I pull down my panties and beg "please, fuck me." He slides a single finger inside and I am so wet, so ready for him. "Please," I beg. He places the finger to my lips, I purse my lips around it, sucking on it just as I would him. Once he is satisfied, he turns me around and raises my camisole overhead, lightly kissing my breasts, then my stomach, and grabs me by my waist, lowering me onto the cool, velvety bed of petals. He buries his face in my neck suckling so softly, making goosebumps rise all over my body.

"Do you want me to fuck you?" The familiar voice asks.

"Yes."

"Hold it."

I put my hand around his girth, it's so hard, so ready. The outline of this beautiful, thick, phallus makes my clit throb.

"Do you want this to fuck you?"

"Yes," I beg.

"Rub it on that beautiful pussy of yours."

I obey.

"Please don't tease me," I beg of the shadowy man.

He slides it in slowly, each inch a new threshold of pleasure. I let out a moan. He slowly winds his hips in and out. My clit engorges, and his slow pace only draws out the pleasure. My nails dig into his muscular back as

38

I hold on for dear life. Then my moans become louder, my breath shallower. I feel hot, and tense all over, I can't hold on any longer.

"Say my name," he says. "Say my name or I'll stop." He holds me hostage with his dick. The moonlight finally catches his face, the light hair and pale eyes, and despite my horror, it's too late.

"Eric! Fuck! Eric!" I cry out into the dark night as he comes inside of me.

❅ ❅ ❅

The immense guilt I feel as I lay awake after the dream is only compounded by the physical aftereffects of the delicious sex romp I just experienced. *It's only a dream*, I remind myself. But goddam that felt real, too real. I should hate this man, and I truly want him to go away, but he has somehow found a way to get under my skin. He has not only violated my body, but he has violated my psyche. Taylor is right, this man is dangerous.

It's around 10:30 in the morning. Taylor is still sound asleep and likely will be for a while since he took his medication so late into the night. I slide out of bed, grab my phone, and take it outside to call Mr. MacAllister.

"MacAllister speaking."

"Hi, it's Shyla."

"Hi Shyla! I was beginning to worry. I have been trying to reach you for some time now."

"I know, I am so sorry. Someone broke into my house last night and attacked me. I suspect it was the person who has been leaving me the messages."

"Are you alright?" He asks.

"Yes, just shook up. Listen, the police are investigating him now. I am not sure I need you to dig into the calls now that they are looking for him. That should resolve the issue."

"Are you certain? Would you like me to pass along information?"

"No, please don't. I don't want you to communicate with the police. I was going to see if we could trace the calls to him so maybe, I don't know, I could get a restraining order or something, but he already showed his hand."

"I would always recommend we look into the calls or at the very least you file the reports as I had mentioned. The more evidence we have against him, the better your chances are of getting him put away for a long time."

I don't want Mr. MacAllister getting involved in the police investigation. Like Taylor said, the less variables, the easier it will be to keep our story straight. We have proof he came into my apartment and that's all that matters.

"I would rather not. My boyfriend doesn't know about the texts and this will get me into more personal drama than I would like. They have plenty of evidence against this person, including video of him entering my home. I would like you to just send me what you have and then close the case. What's most important to me is the other case you were looking into. The one about the cult."

"Yes, this is proving to be challenging, but very intriguing. Do you mind me asking why you want me to dig into this?"

"I can't say, but it is important to me. I know you won't tell Kristin anything, but I have to reiterate, she really can't know about this."

"Of course."

"So you think this woman could be alive?"

"The child is the only person who the police believe survived. His mother, Lyla Bordeau is a mystery. It's possible that she may be alive, or that there was foul play unrelated to the mass suicide."

"Could you explain further?"

"Well, all I know right now from digging into past records is that her son was found alive at the scene. When the investigators identified the bodies, everyone was accounted for except for her."

"And they were never able to find her?"

"No. They used the media, no quality leads. They never considered her a suspect, just a possible witness, since it seemed clear that people did what they did on their own volition. Eventually, the interest faded with the press and she remains a cold case. So it's possible she may have been murdered before the suicide even happened."

"They just stopped looking for her?"

"Unfortunately, yes. A lot of resources went in initially, and then they just figured she may have been killed before the mass suicide. Witnesses stated that she was growing discontent with C.O.S and her relationship with Peters, the cult leader, was getting tumultuous. Police thought he may have killed her which triggered his downward spiral into leading the group into the suicide. Cult survivors supported this theory by saying they believed she was murdered. I have to say though, I get the feeling that there is more to this. I think it's possible she is alive. It's no coincidence to me that her son was the only survivor of the suicide."

"So what's next? If the police couldn't find her…"

"Sometimes time helps. People get comfortable, start slipping up – over time, they leave a trail. They start to tell people secrets. I am going to try to find people she knew, people who were important to her, and I am going to do good old fashioned detective work.

Now, I know you want to keep your reasons private, but if there is something you know, anything that can help me narrow down where she may have headed..."

"I'm sorry, I thought she was dead too. This is a shock to me. If I think of anything, I will let you know right away." Just as I complete the sentence, I hear footsteps approaching. "I have to go. I'll be in touch."

"Good morning. Who was that on the phone?"

"Oh, Chad had a question about work. I'm surprised you're up so early with the drugs and the late night."

"Drugs and late night? You just made it sound way more fun than it actually was. Yeah, well I feel groggy, but I could sense your absence from the bed. It woke me up." Someone who has spent his entire life sleeping alone, banishing people out his bed, can't sleep without me. "How did you sleep?"

The dream. I am so sickened by it, by my infidelity by REM. "It was okay. I couldn't sleep late either, which as you know is a rarity for me."

"That's the truth. Breakfast?"

"Yes, I'm starving. Do you need help?"

"No, just keep me company. I want to make you some outstanding french toast."

"You're kind of perfect." I stand up to kiss him. He wraps his strong arm around my lower back, pressing me close to him. He is already firm and I know the first course won't be French Toast. He lifts me up and I wrap my legs around him as he carries me inside to the great room, seating me on the couch. All I have on is a long, slouchy tank top, so he easily slides it up to reveal my bare lower body.

"Your pussy looks like a juicy, ripe peach. Delicious."

"Thank you," I say coyly.

"Can I have a taste?"

"Of course, sir."

He grins, as usual, he is most relaxed when he is being sexual. Sexuality is his home. Taylor takes his index and middle fingers and purses his lips around them, maintaining eye contact with me. His eyes smile darkly and he sucks on his fingers with his full lips, takes his moistened fingers and slowly and ever so lightly runs them down my labia while biting his plump lower lip. Then he gently separates the them. "Like a flower..." he says under his breath. I feel a tingling and start to snake my hips towards him, begging him with my body to eat me. "Do you want me to eat this luscious little peach?" His bluish eyes looking directly into mine.

"Yes."

"Beg me."

"Please."

"More."

"Please."

"Please what?"

"Please eat it."

"Eat what?" He cocks his eyebrows.

"My peach," I barely get out. He fingers gently message me as I beg. I grab a handful of his hair in my hands, trying to coax him but he resists. Finally, he leans in close, but then he stops just short of contact. I feel his lips graze below just barely.

"Take out your titties." Just a slight adjustment of my slouchy tank top reveals them. "Play with them." I cup them in my hands as my hips still snake towards him. My breathing shallows, and I feel that if I do not get back some control, I could come before he ever places his lips on mine.

"Please, just fucking eat me." I beg, almost pathetically. "Please baby. I want you so bad."

"You taste so good. I am going to savor your juices." He purses his lips and finally presses them against me. I throw my head back, wrapping my legs around his shoulders. He slowly sucks on the clit, doing it with just enough pressure to slowly and steadily tease me. My hips snake towards him with more force and speed until I am fucking his face. Just as I am about to come, he stops. I look at him desperately.

"Wha-What are you...?" I ask.

His pants are off and I don't ever recall seeing him remove them. His thick, hard cock, stands at attention. "I don't want you to come too fast, I want you to enjoy this."

"Trust me, you have no idea."

Taylor dives back in, slowly using his long tongue to penetrate me. I moan all sorts of incoherent things. Finally, he comes back to my clit, which is engorged and just waiting for him to release the explosion of pleasure. He takes his soft, plump lips and purses around her, gently sucking. I take one of my hands off of my breasts and pull on his hair as I moan loudly out into the world, clenching his neck with my thighs, tiny explosions erupting inside of me over and over. I look down at his face, his lips covered in my wetness so that when he kisses me, I taste myself in his mouth. He lies me horizontally on the couch and rests his body over mine, but just as he is about the enter, a panic hits me again. "Wait."

Taylor's eyes change as if I had awoken him from a dream. "Oh...I didn't think."

"No, I'll be fine. I just want to do something for you. Tell me how you want me to suck your cock." Inside, my heart is still going at full speed, and I secretly fear that something inside me might be broken, that something finally gave from all the recent events. But I still want to please him; I don't want to isolate him from the act in which he feels most comfortable relating to me. "Tell me. I'm yours. I want to please you." He stands up and takes me by that hand so that I stand up as well.

"You sure? You want me to tell you exactly how I want my dick sucked? No holds barred?"

"Yes, I want to make you come so hard. I want to please you. I want to do more than please you."

"You are making me rock solid."

"I know," I smile.

"Get on your knees." I take comfort in being commanded. I want to be told, I want my thoughts to only be of him and his dark, velvety voice. "Spit on your hand and put it around the base. Hold it firmly, now put that sexy mouth around the shaft. Uhhhh." He lets out a sigh as I do this, his voice lowers and becomes breathy. "Oh fuck. Yeah. Suck on it baby. Jerk me off at the base with your hand. Oh yeah."

He takes all of my hair in his hand and guides my pace. Then his hips begin to gyrate back and forth towards my mouth. "Run your tongue along the under…yeah, like that." I can feel him swelling in my mouth making it hard for me to contain him, but reinforcing that I am doing it exactly the way he likes it. "Now take your mouth off, but keep your hands on. Keep going, like that." His engorged dick looks like it will burst at any moment. "I want to come on those beautiful tits of yours. I want to filthy them with my cum." With my available hand, I slide my tank off of my shoulders, revealing my bust. "Put your mouth on it one last time, and take me all the way in." I take him to the back of my throat, gagging a little as my throat muscles tense against the head of his penis. "Finish me off baby, all over those beautiful face and tits." It only take seconds as he pumps all over the pale flesh of my breasts, streams of his cum adorning the curvature of my collarbones, areolas, and bust.

Taylor collapses onto the couch. I sit back onto the floor, studying the aftereffects of our encounter. It's the first time I have ever had a guy do that to me, so I don't have a standard procedure about what to do next.

Taylor breaks the silence. "Fuck, that was fantastic baby. Why don't you shower while I make breakfast?"

❋ ❋ ❋

By the time I get out of the shower, Taylor is plating the French toast. Drying my hair with a towel, I watch him from a distance, admiring his shirtless body. His hair is disheveled and he is just starting to grow a 5 o'clock shadow. He appears well rested compared to the way he looked at the hospital. I cherish the moment as I know it is only a brief respite from the reality of our world. There is a lot of pain and anger that needs resolution. I know Taylor won't be at peace until he has avenged me. Finally, he looks up and notices me watching him.

"Well, what are you waiting for? Come eat."

I walk over to the breakfast bar and he passes me a plate with three pieces of French toast, covered in berries and bananas and a dollop of mascarpone cheese. "Thank you so much, this looks great." Taylor stands across from me at the counter, and we eat in silence. "This is so delicious."

"Thank you…Shyla…" He pauses.

"What is it?" It seems that he is going to throw away the question, but I want to know what is on his mind.

"Are you…okay? I mean, a lot has happened. And you, well, the last couple of times we tried anything…do you need to talk to someone? A professional?"

"I'm okay, really. It's just a little soon is all. I'm a little shaken up by the past couple of days. I am sure it'll subside."

"He didn't really do anything at your house, right? You wouldn't hide that from me? I know I reacted poorly the first time—"

"No. I swear. I just think my emotions are fried. There has been so much happening at once. I just need some time to let things settle. I think I might still be in shock."

"Listen, I know it's different, but I know what you're going through. All of this, what we do, the dom stuff, I won't do it until you tell me you're ready. You need to tell me when you are ready to handle something that intense."

"I will, but part of me thinks it might help me. You know, work through everything."

"Are you sure? It's a dangerous road, using sex as a way to work out your issues. I would know." We both laugh a little at his dark joke.

"I understand."

"And maybe it's good that you — I don't know — see someone."

"Taylor, how rich of you to suggest that I see a therapist."

"You're not like me; you can be fixed. I mean not just what happened, but the mutilation..." Both of our eyes dart down to the thin cuts on my arm, and I feel ashamed and conflicted. How much different are the bruises on my body, the cuts on my lips, from the cuts on my arms? I know myself and who I am. I don't need to see a therapist as long as I have him to guide me through the shadows.

"I'll tell you what. Once you start making weekly visits to the shrink, I promise I'll go too."

Taylor sighs and nods his head, conceding to my point. "Point taken, smartass." His phone rings and he excuses himself to grab it. "Hello? Yes, this is. Oh, yes, I'm fine and you? Sure, just a moment." He puts the phone down. "It's for you. Detective Acosta." My phone was taken into evidence and so I gave Taylor's number as my contact information.

"Detective?"

"Hello Miss Ball. How are you feeling?"

"A lot better, thank you. Do you have any news?"

"Yes, actually I do. It's both good and bad."

My heart drops and I instantly become nauseous. "Yes. Go ahead."

"Eric Holden has left the country."

CHAPTER FOUR

"What? How?"

"From the timeline, it appears he immediately headed to the airport. He already had reservations for a flight to Brazil."

"Brazil?" I slump into my seat as I look up at Taylor, who is stoically leaning against the kitchen counter with his arms crossed, boring holes through me with his turquoise eyes. "So what are you going to do?"

"Ms.Ball, policing becomes very difficult internationally. He may have already headed to another South American country through Brazil. At this point the court will be issuing a warrant for his arrest but it is a waiting game."

"So are they going to track him down?" This is getting much bigger than I thought.

"Well, it's not that simple. He's effectively disappeared at this point. The best thing to do is to wait for him to slip up." *He won't slip up.*

"So you mean, he just gets off, scot-free?" I am not sure if this is good news or not. On one hand, he's gone, really gone; on the other he won't pay for what he has done.

"We will do everything in our power to find him, but I want you be prepared for the fact that our search has gotten a lot more complicated and will most likely take longer than we originally thought. We will continue to work leads and see if we can find out his specific whereabouts, working with the FBI and Interpol if we need to."

"I cannot believe this."

"Listen, Ms.Ball, if there is any silver lining to this, it's that he has gone on the run and it is unlikely he will return to this country or ever try to contact you again."

"But he gets to just live his life, as if nothing even happened?" I want to make sure he thinks I am outraged, but in a way I am relieved. Lying was as difficult as Taylor said it was.

"That's not necessarily true. He will have to hide and that is not pleasant. I will continue to be in touch if there are any new developments. He is on every list we could get him on so if he slips up, we will find him."

"You'll never find him. He's smart. He is a security expert. He was in the military."

"Actually, I did want to ask you about that. You mentioned he owned a security firm, but we didn't find any record of that."

"Well that's what he once told me. Maybe he was trying to impress me. His family is rich, he doesn't need to work. He was in the military, Taylor knows that for sure."

"Well, I will be in touch if I have any updates or questions."

"Okay. I'm going out of town for a while visiting family. So, I may be unavailable." It's kind of a fib since I have no official plans yet, but ever since things spiraled out of control I have developed an unusually strong urge to visit my mother. I need a break from all of this, and that includes any more conversations with Acosta.

"Okay, I'll keep that in mind. I know you are frustrated, but we will do our best to bring him to justice, no matter how long it takes."

"I understand and I'm sorry if I sound ornery. This has been very difficult. Thank you for your help." I hang up the phone, and before Taylor can ask, I tell him: "He's gone."

"Brazil?"

"Yes. The detective tried to lay it on softly, but he basically said it's like finding a needle in a haystack."

Taylor rests his forehead in his hand for a moment, and then he looks up. "I can find him. I can pay someone to find him," he says, stabbing his index finger into the kitchen counter.

"And then what? Taylor, he's probably in the fucking jungle somewhere living off of the land with a goddamn indigenous tribe. This is Eric we're talking about, he knows what he's doing. He's the last person you probably want on the lam."

"Goddamit!" Taylor slams his fist into his plate and it shatters. His hand begins to drip blood. "I fucking swear it, I'm going to destroy him! I will wait, patiently; he will slip again, he will make a mistake, and when I get my hands on him again, it will be for the last fucking time!"

His tone and the fire in his eyes paralyzes me. The wrath is not directed at me, but the rage is so palpable, so heavy, it feels as though he could explode at any moment.

"You're bleeding." I motion towards his hand, but he raises the other one to stop me. Taylor walks over to the sink and runs the wound under the faucet. "Let's just try to go back to the way it was. This could be a blessing," I reassure Taylor.

"Blessing…" He says under his breath in a mocking tone.

"I don't mean the situation, but the fact he's gone. We can just move on."

"You don't get it. There is no moving on."

"What do you mean?"

"It's either him, or me."

"Come on. Don't let him infect you like this."

"Why aren't you as angry as me? Don't you want to get him too?"

"Yes! For Christ's sake I just lied-!" I look around and lower my voice to a whisper. "I just fucking lied to the police so we could get him, but I don't want to let him ruin what we have. The bitterness will destroy you."

"Shyla, this is on me...on me! It's because of me that this happened to you, that he came into your life and because I didn't finish the job when I had the chance..."

"Don't say that. None of this is your fault!"

Taylor shakes his head, his vacant expression and pursed lips informing me his mind has gone elsewhere. "I'm going to go work out. I need to clear my head. I'll be downstairs."

"Are you mad at me?"

"No."

"Okay. Please don't go looking for him. He's gone and that's exactly what we wanted."

Taylor begins to clean the dishes, which is something I have never seen him do before. I sit quietly behind him, leaving him to stew in his silent fury. Finally, turns to me.

"Did you say you were going out of town? Did you mean us going to New York?"

"Actually, I was thinking I should go visit my mother. It's been a while, and like I mentioned, maybe this will give me some air so I can absorb all of this." The thought crosses my mind to invite Taylor, but I don't think he's ready for that. In fact, I'm not sure I am, and "meeting the 'rents" right now just seems so trivial.

"When?"

"Well, I was going to make a long weekend of it, take Friday off. I am going to call Chad and let him know something happened this weekend. Home invasion without all the personal details. I'm sure he'll cut me some slack."

"Do you want Harrison to come with?"

"Harrison? No, Eric's really gone this time. I just want to be normal, no security, no stalker step-brothers…"

"No ultra-kinky dom boyfriend with a sordid past?" I think he says it jokingly, but I am never sure with him.

"No…you're welcome to come. I didn't mean it that way. I didn't think you would be interested in meeting my mother."

"No, you should go see your mom alone, have a chance to be a kid again and escape all this madness." And with that, Taylor throws the dishrag on the sink and heads downstairs to the gym.

I watch him walk away, saddened by the guilt I know he holds for what happened to me. Things are so tense now that it never seems like the right time to tell him what I've learned about his mother. At best, he will feel betrayed by my snooping around, and rightly so; at worst, he will never trust me again. Eventually, I will have to tell him. He needs to know the truth whether he wants to or not. Some time away at my mom's will allow me map out how I will break the news to him. I call Chad.

"Hello? Chad speaking."

"Hey Chad, it's Shyla. Sorry, I'm calling from Taylor's phone."

"No problem, what's up?"

"Well, everything is okay and I don't want you to freak out, but someone broke into my condo and attacked me."

"Attacked? Oh my god! Are you alright?"

"Yes, I'm fine. Everything is okay, I was with the police until late into the night." Then I hear Kristin's familiar voice in the background.

"Okay…Kristin is freaking out, I'm gonna pass the phone to her before she rips my face off…"

"Shyla! Oh my god! You were attacked? What the fuck happened? Are you okay?"

"Yes! I was going to call you next, I swear. I didn't know you were with Chad. You two are spending a lot of time together." I hope her budding relationship is not nearly as tumultuous as mine.

"What happened?"

"Someone snuck into the condo, I guess to steal something, and I walked in. We struggled so I am a little beat up."

"Oh my god," Kristin's voice sounds shaky on the other end.

"I'm okay, really. Don't worry about me."

"Do the police know who it was?"

"Can we talk about this another time? I love that you're with Chad, but he's still my boss and I need a little privacy."

"Of course! Can I come over today?"

"I don't have any specific plans, I'm at Taylor's for the time being."

"Sure. Do you want to do dinner?"

"Yeah, let's. I'm going to see my mom later this weekend. Actually, that's why I wanted to talk to Chad."

"Oh yeah, I forgot you called him," she laughs. "I'll pass the phone back to him. Love you, and I'll see you later, okay? I just cannot believe it."

"I know, it's crazy. I'm fine though, really."

There is the sound of the phone bumping around a bit, then Chad gets back on the line. "Hey Shyla, it's me again."

"Yeah, so I wanted to let you know because I am a little beat up. There was a struggle…I didn't want to freak you out tomorrow."

"You're coming in?"

"Well…I'm okay."

"Take tomorrow off, please."

"Actually, I was hoping to take Friday off to visit my mom in light of this disaster. So I don't want to get too far behind."

"It's up to you, but you can do most of your assignments from home this week. It's all about your comfort level. I know it can be hard to have to rehash the story to people and with any visible injuries, people will ask." I wonder to myself if Chad would be this understanding if he wasn't crushing so hard on my best friend, but I am grateful for the latitude.

"Okay, well I'll see how I feel tomorrow. If I stay home, you won't miss me, I'll be in touch and get everything done."

"I know you will."

"Thanks so much for understanding Chad. You're the best."

"Don't mention it. I'll talk to you soon."

I wasn't expecting to be able to stay home all week, and the surprise is welcome. The thought of showing up to work with a busted lip, a bruised neck, and cuts on my arms wasn't something I had fully thought out. And while I know intellectually that Eric is gone, I can't shake the feeling that I am being watched. Hopefully working from home this week will let the fact that Eric is gone for good register.

Instead of calling my mom next, I choose to surprise her with my visit. My mother now lives in Massachusetts. She moved about three years ago when she was offered the position of executive director at a drug rehabilitation center. It was a very proud moment for her and me. She suffered greatly from the loss of my father and it took many years for her to get back on her feet and regain her independence. Since my father's family wanted nothing to do with me, the only family we had was my aunt, her sister, who lived out of state. It made for hard times growing up. I never could afford the perks that a lot of my friends had; no vacations, no nice clothes, no allowance. During the really bad times, food was scarce. Most times, we had each other and only what we absolutely needed.

When I saw my mother struggle, I often felt like I was a burden, even though she never expressed that I was ever anything other than the person she loved most on Earth. Yet, I could see the weight on her shoulders, the heaviness in her eyes and I knew I was at least partly responsible for her troubles. Then, after years of trying to hold it all together, she too turned to the bottle. I was crushed in high school when I saw my mother slowly fall apart under the loneliness and responsibility. That's when the cutting started. A side of me felt guilty about my presence, the fact that I was a daily reminder of my father, but another side of me was angry with her, for allowing herself to be so weak and for abandoning me for her own brand of escape. She was all I had and then she left me just like my father; maybe not physically, but in every other way. I felt so numb to my predicament and the cutting made me feel; it was my personal brand of coping. Something about brightness of the red blood was a thrill, and the danger made me feel alive. I didn't want to drink, because that only numbed me more. I wanted to feel, I wanted to feel things with intensity. Pain seemed to be the only thing that could bring me that.

Luckily, around that time I met Kristin, and something about her and I just clicked. I didn't feel so alone anymore. I started laughing again. When she found out about my morbid tendencies, she didn't treat me like a freak, while at the same time making it clear that she was not okay with my self-harm. When my mother decided to turn her life around, it created a crack in the wall of my self-loathing where I could break through. She started to smile again too. Slowly, over time, the need to cut was not so great and by the time I was a freshman in college, newly in love with an adorable, tall, lanky, amber-eyed boy, the urge had all but entirely disappeared. The stability was great, I felt so "normal," and "adjusted," but after so many years of stillness, I began to miss the rush of danger, the thrill and the pain of that first cut. It was right around that time that Taylor walked into my life and I could smell the danger on his skin. It smelled delicious.

After the call, I find myself with nothing to do. I could attempt some work, but am just too full of nervous energy to accomplish anything of significance yet too jittery to sit and watch TV. I wander around the house; strangely enough, there are some rooms I have yet to explore. During my tenure at Holden Industries, I never went into various rooms for professional reasons…well, except for that *one time*. After Taylor and I started our relationship, it just never happened. We were always together doing our thing and never really got around to the grand tour. I make my way upstairs, finally using the staircase to climb to the second level. First, I poke my head into a few bedrooms, which are decorated in a minimalist fashion. I smile to myself wondering why this extreme introvert would have so many guest bedrooms. I think of his subs and where they might have stayed. That hot and jealous sensation creeps up, but that only makes me think of it more. *Did he leave them upstairs here until he was ready to beckon them?* There is one very large bedroom with its own huge bathroom. I imagine this would be the preferred bedroom of a longterm guest such as a sub. *Ugh.*

Eventually, I make my way to an office. It's smaller than the one downstairs, but still bigger than the living room of my old apartment. The shelves are lined with books and photos. There is one photo, tinted with age, in a frame on the desk. A man and a blond woman, smiling, standing next to a beautiful dark-haired boy. *Oh my god, that's Taylor!* It's so hard to imagine the tall, brooding man I am completely enamored with as this little boy. And while he should be smiling, engulfed in the embrace of these people, he is off to the side, alone, not a speck of joy in his expression. His father, tall and strikingly handsome, tries to hold in a mischievous, crooked smile. Taylor's right, he looks so much like his father, except his father's brow is much darker, heavier. The platinum blond woman with bone-straight, shoulder-length hair must be his stepmother, based on what I know about his life and his age in the picture. She smiles, but it appears forced, as if some invisible force is tugging down at the sides of her mouth. A small hand peeks in from the corner of the picture, separated from its owner by the composition of the photo. *It must be Eric.* I wonder if he was left out of the photo entirely or cut out later by Taylor.

Gently, I return the frame to the desk and scan the bookcase. It is full of very old books, and I make a note to later ask Taylor if he collects them. Then my eye catches something out of place. The spine clearly does not belong to a book. I carefully glide it out of the bookshelf and see it's a photo album. My heart skips with glee and curiosity. I am so hungry for knowledge about Taylor's life and his family, I open it without hesitation. A photo slips out of the album and floats to the floor, landing face-down. I carefully pick it up, hoping not to bend it. When I flip it over, it feels as though someone has stuck their hand in my chest and clenched my heart.

A tall, thin blond girl with a bright, wide smile tucks her chin away from the camera. Her hair is long, nearly down to her lower back. Her golden waves are occasionally interspersed with light brown locks, and adorned with a single flower by her temple. She wears a loose-fitting white dress peppered with faded blue and pink flowers. Her bare feet bury into the grass. The bushes that surround her hold the same flower as the one she is wearing; the innocence of a girl picking a flower from a bush and placing it in her hair breaks my heart. I know what her future has in store, and from the hopeful look in her glimmering blue-green eyes, she has no idea. *Those eyes*. Sometimes I think they will be the death of me.

"What are you doing?"

I let out a loud yelp, still shaken up from yesterday's events.

"Uh, I — I was just looking around."

"Do you have any concept of privacy? You're just snooping around?"

"I wasn't snooping around."

"Well, you could've fooled me."

"I didn't think there was a problem. I mean this was just sitting in a bookshelf, out in the open."

"Those concepts are mutually exclusive, Shyla."

"I wasn't snooping, like looking for stuff, I was just curious about the parts of the house I hadn't seen and then I came upon this office."

"I doubt that."

"What the hell is that supposed to mean?"

"You know exactly what it means."

"No I don't. Please don't play games and tell me exactly what you are referring to."

"You're looking for the journal."

Honestly, the thought had not crossed my mind, and I can't believe how offended I am by the accusation even though it's pretty logical. Sure, most women would be obsessed with finding the mysterious book of her boyfriend's ex-lovers, but Taylor's stalker brother, my new hobby as a detective of cult murders, and my new job have left little time for trying to find sex diaries. I guess it says a lot about my predicament that that task has fallen so low on my list of todos.

"Seriously? That's what you think I was doing? After all of this, all that I am willing to go through, you think I am sneaking around behind your back?" *Oh no, here come the waterworks.* This is not the time to come at me with anything that might even remotely touch anything having to do with emotions. I am just a hot mess. "That is so fucked up, Taylor. I just wanted to find out more about you, learn about your family when I saw the photo on the desk and you think that I was looking for what? Incriminating material? You can be so hurtful sometimes. Why are you so protective of that journal? Are you hiding something?"

"No, I destroyed it. Not because I was hiding anything, but because I don't want to hold onto it. I thought it was a way to protect myself, but it was just another burden, having that thing around."

"Well I guess I'll have to take your word for it. But what about the other way around? You have to do the same for me," I say, clearly heartbroken by his tone.

Taylor watches me hold back tears in silence, seemingly dumbfounded by my emotional reaction. "I didn't mean to hurt your feelings. You did snoop around once before, remember? It's not like I just pulled this out of my ass."

"I'm sorry I did it that one time. It's not like me, I just had a hunch and I had to know. I'm sorry, okay?" He grabs my arm and pulls me close to him. He hasn't showered yet, but I find his natural scent intoxicating. "You smell yummy."

Taylor laughs. "Really? I just worked out."

"I know, that's why you smell so yummy."

"Am I gonna find you sniffing out my shoes or something? Do you have some sort of odor fetish?"

"Oh you should talk, Mr. Dom!"

Taylor lets out a faint smile and sighs. "I didn't mean to snap at you, I'm just stressed, and I know you are too, so it's not okay for me to take it out on you. I'm not used to living with someone all the time, even as much as I love having you around, I am not used to navigating what that's like."

"I know," I say tenderly.

"Why are you smiling?"

"Nothing, it's silly."

"No, tell me."

"When you were a kid, did you ever watch Beauty and the Beast?"

"No, I was too busy being a badass."

"Oh, nevermind."

"I'm joking!"

"Oh, god, I can never tell with you! Well, you remember that scene when the Beast finds Belle in the west wing?"

"Oh christ, so now I'm the Beast?"

I start to laugh uncontrollably. "Nevermind...that's why I didn't want to mention it. You're way too hot anyways."

Taylor looks down at me warmly. "You know, if you want me to show you stuff, you can just ask."

"Well, I know how you hate to talk about things from the past. Plus, I never took you as someone to have pictures around."

"You're right, but you can still ask me." He steps away for a second and then leads me by my hand to a large leather chair, pulling me onto this lap. "Did you look through the album?"

"No, I just pulled it out when you came in."

Taylor's eyes glance over to the single picture I hold in my hand. "So you found her?"

"Yes. Sorry to bring her up. She just slipped out of the album."

"No, it's okay. I've seen that picture for years. It was the one my dad kept in my room growing up."

"She was beautiful."

"Yes."

"Do you know when this picture was from?"

"No, I never asked."

"You have her eyes."

"I know."

"Can I ask you something?"

"Well, I guess I have no choice, now that I said it was okay to ask me anything."

"Why did you keep the photo all these years? I mean you say you hate her, that you want nothing to do with her, but you held onto this."

Taylor rests his face on the back of my shoulder and sighs.

"You know, I never thought about it. I guess it does seem odd that I would keep it."

"Well, any boy would want to keep the last memory of his mom alive. But the way you speak about her is what makes me surprised that you kept it."

Taylor sighs again. "You know when I was in the hospital today, I remembered something that I hadn't thought about in a long time. Something I never told anyone."

I turn to face him, bringing my feet up in the large chair as he cradles me in his arms. "What was it?"

"The person who discovered me after the suicides was a woman. I don't remember much about her, besides that she was a friend of my mom. I remember she was familiar, someone I trusted at the time. The room was really dark because they had drawn all the shades and so I had been in the dark without light for days."

"Oh my god."

"When she opened the door, my eyes were so sensitive to the light and she was engulfed in it. At first, I thought that I had died and she was an angel. She was beautiful, she had long dark brown hair." He slides a tendril of my hair between his fingers. "She started to cough, I presume because of the smell. And she kept mumbling something over and over. I think she was panicking, calling out names of people she knew. She was definitely crying."

"I can't even imagine."

"I started to cry out, but I was so weak, I could barely make a sound." Taylor's eyes look out into the distance, as if he can see the scene replaying in front of us. "Then she spotted me and ran over. I remember her tripping over the bodies, then she started to crawl towards me. She scooped me up and I hugged her so hard. I mean a tornado could have ripped through that building and I would have never let her go." I try so hard to hold back the emotion, but a single tear drops down my cheek. Then another. Taylor snaps out of his trance for a second and notices the second tear. He wipes it off of my face and pushes some hair behind my ear.

"So what happened next?" I ask.

"Well, it's kind of blurry, but the next thing I remember is being in the hospital, which is why I fucking hate them, not just because of all of the people. I didn't want to let this woman go, she was the only person I knew, everyone else was strange. I had spent my entire life up until that point at the commune. I didn't know what hospitals were, or the police, I didn't know these people were there to help me. So many adults had hurt me up until that point. Eventually, they had to pull me away from her and I screamed, I bit, I kicked, I cried. She cried. It took several people. All these strangers, putting their hands all over me, ripping me from her arms." He stops.

"That must have been really hard and scary for you." The act of speaking distracts me from holding back my tears and they begin to drip down steadily. He simply nods. We are silent for a few moments, and I lay my head on his shoulder.

"She held me the entire time, until my dad showed up, which is when they ripped me away. He left for the first flight out to get me as soon as he found out. Before I was to leave with him, they gave her one last opportunity to speak with me. So this woman crouched in front of me, as I sat there with my head down, and she whispered to me. 'Taylor, I may never see you again, but it is important you never forget this. Your mother loved you very much. People may try to make you think otherwise, but I know she did. Don't let yourself forget that.' Then she kissed me on the forehead and left. My dad took me immediately after. She was the last person who I ever let hug me, until I met you."

"Do you know what happened to her?"

"No idea. That was the last I ever saw of her. But I guess that's why I kept the photo. In a way, it was the last wish of the woman who saved me."

CHAPTER FIVE

Taylor's story is so overwhelming that I have no words for him. Instead, I use my touch to express my love for him by laying in his arms. Now I understand what that loss, his inability to physically connect, has meant all this time. When they ripped Taylor from the arms of the only person he knew, into a strange and unfamiliar world, however better it really was, he was lost. In this new and strange world, the people laid their hands on you to take you away from the people you loved, and if you gave up your heart to someone and embraced them, you could be setting yourself up for another heart-crushing loss. We both nod off, not having had much sleep the night before. Eventually, I wake to Taylor shaking underneath me, swinging one of his arms. Luckily, the other arm is pinned down by my weight. His eyelids flutter, the whites exposed with each movement of his eyelids. It's been a while, but he must be having one of those dreams again. Quickly, I rise off of him to keep a safe distance. I heard once that you shouldn't wake someone up when they are sleep walking, so I don't know if I should interrupt him. It's not exactly sleep walking, and I debate what would be the better of the two evils. Suddenly, he starts to speak. "No...no...no!" Each "no" gets successively louder, starting as a mumble and eventually to a yell, as if he is fighting someone. The level of distress he is under freaks me out, so I begin to softly call his name.
"Taylor."

"No…no…"

I try a little louder.

"Taylor."

"Stop…please no."

It's clear that unless I scream, I won't wake him up from his terror.

"Taylor! Taylor!" He jumps up, startled. He wildly looks around, trying to register his surroundings. It's as if he still can't see the world in front of him. "Taylor, it's okay…it's me. You're okay, you're home with me. It's okay."

He scratches his head and says something incoherent.

"It's me…Shy. You were having a bad dream." He squints at me (clearly he was in a very deep state), lets out an exasperated sigh, and buries his head in his hands. His hair is wild and he looks like he's just been through a battle, which in a way, he has. "Taylor?"

"Gimme a sec," he says while keeping his head down. "What the fuck?" he murmurs to himself. After 30 seconds or so, he looks up at me and sighs. "I am so fucking out of it. Did I freak you out?"

"No, I was just worried about you. You seemed terrified. I wasn't sure if I should wake you."

"You did the right thing. It's just that it's really confusing to come out of it, it takes me a while to figure out where I am and shit. I shouldn't have napped like that."

"You should be able to nap."

"Not with you around. I can't risk it. Besides, I never nap, your sleepiness is contagious."

"Hey!" I say defensively.

"Well, I am going to shower and get out of this daze I'm in."

"Can I join?"

"Sure, pretty girl."

"Oh I forgot to mention, is it okay if Kristin comes by for dinner?"

"Mi casa es su casa, but are you sure you want her to see you like this? What did you tell her?"

"I told them someone broke into my house. She is going to want more details regardless."

"You're not going to tell her about Eric?"

"Which version?"

"I don't know. That's my point, this shit gets twisted fast."

It occurs to me, in both versions of the story, Eric rapes me. I can't tell her the real story and put her in any position to have to lie to the cops or betray me under oath, but the second version is so violent, and I don't want her thinking that's how it happened.

"You're right. I'll wear long sleeves so she doesn't see the cuts, she knows all about that and will know I relapsed. I'll just say it was a robbery attempt, that's what I implied over the phone anyway. I don't want her to worry about me and it's not fair to get her mixed up in this."

"I'm glad you agree. Oh, just so you know. I called someone to find out what's going on with Em. I am sure she is off living her life happily married with 10 babies by now, but you asked." *Em? I'll admit, his little abbreviation of her name makes me jealous. It's intimate, in a way.*

"Thank you."

Instead of showering, Taylor and I grab a bottle of wine and take a nice long soak in the bowl-shaped tub. *Finally!* We lay in the water for about an hour, talking about anything but the heavy topics we've been forced to confront these past few days.

Taylor insists on picking up dinner from our favorite Italian place so that we don't have to cook, which is fine by me. While he is out, Kristin arrives at the house.

"Oh my god, your lip! Thank god you're okay. Okay, now tell me what happened?"

"I walked in on a robbery. He freaked out and we struggled, but then he panicked and left."

"I just can't believe this happened. Do you think it's because of Taylor? Like people know he's rich?" *Well, you've got half of it right.*

"It might be, the police are looking for him, but since he didn't take anything, unless he confesses, it will be hard to find him. I didn't see his face."

"You seem to be taking it so well. I would be freaking out if I were you. That is so scary. Are you sure you're okay?"

"Oh trust me, I was. Taylor has really helped me though, he makes me feel protected and I'll be staying with him for a while."

"Awww. You two are so cute. I'm glad you're okay and please be more careful!"

"So are you and my boss! Please tell me what the deal is. You two have been spending so much time together."

Kristin lets out a gleaming smile. "Yeah, we've been spending the night at each other's places. I really, really like him. You know, I've dated so many jerks, and I used to look at you and Rick...oh sorry, too soon?"

"No it's fine, I get what you're saying. You always dated the bad boys, and I had the nice guy." *My how the tables have turned.*

"Yes, exactly. It wasn't that I didn't like nice guys, but I never found one who could hold my interest, but Chad, he's fun, and sweet, and stylish, and smart..."

"Wow, you really, really like him. I guess I'll have to prepare for the fact that you two are going to be a thing.

Just don't break his heart, or he'll hate me for introducing you two."

"Never! He thinks you're great by the way."

"Tell him I want a raise." I wink and we both laugh. "Seriously though, I am happy for you two, Chad has a big heart."

"I don't want to count my chickens so to speak, but yeah, he's kind of awesome. Where's Taylor?"

"Oh, he went out to get dinner. You don't mind if he hangs out with us, do you?"

"No, not at all! I had a lot of fun last time."

I remember how nervous I was for them to first meet, which then reminds me of the awkward hug. "Hey, I know this is going to sound weird, and please don't take this personally…but could you not hug him when he comes back?"

"Ummm…okay, I guess."

"It has nothing to do with you, or me, he has a thing about people touching him."

"Really? Why?"

"I don't really know…well, just between you and I, some stuff in his childhood. He gets like anxiety about it. Please do not repeat that to anyone."

"Oh course not. That's really sad. What about you? Does he hug you?"

"Yes, but it's different. He and I, you know…we have something."

Taylor walks in with Harrison, who is holding several take-out bags of food. Harrison places them on the counter, nods at me, and walks out.

"Jesus Taylor, are we feeding the entire city?" I ask.

"I didn't know what Kristin would like, so I went a little crazy. Kristin, good to see you again."

"Same here!" she says, a little googly-eyed by his presence. I'm sure she'll get used to him after a while.

He opens up the various containers and lines them up on the breakfast bar for us to help ourselves, which fills the room with appetite-inducing aromas. I pour three glasses of red wine for us, and Kristin and I sit in stools on the breakfast bar while Taylor stands at the counter facing us.

"So, you must have been freaked out by what happened to Shyla, huh?" Kristin asks.

Taylor's face tightens, Kristin doesn't realize how personal that question is. Taylor finishes chewing his bite. "Yes, it's really upsetting. I'm just glad she's okay now and I am not going to let anything like that happen to her again." The room gets uncomfortably silent, Taylor emits a tense energy. I choose to take the conversation in a lighter direction.

"So, Kristin is officially dating my boss!" Taylor nods and lets out a hesitant smile but seems distracted, I know it's because he can't take his mind off of Eric again. I turn to Kristin, "Have you heard the surround sound in here? Let me get some music going, it's incredible, it'll feel like we're in a restaurant. As I hop up to grab my laptop, which connects wirelessly to the speaker system, Taylor's cell phone rings. He picks it up, something I am used to with Taylor: when dating a CEO, the cell phone gets answered no matter the time or setting. While I am surfing for songs on my laptop, his face drops a bit as he quietly exchanges some words and then hangs up.

"Ladies, I'm afraid I have to run out for a bit, some last minute business came up." My gut tells me there is more to the story than this.

"Is everything okay?" I ask.

"Yup, everything is fine. Have fun, take any car you want out for a joy ride." His eagerness to allow me to take any of his cars only adds to my suspicions. *What is he trying to distract me from?*

"Let me walk you out." I say.

"It's fine, no need."

"I insist," I say sternly.

I follow him through the foyer and once we are out of earshot, I ask "Is everything okay? This doesn't feel like business."

"Yes, everything is fine. I might be in the office for a while. I'll be back later tonight. Nothing to worry about, okay?"

I sigh, knowing further conversation is pointless. He'll tell me what he wants, when he wants. He leaves in a rush, without giving me a kiss goodbye.

When I enter the great room again, Kristin asks, "Is everything okay? Did I fuck up again? First the hug, and then I think I upset him by asking about the break-in. He must hate me!"

"No! Not at all, he likes you! Trust me, if he didn't like you, he would never have you over. He's just stressed with work. It's the downside of being Mr. Big Shot."

"So what did he say about a joy ride?" Kristin asks inquisitively.

"I don't know…" Normally, I would jump at the opportunity, but I have an unrelenting residual sense of fear of leaving the house without Taylor since my encounter with Eric. "I'm tired and literally beat up."

Kristin pauses for a second, and then asks hesitantly, "*Can I see?*" Intentionally, I wore a long sleeved chiffon button down shirt with jeans, to cover up as much of the bruises as possible. I can see however, how that would leave a lot to the imagination. One thing is for sure, I cannot show her the cuts on my arms. "Sure," I say, opening up the top buttons of the blouse to reveal the bruises around my neck.

"Oh my god!" Kristin reveals a look of horror. "That son of a bitch." *If she only knew the real reason behind those bruises.*

"There are more bruises on my legs, from banging into stuff."

"Can I just say, you're a fucking badass? You wrestled an intruder!" *No I cowered in fear, and stood there as he kissed me.*

"I am hardly a badass, just lucky…I never showed you around, have I?" Instead of going for a joyride, I take Kristin around the property. Eventually, we find ourselves at the pool.

"Is this thing heated?" Kristin asks as she kneels over and puts her hand in.

"I dunno, you tell me."

"It feels warm," she says, in a mischievous tone.

"You want to go for a swim?" I ask in disbelief.

"Hells yeah, this pool is fucking awesome!"

"I don't have bathing suits here."

"So?" Normally, I wouldn't worry one bit, but the cuts and the bruises would lead to more questions. "Oh come on, you need to have some fun, get your mind off of the bullshit."

"Okay, but only if we turn the lights off, since Harrison might see us otherwise." I fiddle around with the lights a bit until I find the dimmest possible setting. "Check this out," I yell from the pool house. Music begins to play.

"Oh yeah!" Kristin shouts as she pulls her shirt off overhead, swaying her hips to the music. Kristin is taller than me, and has a beautiful, curvy, voluptuous figure that she wears with full confidence. Sometimes, I feel like I disappear next to her with my petite figure. Her excitement puts a big smile on my face, she has always known how to take me out of a funk. I dance inside of the pool house, wine in hand as I sashay out onto the pool deck. Kristin unclips her bra, and I can barely make out the outline of her breasts in the dim light. "What song is this?" she asks.

"It's called Royals," I say side-stepping.

"How fitting," she says sarcastically, then she dives in. "Come on!"

"If you see bruises, don't freak out."

"I can't see shit, you made sure of that!" I pull off my clothes and do a running cannonball into the water. "Shyla, why would you ever want to leave this house? This pool is awesome!"

"Honestly, it's my first time in here! Taylor always swims these perfect laps, he makes the pool look so un-fun."

"Do I?" Taylor's voice asks from the deck.

"Oh my god!" Both Kristin and I exclaim.

In the darkness, I can barely make out his devilish smirk. Strangely, I feel like we've been busted by one of our dads; it might be because Kristin brings out the kid in me.

"Should we get out?" I ask.

"No please, enjoy. Apparently I haven't been making good use of this thing," he says sarcastically.

"You have to join us then," Kristin declares scandalously. If any other girl invited him into the pool while naked, I would have given her a Vulcan death-grip, but it's Kristin, whom I trust wholeheartedly. I expect Taylor to politely decline, but he shrugs and then starts to unbutton his shirt. I lean over to Kristin and whisper, "brace yourself," in her ear.

Taylor removes his shirt and then pulls his undershirt overhead. He slips off his pants. The vague outline of his penis is visible once he removes his boxer briefs. Watching him from a distance, being just a spectator to his statuesque physique instantly makes me horny and giddy. At this moment, I realize this scene is only unfolding in front of us because Kristin and I have polished off most of a bottle of wine. As for Taylor, this side of him is a surprise to me, and it excites me thoroughly. He dives into the water and disappears for a few moments, popping up in front of me. I let out a yell and he picks me up out of the water, then throws me a surprisingly long distance.

"See, I know how to play," he says, swimming towards the edge of the pool to steal my wine.

I look over to Kristin, who hooks her hand over her mouth and mouths an, "oh my god," to me as she points to his flawless, bare ass. I smirk and nod in agreement. "I'm going to get another bottle," Taylor says, pulling out of the pool, his muscular upper back dripping wet and gleaming in the moonlight as he walks, completely to my surprise, butt-naked into the house. It is completely lit and through its glass facade, his naked body is completely visible to us.

"I cannot believe him," I say, shaking my head in disbelief.

"It's fine by me," Kristin says with a smirk.

"Oh shut up!" I say as I splash her. She and I are engaged in a vigorous splash fight by the time Taylor comes back.

"It's like a cheesy soft porn," he says, sliding back in. He fills his glass all the way to the top, which strikes me as unusual, but perhaps like me, he feels the very strong need to unwind. "So whose idea was it to skinny dip?"

"Me..." Kristin, raises her hand hesitantly.

"I have an idea." Taylor says. I know from the tone in his voice, he means trouble.

"What?" I ask with an eyebrow raised.

"Have you ever dropped E?"

"Ecstasy?" Kristin pops in.

"Yeah."

"No," I say and the exact same time as Kristin says "yeah."

"Well have you?" I ask Taylor in disbelief.

"Yeah."

"I thought you never did drugs."

"E is different. You don't feel altered. You just feel happy. I mean I do it once every couple of years. It just seems fitting tonight."

"I'm down," Kristin says.

"You guys...really?" I ask again in disbelief.

"He's right, it's not like shrooms or anything else, you don't feel out of it. You should at least try it once. Come on, you've smoked weed."

"My grandma does weed. I've never popped pills. I don't know."

"No pressure, doll." He says, taking a swig of wine. I give Taylor a strange look, I don't recognize him right now.

"Hey-oh!" Another male voice comes from the pool deck. *What the fuck is Henry doing here?*

"Henry! What are you going here?" I ask.

"I invited him," Taylor interjects. *There is officially some tomfoolery amidst.*

"Oh...well okay. Um, Kristin, this is Henry. Henry, Kristin."

"I have the goods," he says, pulling a small baggie from his pocket. Taylor had this planned before ever mentioning it to us. Without skipping a beat, Henry rips his clothes off. This night has taken a wildly unexpected turn.

Taylor turns to me and leans into my ear. "You don't have to do anything, but it would please me greatly if you did. Remember what I said about giving you unimaginable pleasure?" As soon as he pulls away, Kristin pops a pill.

"Kristin!" I say.

"What?" she shrugs innocently. Taylor is next. Now I am the only one not doing it.

"Come on Shyla, we wouldn't make you do anything that wasn't great. You can't be the only one not rolling." Kristin says.

Under the water, Taylor places his hand on my ass and gives it a hearty squeeze. *I'm too old for this shit.* "Okay, but if I like start to think I am an eagle or some shit, I am going to be so fucking pissed at you guys." They all laugh, and Henry hands me a pill. This is my first time seeing him since the "elevator pitch," when he drunkenly tried to make out with me in St. Petersburg, and there is some residual awkwardness. I wash the pill down with wine and expect some sort of instantaneous, magical effect, but there is nothing.

"This is it?" I ask the group.

"Give it a bit," Henry says through a smile. We decide unanimously to spend some time in the hot tub. As we walk over, I lean into Kristin's ear and whisper "I am so going to kill you for this." She gives me an innocent shrug and slides into the hot tub.

Taylor sits next to me with his arm around my shoulders. Henry and Kristin sit on the opposite side, but at a comfortable distance from each other. I quickly come to the conclusion that Taylor is trying to set them up and I want to be furious with him, but for some reason, I just can't. Then I look at Henry, and I am filled with an overwhelming sense of love and forgiveness. Out of nowhere, I blurt out "Henry, I just want you to know that I think you are an awesome beautiful human being. There is no awkwardness, and I completely forgive you. I love you. I love you guys." There is half a second of silence where Taylor, Kristin, and Henry look at each other awkwardly and then they all burst out into laughter.

"You're rolling out of your mind!" Henry says in an especially jubilant manner.

"*I am?* — I am!" Suddenly the world feels like a beautiful, limitless place, full of wonder and love. I feel so...so...happy. Unadulterated euphoria; I don't think I've felt like this since Christmas morning as a child. And while I know I took a drug, it feels so real, I don't feel like I'm on anything at all. I can genuinely say I love everyone from the bottom of my heart. The world is a perfect place right now.

Henry addresses my statement. "Thank you and I'm sorry, and I love you too. I love Taylor like a brother and I am happy that you two are together." We are in a supernova of love, riding on a space-unicorn into a cloud of cotton candy. The next hour or so, it might have been two hours, because time seems to move independently from us, consists of us singing and taking turns jumping into the pool and the hot tub. During this time, I notice Henry and Kristin becoming more and more comfortable with each other. Instead of wanting to stop her, or talk some sense into her, I want them to continue, to share their love and beauty with each other. It all seems so harmless. *How can spreading these wonderful feelings be a bad thing?* Finally, I spot them, together in the hot tub, making out.

"Taylor, oh my god, look!" I point.

"I know," he says with a big smile. "Not sure why I didn't think of it sooner." Taylor leans in and kisses me. I feel so much a part of him, as if we are the two lovers in Klimt's "The Kiss". I get so hot, so horny. After a while, Taylor stops me. "Looks like things have escalated," he whispers. Laying on one of the outdoor beds on the deck, under the moonlight, Henry's head is in between Kristin's legs.

"Oh my god!" I let out one of those shout-whispers. "He's going down on her!"

"They'll probably end up fucking."

"This is bad," I say. "Chad."

"Oh they'll be fine. They're just having a little fun. Kristin and Chad just started seeing each other. Watch." Taylor says, turning me so that I am sitting between his legs with my back to him. We watch in silence as Taylor glides his hand down my belly under the water, and begins to fiddle with my clit.

"This is so bad." I say.

"Shhh…" He whispers into my ear. "There's no such thing if it makes you feel good."

I moan as he plays with me. It surprises me how attractive I find Henry's body as he thrusts into Kristin, but I'm not sure if it's me or the E thinking that. Taylor softly kisses my neck, one hand fondling my breasts, the other massaging my lips. Such a simple act feels outrageously pleasurable. I'm not sure why. *Is it because I'm rolling? Is it because this is so naughty? Is it the presence of the two really good-looking naked men?* Taylor bites my earlobe and tugs on it with his teeth just slightly. Henry and Kristin seem to have no idea that we are watching and are very much into their own sexual adventure. In an effort to keep our little secret I presume, Taylor covers my mouth so that when I come, the sounds of my moans are muffled. I didn't think it was possible, but I feel even more joyous, more bold. I turn to Taylor.

"I want to see you touch yourself. I want to see you hold your dick and make yourself come." I beg.

Taylor cocks his head. "Oh really?"

"Yes, something about you holding your dick is so hot."

"Come on," he says, guiding me out of the water and into the pool house. "Lie on your back, keep your legs spread. I want to see your pussy." I lay down, obeying his commands. "Spread the lips open, I want to see the ripe, pink flesh."

"Okay," I bite my lip.

He stands over me. From this angle can fully admire his chiseled, long torso, and his thickness as he grips it with his large hand. He begins to jerk himself as he rolls his eyes back for a moment. Then he stares at my naked body like a hungry animal, with every second his breathing becomes shallower. Finally, his knees become weak.

"You look so fucking hot right now baby. Your cock looks so hard and thick. Come on my pussy, let your load out on it." I keep the lips spread open, ready to catch his cum.

He drops to his knees so that his dick is level with my groin and lets out a deep sigh as he comes all over it, releasing an especially large load. I think he's done, but he takes it a step further.

"Taste it," he says. I hesitate for a moment, but then I take my index finger, and run it along my labia. Then I place my entire finger in my mouth and slowly suck it to the tip. "Mmmm." I say with a smirk, biting my lower lip. Taylor collapses to my side with a huge smile.

"I love it when you act slutty with me. See, I told you you wouldn't regret it."

❊ ❊ ❊

The feeling of complete and utter lowness I feel when I open my eyes the next morning is only amplified by the incredible heights I was soaring the night before. None of it was real. I will never feel that completely relieved of burden, of pain, or doubt. It was all just a magical little pill, a chemical reaction. Taylor is not by my side; I peek my head out of the pool house and Kristin and Henry are no longer there. My clothes lay on a chair in the pool house, it seems Taylor was kind enough to spare me the embarrassment of trying to find them in broad daylight. Sluggishly, I pull myself out of the pool area and walk past the sliding glass doors into the great room. If yesterday felt like a unicorn was shooting me out of its ass, today it feels like I am attending that unicorn's funeral. Taylor is reheating leftovers on the range.

"Hi," I say groggily.

"Good morning," Taylor says, almost formally. It seems he too is no longer floating in the cloud of universal love.

"Where is everyone?"

"They were gone when I woke up. I think we fell asleep around four in the morning."

"Fuck, I cannot believe Kristin and Henry hooked up. I have to call her. I feel like total ass. Like a five-foot-plus turd. Do you?"

"Well I am a little down from yesterday. It hits some people harder than others."

"I feel really depressed, and stupid. Really, really, stupid. The shit I was saying last night. It wasn't me. You didn't say as much stupid shit."

"I comport myself differently is all. Trust me, I felt it. It's actually nice to feel joy the way other people do. At the same time, it's a great reminder that what we feel is really just a constellation of neurochemicals acting in concert."

"How romantic of you. Seriously, I feel like I hate myself."

"Eat something. Chill out today. You'll be fine. You had fun, that's the kind of fun you would have if you had no inhibitions. It's nice to experience that once in a while."

"I'm not sure how I feel about you plotting out Kristin and Henry."

"That was all them, I simply didn't want her to feel like the third wheel and since Henry is so affable, I thought he would make for good company. Henry mentioned he had the goods, but I never set the expectation that he was going to get laid. I'm not surprised though, they're both outgoing, attractive people. They're both adults Shy, don't put that on me."

"Where did you go last night? I know that wasn't business."

"You're in a funk." He turns to put some food on a plate.

"You're dodging the question."

"Considering your current mood, it might not be the best time to talk about anything."

"Well now you have to tell me!"

Taylor's face suddenly drops and becomes very serious. I know that look and he only reserves it for painful news.

"You sure you want to hear this?"

"You know me well enough to know the answer. Spit it out."

"So, like you asked, I had someone look into Em." *There he goes again, calling her Em. Vomit.* "Actually, it was Harrison, he knew I had company over, so he didn't want to walk in and tell me, he called instead so we could step away for a bit and talk it over."

"Tell you what? What is it Taylor?"

Taylor takes a deep breath. "Em is dead," he says, looking down at the kitchen counter, trying his best to avoid my eyes.

CHAPTER SIX

"She's dead? How?"

"Car accident. Drunk driving. A few months ago."

"Oh my god. She was drunk driving?"

"Yes."

My mind races. Maybe there is some validity in Eric's claim that I check out her story. On the other hand, it seems Taylor is being honest about what happened to her, I mean death *is* a worst-case scenario.

"And you didn't know that she died before yesterday?"

"Of course not, no idea until yesterday. I've had no contact with her since we parted ways, like I have said countless times."

"So you found out this news and then you decided to have a pool party?"

"I'm not sure what you're getting at with that question. I wasn't celebrating her death with a pool party."

"Your ex-girlfriend is dead and it's like nothing happened. You don't even care." I realize, it might not be so much that I care about how he feels about her, but that I have always feared that I could be the next Emily Brown.

"She's not my ex-girlfriend, at least not in the conventional sense. And if you must know, I did find the news upsetting, but what was I supposed to do? Walk in crying? Begging for hugs from you and Kristin? You know me better than that."

"I don't know, maybe show some human sympathy?" I say.

"People deal with death in different ways and you should know not to expect a typical reaction from me by now. You were having fun, you looked relaxed. It was nice to see that after what you've been through. I figured waiting to tell you was a good idea. You had fun last night, didn't you?"

"Any fun I had was because I had no idea that Emily was dead."

"You didn't even know Emily and she's been dead for months now. Maybe you should step out of yourself for a second and think about how the people who actually knew her felt."

"You felt good enough to watch your best friend fuck my best friend. My god, what the fuck did we do last night?"

"Aw, now you're going to get all self-righteous on me? No one put a gun to your head. You were *begging* me to cum on you."

"No, but everyone was begging me to do the E."

"That included Kristin, who seemed to be enjoying herself."

"Don't talk about her!"

"I'm not judging her. I think what she did was totally fine. You're the one freaking out!" Taylor says in frustration.

Eric's claim replays in my head: *You know you're slowly changing, to be the person that can fix him, but you can't…you may think the person you are becoming is by choice, but nothing around Taylor happens by choice.*

"What did you do to her?" I ask.

"Who are you talking about? Kristin?"

"Emily. What did you do to her?"

"You need to watch what you are about to say next Shyla. There are things that cannot be taken back once you say them."

"I don't mean that you killed her, but you changed her, didn't you?"

"Are you saying I drove her to drink and drive to her death? It was a freak accident."

"I don't know, but Eric —"

"Eric? Do tell, what did Eric say?" Taylor asks sarcastically, throwing his arms up in the air. "It's enough that I looked her up based on his bullshit suggestion to you. I cannot believe you are about to quote him. I mean, if you are trying to somehow prove to yourself that I have a heart by breaking it, then go ahead, say you believe what Eric has told you about me."

Something about the last thing he says, the vulnerability in it, stops me in my tracks. *What am I doing?* I am reacting hysterically. I steeple my fingers over my lips and take a deep breath. "I'm sorry. I should have never brought Eric into this, that was low of me. I don't know what I was thinking. I think I have just had more than I can handle as far as emotional stress, and each thing that happens seems to rattle me easier than the one before it. You're right, I didn't even know Emily and she had a life after you. To even think of blaming you is wrong. It's ridiculous." It seems my words have come a little too late into the conversation. His eyes look haunted, I should feel some sort of power being the only person who can hurt him, but instead I feel like an enormous asshole. "Taylor, I don't feel like myself right now. I mean it, I think my brain chemistry is fucked up from the E."

"Like I said, you'll be fine by tomorrow. You never have to do it again, I just thought you would have fun. I'm going to do some work in my office for a while." He takes his plate with him, which is something I have never seen him do, and walks down the hall, his normally proud posture displaying a slight slump.

I pull up my laptop and book an earlier-than-planned flight to see my mother. Now that I know I don't have to show up to work this week, and I can work from anywhere, I book something for Wednesday afternoon instead of Friday.

Next I text Kristin.

Shyla:
Hey, how's it going?

Kristin's response is almost immediate.

Kristin:
Not sure.

Shyla:
Things got a little wild, huh?

Kristin:
Yeah. Henry was a lot of fun. I'm not sure if I should tell Chad.

Shyla:
Would you want him to tell you?

Kristin:
We haven't declared exclusivity, per se. So probably not. That would make it awk.

Shyla:

There's ure answer. If you both are seeing other people, you didn't do anything wrong and confessing would only make him feel shitty.

Kristin:
I don't think he's seeing other people, but I get ure point. Did you speak to Henry?

Shyla:
No, when I woke, you were both gone.

Kristin:
We both cut out at around 6. I gave him my number. Yikes. I hope he doesn't call.

Shyla:
Do you feel like you said stupid shit last night? I do, and I feel really shitty today, super depressed and sad.

Kristin:
Don't sweat it. That's how it is, everyone loves everyone and everyone wants to kiss and touch everyone. We were all in the same boat. I think I am the one who should feel stupid : \

I'm relieved that we didn't sabotage her relationship with Chad and that maybe I wasn't as creepy as I felt. Then again, I don't think she knows that Taylor and I had our own personal porn show on their account. Never in a million years would I have done that if it wasn't for the E, which made me feel like we had no boundaries with one another.

After I am done with Kristin, I start to work ferociously to minimize my work needs for the rest of the week and distract myself from clinging all over Taylor. *Will I ever get used to Taylor's seeming lack of connection to humanity? What does it even matter as long as he feels connected to me? Does he even care about his friends, or is that all part of his cover, so that people don't know how damaged he really is?*

When three hours pass and Taylor does not emerge, I start to worry. *Have I pushed him away during a time when I need him the most?* Contrasting this is a lingering voice of doubt that will not let up. It is low, overshadowed by the stronger, more reckless voice that has taken over as of late, but it is still persistent. *Should I take what Taylor says at face value or should continue to look into Emily's life, just to clear the record?*

Another hour passes and finally I hear his office door open. He emerges with an empty plate in his hand. The tension between us persists.

"Please don't be mad at me," I beg as he sets his dish in the sink. I can't take the heaviness in the air between us.

"I'm fine Shyla. But I have to admit, you bringing up Eric against me, that was a low blow. It's like everything he's doing is starting to work. He's turning you against me."

"No! Please don't think that. Like I said, I was reacting to another piece of shitty news on top of the never-ending list. Please, I'm sorry. I never want to be the person who hurts you. I didn't know my words could have that effect."

"Well, now you do."

I walk over to him and wrap my arms around his waist and look up into his gorgeous eyes, the same eyes I saw in the photograph of his mother. "I love you. No — I more than love you. I'm losing my mind over you; I'm sick over you. And I keep trying to beat around the bush about it, as if by keeping it to myself I'll have some leverage like this is some sort of power play, but it's not. If I act erratic or emotional, it's because the intensity with which I feel for you makes everything else more intense. Being in love with you is like a drug, it's changed my view of the world, my reaction to things. It's an incredible feeling, but it's maddening, it's like a never-ending high."

With those words, the spark appears in his eyes again. How many times in his life has he been told that he has been loved like this? I am certain very few. Maybe just me and the woman who saved him from C.O.S. I don't say it expecting him to say it back. I know it's hard for him to say those words, but I know what we have, and I don't need to hear him recite a collection of letters to reaffirm it for me.

He smiles warmly and pushes my hair out of my face. "Where did you come from? Who are you? You're like that angel that emerged from the light to save me."

Taylor insists that he take me for a joyride since I haven't left the property since the hospital. We spend the afternoon with the wind in our hair, simply enjoying each other's company with very few words between us.

Later that night, Taylor reads a book in bed, when I emerge from the shower in a little silk nightie. Still not 100% myself from the previous night's festivities, it is almost scary how hard it has been to regain my normal temperament. It's as if I used up all my joy the night before. I am beat and eager to sleep, hoping that when I wake up tomorrow, I'll be myself again. As soon as I slide into bed, I feel Taylor roll over, pressing his firmness on my backside. We haven't had intercourse since before we were last in the darkroom and I know rejecting him is more than just saying no to sex. This is how he relates, how he loves, but I can't. I'm not ready and after finding out about Emily, it's stirring up my emotions about Eric and what he did to me.

"I'm sorry, I can't." I say as kindly as possible.

"What's going on, Shy?"

"I just, you know…I'm not myself."

"When will you be yourself again?"

"I don't know…I'm trying to deal."

"You don't want to get help, so you're just going to let it get between us?"

"Taylor it's hardly been a few days, and we've done other things. Other amazing things I might add." He nods in acceptance, but I can tell he's bothered. He gets up to leave. "Where are you going? I'm sorry, but this is not easy for me."

"I know it's not, Shy. I just get so fucking pissed about him, about what he did and I just can't fucking lay here anymore. I'm not used to being told no, and I respect it, but it's hard, because I want you all the time. Honestly, I want to tell you to shut the fuck up and take my cock, but you're not like my other relationships, and then sometimes you are and it's fucking confusing as hell."

"I'm sor-"

"Don't be fucking sorry. Don't." And with that he leaves the bedroom.

The rest of the week is full of me cramming work as I try to prepare for my trip. Taylor insists that he stay at home, but locks himself in the office telling me my presence is a major distraction from getting work done. I can sense his sexual frustration and the wall it is putting up between us, but something is blocking me, and I don't know what it is exactly. I guess I am scared to revisit the conflicting feelings I have about what Eric did to me.

While I am still in town, I go to Rubix every evening at around 6 o'clock when most people have started to head out to have a quick recap meeting with Chad. He still has that glow of someone in a new relationship and I am so glad it won't be ruined by the knowledge of Kristin sleeping with Henry.

By the time Wednesday rolls around, I am ready to enjoy a few days in fresh surroundings. I know as soon as I get to the airport, I'll want to turn around and run back to Taylor, but it's the only way I can think of to get some clarity and balance back. Taylor insisted I take the corporate jet, but I had already bought a first class ticket, since the thought of asking him for a jet to visit my mom seemed just mildly ridiculous. Before heading to the airport I called my mom to tell her I was on my way, and she was very excited. Taylor escorts me all the way to security. We pause for a moment, and I look up at him and admire the dark lashes against his bright eyes. I never tire of admiring his face. I want to apologize for my distance, for my inability to fully surrender myself to him since Eric and finding out about Emily, but I don't. I just stare into his eyes for a few extra seconds than normal, and then I kiss him tenderly.

"Take care of yourself, kiddo," he says, with the slightest hint of sadness in his eyes. "I hope you get some much needed peace."

"I think you need a break from me," I say.

"Never."

Then, sadly, I watch him walk away.

❊ ❊ ❊

Shortly after the plane takes off, I begin to feel under the weather. I can't quite put my finger on it, other than it being that out-of-it feeling I usually get before a bout with a bad cold or fever. By the time we approach the descent, I shiver, despite being wrapped in several blankets provided by the flight attendant. When the plane lands I am too weak to grab by bag from the overhead compartment.

"Ma'am are you okay? You don't look so well," one of the flight attendants asks.

"I don't think so..." I say between chattering teeth. She is kind enough to have someone drive me out in one of those golf carts. I know I look terrible when I see my mother's facial expression.

"Shyla! Oh my goodness, what's wrong?" By this point, every bone in my body aches. Two times on the way to her apartment, my mother pulls over her car for me to puke on the side of the road. "We should take you to the hospital," she insists.

"No mom, I want to go home," I say, weakly. "It's probably just food poisoning."

Once we arrive, she helps me undress and tucks me into bed. Three comforters do nothing to stop the shivers despite my body being drenched in sweat. I don't ever recall having been this sick before, it's as if my body is finally crumbling underneath the weight of the stress it has endured. I sleep for hours and whenever I wake, I am still so tired that I immediately fall back asleep.

On Thursday evening, my mother peeks her head into the bedroom. "Shyla, doll, you're phone has been going off a lot. Should I answer it?"

I rouse my achy body up from underneath the mountain of comforters. "No, gimme, I'll look," I say, barely able to keep my eyes open.

"If this fever doesn't break by tomorrow, I'm taking you to the doctor, I don't care what you say." I am too weak to even try and resist. She hands me the phone and brushes my sweaty hair out of my face. "My god, you're boiling up. I'm bringing you some soup. You need to get some fluids in you."

"I'm too nauseous, mom."

"Just try a few spoons, okay?"

She steps out and I take a deep breath to conquer the normally simple task of trying to check my messages.

There is a voicemail from Chad, so I quickly call him to let him know how terribly sick I am.

From there, I see several missed calls from Taylor and then several unread texts.

Mr. Sexypants:
You're not answering my calls. What's going on?
— —
You've got me worried here. Please message me.
— —
Okay I'm going to get your mother's number from Kristin and call her.

The last message was sent just minutes ago. I laboriously press the touchscreen to call Taylor.

"Shyla, what the hell? You said you would call me once you landed. It's been an entire day."

"I'm sick," I utter. It must sound pretty awful, because he seems to understand how much so right away.

"What's wrong? You sound terrible."

"Everything, I can't get out of bed, everything hurts, I have a fever, I can't hold any food down."

"Are you going to the doctor?"

"I don't want to move."

"I wish you would have stayed home. I would have taken care of you. Should I have a doctor go to your mother's house?"

"I'm so tired…I'm going to sleep."

"Shyla, you sound out of it. Do you know how high your fever is?"

"Taylor don't worry. My mom is watching me, okay?" Mom comes back into the room with the chicken soup. "I have to go eat soup," I say like a child who has no other choice but to obey her mother's commands.

"Call me as soon as you feel better, okay?"

"Yes." I hang up the phone pretty rudely, no strength remains for manners or pleasantries.

Mom hands me the bowl and I take four slurps of soup before I am so tired that I can barely keep my eyes open. "Honey, I hope you don't have mono," is the last thing I hear her say before I doze off.

The following morning, a ray of sunlight peeks through the shades right onto my eyes, awaking me. Finally, I feel human again as I sit up. My cell phone is dead, rendering me unable to find my bearings by checking the time. I walk out of the bedroom and notice that I am in a pair of my old Christmas footies littered with dozens of jolly Santas.

"Mom?" I call out.

"In the kitchen!" She calls out. "Oh you look so much better," she says as I turn the corner.

"Wow, I don't know what that was."

"You pretty much slept for 36 straight hours."

"What time is it?"

"It's 11:13 on Friday."

"Wow! Whatever it was hit me like a freight train. I was fine and then all of a sudden-bam."

"I thought maybe food poisoning, and then I started to worry something like mono, but it looks like you've turned a corner."

"Well, sweet trip this has been, showing up so I could puke and sleep."

"It seems like you needed your mama." She couldn't be more right.

"Is there anything to eat? I might consume my own foot if I don't get something in me." There is never a shortage of food when I visit mom's. She pulls out some leftover meatballs she had prepared the night before and makes a sandwich. "This is heaven!" I proclaim between giant bites. Afterward, I take a much needed shower as I have been marinating in my own sick sweat for days now. After my cell phone recharges, I call Taylor. He answers immediately.

"It's good to hear your voice," he says.

"Same here. I don't know what that was. It was a huge blur. I ached to my bones."

"It's probably the stress. Takes its toll on the immune system."

"Maybe. I never get sick. The good news is now I feel like a million bucks. Who wouldn't after sleeping for a few days?"

"Come home."

"I will! I'm leaving tomorrow morning. My poor mom has been stuck taking care of me. I at least have to give her a day of conscious Shyla."

"Well I guess you were able to be a kid again in a way. Your mom nursing you and all."

"I guess you're right, but not in the way most people idealize."

I surprise my mother with a shopping spree (shopping is our favorite bonding activity). At first she relents, but eventually, I get her guard down and we shop for several hours. When we return to her home, we order take out and rent a movie, our second favorite bonding activity. While we are waiting on the food we chat for a bit.

"I promise, I wasn't being nosey, but you kept getting calls from a Mr. Sexypants. That couldn't have been his real name."

"Yes mom, it's his family name, the Sexypants clan," I say sarcastically to hide my embarrassment.

"Is this a new boyfriend?"

"Yes." *Don't give me that look mom; that I'm-so-concerned-you-are-moving-too-fast, but I'm trying to hide it look.*

"Is it serious?"

"Yeah, it is. I wasn't expecting something serious so quickly after Rick, but he's amazing mom. He's everything -- gorgeous, funny, smart, caring, attentive…" *What am I doing?* I am supposed to play it cool, but I want her to love him as much as I do and even more than she loved Rick.

"So were you going to tell me about him or were you going to wait for me to ask as usual?"

"I would have had I not been comatose these past couple of days. His name is Taylor."

"Taylor? Where'd you meet?"

"A coffee shop. I spilled coffee on him, just like a cheesy rom-com."

"What does Taylor do?"

"Have you heard of Holden Industries?"

"Holden Industries? Yes, I have."

"He's the CEO."

"The CEO?" My mother sits back a little bit. Her facial expression goes blank for a moment. I wasn't expecting her to tap dance, but still, her mood change catches me off guard.

"Yeah mom."

"Is his last name Holden?"

"Yup."

"Oh. Well, that's nice."

"Something wrong, mom?"

"Honey, I wasn't going to say anything, because I know you don't like to talk about it, but I just can't ignore it. When I was changing your clothes…" *Shit, she saw the cuts. Fuckfuckfuck.* "Your arms, and the bruises. What's going on?"

96

I try to think of any story that could possibly cover all of it, but there is nothing. If I tell her Eric attacked me, she will lose it, I mean lose her fucking mind. "Mom…I'm fine. The bruises were from a minor car accident. A fender bender. Some idiot behind me was texting." *I am such a piece of shit liar.* "I meant to tell you about it, but well, then I got sick."

"Wow, you had lots to tell me. And the cuts?"

"That's why I wanted to visit, to catch up in person. The cuts? They…they are what they are, but I am fine. I swear mom. It was the first time in so many years."

"But why?"

I remain silent.

"Is it your new boyfriend? Is he hurting you?"

"No! No, mom. It's not Taylor. It's not anyone. It's just me and I have dealt with it."

"I can't just take that for an answer."

"Yes you can. I am an adult now mom. I'll be fine. I am actually happy, I feel more alive than I have in a long time. A lot of that has to do with Taylor. You'll just never understand why I do it. I know it looks horrifying to you, but I'm not trying to hurt myself."

Her eyes shift around, as if she has a million thoughts running through her head and is desperately trying to contain them. She then abruptly stands up and marches to the bathroom. After a few seconds I follow her. "Mom? Is everything okay in there?" I ask through the door.

"Yes , I think I am feeling a little out of it. Hopefully, I didn't catch anything from you."

"Oh no! I would feel so bad." I expected more of a fight, but her running off like this - seeking refuge in the bathroom - is uncharacteristic of her. She usually pushes and pushes and pushes. It's why I find myself avoiding her sometimes.

The doorbell rings and I retrieve the takeout. She emerges silently from the bathroom with a defeated smile on her face and we enjoy Paranormal Activity 2 in her dark apartment. The movie allows us to move on from the tension of our previous conversation. Normally, I don't get frazzled by even the scariest of movies, but I wonder with my newly developed edgy nerves, if a horror movie was a good idea. Once it's is over, I look to her, find she is asleep on the couch, and cover her with a throw. As I silently tip toe away, she faintly calls my name.

"Yes?"

"You should really think about what you're doing. This Taylor guy may seem exciting, but all new shiny things do. You may have a chance with Rick again, but if you go too far in with this young man you're dating, there will be no turning back." Rick is safe, he is kind, he is stable. This I have always known. But I want the man who makes me feel the exhilaration of teetering off the edge of a cliff.

"I know mom," I whisper to assuage her. The truth is, there is already no turning back. There was no turning back the very moment Taylor and I locked eyes in the coffee shop. When Taylor laid his hands on me in the car, I knew that Rick's touch would never have that effect on me. When he offered me the job, it was an invitation: *Leave it all behind, come on this wild ride with me.*

I accepted without looking back.

CHAPTER SEVEN

The drive to the airport is quiet, almost tense. I believe it's because my mother is upset about the cutting. Despite the visit not going according to plan due to my dengue fever or whatever the hell it was, it was exactly what I needed. I feel lighter, like I am ready to re-enter the world. *My god do I miss Taylor; down to my bones.* I don't mean just his physical absence, but there was a distance between him and I before I left. He is in a constant battle of trying to respect my needs versus his strong physical desire to connect with me and make me submit to his sexual desires. And because I won't open to him fully, because I have cocooned myself, the only way he can avoid the sting of my rejection is to stay away.

There we were together in his study, as he told me one of the most intimate moments of his life, being ripped away from the woman who saved him, and I return this by shutting him out, telling him I was fine when I wasn't. Telling him I was his, but then snatching it all away just as abruptly. I imagine in a way for him, he must be like a teenage boy in his first intense relationship: experiencing all of the same confusion, intensity, and insanity. Having to talk to my mother, try to explain to her who this man is, and how he understands me in a way that she never will, reminds me just how incredible our bond is. Taylor never made me feel like a freak for cutting, he gets it, he understands the compulsions. I don't have to make excuses like I do

99

with everyone else. I don't have to reassure him it's not really me like I do with the others.

And now I am ready. I am ready to swim back to shore after floating adrift.

"Alright, here we are," my mother says as she pulls up to the departures area.

"Thanks for taking care of me."

"That's what mamas are for!"

"You should come visit soon. I'll pay for the ticket."

"Oh you don't need to do that. As soon as work dies down, I will."

I give her a kiss and grab my carry on. She steps out of the car to hug me. "Remember what I said to you last night? Make sure you really think about what you are doing. I mean for the long haul. So often the things that seem good in the present may not be the best for us in the longterm." *There she goes again, with her meddling. You'd think she had lived with Rick all these years.* "And if things get hard, or if you need someone to talk to, I'm here."

"Mom, I'll be fine. I promise. You don't have to worry about me." I believe she held hope that the breakup between Rick and me was just a phase, and now she is seeing that it really is over. She credits Rick for "healing" me, but it was never really him, it was always me.

As I sit in the plane, my anxiousness to see Taylor builds with each minute. It's like waking up on the other side of that fever has purged me from the fog, I feel strong and clear, ready to take my life back from Eric's haunting presence. I want to give Taylor everything I have been holding back, let him know that *I am his*. I must overthrow Eric's conquest of my body.

When the plane lands, I am frenzied. Seeing Taylor is now an emergency; it won't wait another second. We have worked so hard to get him to open up. I won't abandon him like people have done in the past or let Eric rip me out from his clutches the way Taylor was ripped out of the mystery woman's arms so many years ago.

Once the flight attendant gives the signal to disembark from the plane, I hastily rip my carry-on from the overhead compartment. It's stuck enough that when I whip it out, it sends me back onto the belly of a middle-aged man behind me. "Atta girl," he says. The embarrassment doesn't stop me from escaping the plane like a caged rabid cat. I do one of those controlled "runs," not swinging my arms, but moving my legs as fast as they can go, looking like I have a very long stick up my ass as I roll my bag out of the gate. I take a quick glance at a reflective metal panel on the wall. *Crap.* I kind of rolled out of bed, threw on sweats and made a ponytail. My original plan was to go home as Taylor had to be in the office until mid-afternoon. I roll into one of the airport bathrooms and rummage through my suitcase, attracting the stares of travelers passing me as they enter and exit the lavatory. *My makeup bag, perfect!* Quickly, I apply some blush, cat-eye eyeliner, mascara, and red lipstick. I pull my hair out of the ponytail and shake it vigorously, spraying it with some leave-in conditioner to get out the ponytail bump. This attracts the stank-eye from a teenager next to me, washing her hands at a sink, presumably because I got her in the eye with the spritzing. *Too bad kiddo, one day you'll get it.* Next, my outfit. *What the hell did I pack?* No sexy undies, I was with my mom after all. Instead, I grab a blue midi dress for my unfulfilled plan to go out to a nice dinner with mama-dukes. I dress in a stall, removing all of my underwear. I take a deep breath and fan myself as I emerge. All this vigorous public bathroom makeover shit is making me sweat.

"You clean up nice, mama," the bathroom attendant says to me.

"Uh, thanks!" I reply, nearly out of breath.

Harrison is waiting for me outside of baggage claim. I apologize for my tardiness.

"Is Taylor at H.I.?"

"Yes, I believe his plans where to be there all day until he met up with you."

"Okay, take me there directly."

"Do you want me to tell him we're on our —"

"No. I want to surprise him."

I arrive at about 11am, hoping he is not in one of those meetings that required him to be in the office today. The elevator seems to move impossibly slow to the 45th floor. I find Marsha at her usual place in the reception area on my way to see Taylor.

"Shyla!" she says warmly. She was always one of my favorite people at H.I. One of the few people I have ever met that is sincerely nice, no bullshit motives behind her enormous kindness.

"Marsha, so good to see you! Sorry to be in a rush, but is Taylor in his office?"

"Um, yes, but he's in a meeting."

"Oh. Who's it with?"

"Henry."

"I'm going in."

"Um, I don't know if I'm supposed to —"

"Don't worry about it. I got this."

"Oh, on your way out, I have something for you!" She tells me as I charge towards his office.

I abruptly let myself in through the large cherry doors. Both Henry and Taylor jump in their seats. Taylor stands up. "Shyla, what are you doing here? Is everything okay?"

"We need to talk," I say as I look out of the corner of my eye at Henry, who I am sort of pissed at again for fucking my best friend.

"Okay…let's just…you and I," Henry awkwardly points to himself and then Taylor. "Okay…yeah…we'll pick this up later," he says as he slithers out the side of his chair and closes the door the office behind him.

"What's going on?"

"I've missed you. A lot."

"Well, uh, yeah I've missed you too. Is this how you usually act when you've missed someone? Like you're going to kick their ass? Did I miss that memo?"

I lock the office door and walk over to his desk, resting my hands on the edge. "I need you to fuck me. Here. Now."

He is taken aback for a moment, and then I see the "sex switch" flip on. It's always in his eyes and his sly grin.

"So you want me to fuck you? That's what this is about?" He says, calmly walking to the side of the desk as he trails a finger over its edge.

"Yes. I'm sorry I've been distant, but I need you." I gulp. As soon as he turns it on, I melt into warm pudding and completely lose the dominant sex empress act.

"I've never fucked anyone in here before." *I find that hard to believe.*

"Well, there's a first time for everything, they say."

"They say," he repeats in a mocking yet seductive tone. "I've always wondered who is this mysterious *they* that people reference?"

"Uh, I don't know." *Is he really fucking with me right now?*

"Is there some sort of organization that is the authority on platitudes and philosophy-lite that goes by *they*?" He inches closer.

"No, not that I know of. I can google it for you if you'd like."

"You're a smartass," he says as he pulls me by my waist against his body. He is hard; granite hard. It must be the sexual frustration.

"I'm gonna fuck you, but you'll have to be quiet, you know that?" I nod. He pulls up my dress. "Ooh, no underwear, you're really trying to get fucked. You have your pussy ready and waiting for me, huh?"

"Uh huh." He picks me up and seats me on his desk, leaning past me to reach for the speaker.

"Marsha, reschedule all of my afternoon meetings," he turns his attention back to me. "I'll fuck you, but you're gonna do what I say. Then I'll reward you with my cock." I shake my head in jittery agreement. He's making me pay for making him wait. He rips a cord from his computer and ties my hands behind my back. "You look hot. Sexy as hell. Did you dress up for me?"

"Yes."

Taylor pulls my breasts out over the neckline of the dress leaving them propped up and exposed. He leads me by the restraints and presses me against the glass window of his office. Then he bends down, and while I expect the requisite licking, I am stunned when instead, he bites the back of my thigh so hard I jump and let out a moan. "Shhhh…" After the initial shock wears, a tingling emanates from the spot. He does it again, biting the sensitive flesh of my inner thigh, tugging on it for just a moment, then releasing so that the flesh bounces back. The pain is sharp, it hurts like hell for half a second, but then it tingles like a million little explosions. I can't help but let out a little squeal again. He pulls his tie off, rolls it up and shoves it into my mouth. "No noise, baby." That is followed by a mix soft kisses and aggressive, teasing bites around my groin and inner thigh. I have no view of Taylor, only the city in front of me, so I don't know what is next; each one is its own surprise. The sting of the bites complement the softness of the kisses too perfectly. Eventually, Taylor's tongue works its way up between my legs and he bends me over for easier access, pressing my cheek against the window panel. Unlike the harsh bites, his tongue is gentle. With my face turned, I am able to watch him on his knees from the corner of my eye. His hair is disheveled, his shirt wrinkled with the top few buttons undone, allowing his undershirt to peak out. Something about him taking me in his business attire in his high-rise office makes me so hot, like a queen being taken by her king right on the throne.

Taylor then stands, reaches over my shoulder and pulls the tie out of my mouth from one end so that it forms a long trail until it slides out completely. He reaches his other arm over my other shoulder so that I can see both hands with my peripheral vision. Simultaneously, he winds each end of the tie in his hands, so that he has a firm grip on it. He wraps it twice onto my neck as if he is about the strangle me, but instead uses it to guide me over to the desk, like a makeshift collar. "Get on your knees on the desk." As I do, I knock over various folders and way-too-modern desk knick knacks. He presses my face down, and it rests on a manila folder. When I move slightly, I can see the imprint of my lipstick against it. *He'll smile to himself when he sees that later.* "I'm gonna savor this. Being inside of you. No one fucks you like I do." He slides into me and feels so intense from that angle. I try my best to keep my moans low, but with his rock hard erection in this position that is asking too much of me. He moves slowly, rhythmically. Eventually he leaves the tie hanging around my neck and grabs my ass with his hands, roughly kneading each cheek, pulling them apart so forcefully it hurts, but then releasing just before the pain can linger. "One of these days I am going to fuck you right in the ass. Not today, you have to earn that. And you are going to fucking howl like a banshee when I stuff my cock in your tight little asshole." The dirtier he talks, the more I feel that surge of energy inside of me. He then reaches under and grabs my breasts firmly as he massages each one. "Tell me when you're about to come." He slides a hand under me and guides me up, so that my back is touching his chest. He is at a new angle inside of me, forcing my bodyweight to accelerate the inevitable.

"I'm gonna come. I'm gonna come!" I declare. He reaches for each end of the tie wrapped around my neck and yanks relentlessly without missing a thrust. In a second, the tie is cutting off my airway.

"Come baby, come for me, I've got you." I look forward and see our narrow reflection in the frame of one of his paintings hanging on the office wall. My naked pale breasts, plump and perky, my hair wild and sensual, my arms tied behind me, a dark tie adorning my neck like a choker. Just to behind me is that gorgeous man, with the thick, silky dark hair and eyes that pierce me, even through a reflection. He engulfs me, he devours me, he owns me. From a distance I hear weak gasps for air from a wounded creature, and then I realize it is me. And I fall apart, but more so now than ever before. I release my body, my soul back to him. It shakes me on the surface and deep inside; I quiver and I contract around his cock over and over and over.

He releases his grasp and I swallow a huge gulp of air. "Get up."

"What?" I ask, still in a daze from the orgasm and lack of oxygen.

"Stand on my desk and face me."

"Wha—" I stop myself from questioning him, I am learning to just let go and trust him.

As I stand and face him, he swipes an area of the desk just in front of me.

"Now squat down." I do so cautiously, as my coordination is not nearly as keen as his, plus I am wearing these fucking stilettos.

He rolls over his executive chair in front of me and waits. I wait in silence, my thighs burning, knowing that asking him what's next will ruin the moment. If he wanted me to know, he would tell me.

And then it happens, his cum begins to drip out of me onto the desk. His eyes narrow as he tugs his lower lip while rubbing his crotch. He walks up to me and says in my ear in a low, raspy voice.

"Whenever I look at this spot on the desk, I will think of your pussy, dripping wet from me." Then he kisses me, slowly, sensually.

Taylor has reclaimed me.

✿ ✿ ✿

I lie on Taylor's desk for some time to regain my composure. Much like our romp at the racetrack, I believe it's possible a person or two might have their suspicions about what just occurred in the office and so I delay facing the world outside of this safe room. Taylor pours me a glass of ice water and pulls out a fresh shirt from his back up stash in the office closet.

"I'm glad you're feeling better. You really had me worried," he says as he buttons up.

"I might have been worried myself if I wasn't sleeping the whole time. I think it's the stress. In college, I would always get sick right after finals."

"I mean even before that." He adjusts his cuffs. "Well besides that, how was your trip?"

I don't want to bore him down with my mother's meddling, so I omit that part. "It was good. We went shopping, saw a movie…I told her about you."

"You did?"

"Yeah, you don't have a problem with that, do you?"

"No, she's your mother. That's between you and her." He takes a drink from his glass. "My father knows about you."

"He does?" The thought of him telling his father about me never crossed my mind. "When did you tell him?"

"When I visited him. To talk about, well, you know. I explained that Eric was bothering you, and that you were very important to me. And that if he knew anything, he needed to tell me right away."

"Did he?"

"My father swears he didn't know Eric's whereabouts until he showed up recently. Eric has had a tendency to disappear and reappear in my father's life since he agreed to leave town years ago. Apparently, he had gone MIA for a little over a year. He said Eric wanted to be back home, he was tired of being away, that that was his reason for coming back. I don't buy that. I still think he came back specifically to fuck with me. Maybe he was sick of being away, but instead of doing anything to redeem himself, he decided to get back at me for it. Randall, my father, agreed to tell me where he was as long as I promised not to hurt him."

"But you already did. When he chased us."

He shrugs.

"What happened?"

"Do you really want to revisit this?"

"I know I have been avoiding talking about him, but I'm ready. What next? How was he able to get me in the hotel room if you had made arrangements for him to leave?"

"So, my father had been in touch with him ever since he returned, says he has no idea Eric had been hounding us. Of course, my dad didn't tell me a damned thing about him being around. He was hoping to have us both again, but he should have known better. Eric agreed to leave the next evening, but wanted some time with my father before he did so. I agreed for my father's sake and because I thought that would be the easiest way to get rid of him. So, I stayed with my dad until the next afternoon and we parted ways. He went to say goodbye to Eric. I didn't go along because I didn't want to see him ever again. I never thought for one second you would be in his path that morning or afternoon; you were with Harrison. What my guys told me was he had a brief dinner with our father. Then my guys took him to the airport, watched him enter the gate. They waited until the plane departed. But there was that window of time, after he agreed to turn himself in and before he had dinner, almost 24 hours…that he fooled us all. He knew I was at Randall's and that you would be alone." It weirds me out that Taylor refers to his dad by his first name. The conversation has taken a bitter turn and I try to steer it in a different direction.

"He looked really beat up. Even more than the beating you gave him."

"Well, that's too bad," Taylor says mischievously.

"I wonder how that happened."

Taylor shrugs innocently.

"What did you tell your dad about me?"

He sits on an empty spot on his desk, just above my head, and takes another sip. "I told him that he wouldn't have to worry about me anymore. About me being alone. He had always worried about that, that because

109

of my — *condition* — that I would be left alone once he died. I told him I'm not alone anymore."

"Did you ever worry about that, being alone?"

"No. I didn't know something — someone — was missing."

"What did he say?"

"Nothing. He knew there was not much else to say. We don't talk much about those kinds of things, I just told him that and left it there. He deserved to be told that, to know that between Eric and me, one of us will be fine. He just smiled, but at the same time I could sense a great relief in his body language. I know he thinks he fucked up with me, and Eric too. For all of his intelligence and wealth, he could never figure out his own sons."

"I didn't expect that you would tell your dad about me."

"Honestly, I didn't plan on it, but it just seemed fitting at the moment. It felt honest. So much of my life is putting up a front, even with my own family, and this was a simple act of gratitude towards the man who with all of his faults, did his best to raise me."

His desk phone rings. "Sorry doll, I have to grab this."

"Of course."

"Yes, okay, put him on hold for a second. I'll tell you when to patch him through…Shyla, I gotta take this."

"No problem. I'll go home and see you later?"

"Yeah, I might be a little late since you threw off my schedule." His eye twinkles when he winks at me. When he gets on the phone, I attempt to pick up the papers and table decor I knocked over. Taylor motions for me to stop, mouthing he'll get it later, but I insist. Once I am done, I kiss him on the cheek and head out.

As I reach the end of the corridor facing Marsha's desk, I recall that she had something for me.

"Yes, here you go." She pulls up a box from behind the reception area and plops it on its surface. "This was all stuff from your old office. I wasn't sure where to send it. Taylor kept saying he'd take it to you personally, but you know how busy he gets."

"Thank you! I am such an airhead, thanks so much for holding onto this for me." Floating on the surface are some of the books I purchased when I started the job and a cardigan I had been looking for. "Yay! I have been looking everywhere for this sweater!"

"It's so cute. I was tempted take it home," Marsha jests.

As I emerge from H.I. with box in hand, there is a text from Taylor:

Mr. Sexypants:
I forgot to mention. Lizzy and Henry are coming over for dinner. A chef will be coming into the house at around 3, so don't karate chop her or anything. She's friendly.

It's been a long time since the four of us have hung out and even longer since we just had friends over for dinner like normal folks. Upon my arrival to Taylor's, I plop the box down in the foyer and immediately head to the bowl-tub for a nice long soak. I load about ten different bath potions and salts into the tub as it fills. My naked reflection stares back at me from the full length mirror, prompting an inspection. Most of the bruises on my body have faded completely, but there are a few that are turning in color. The shallow cuts on my arms are also healing over, except for the deep one I created to draw blood for the crime scene. I vow to myself not to do it again, not to put the razor to my flesh and watch the blood run. But it's not the first time I have made that vow. The problem is, it is easy to keep until the moment comes when I need it, when I have the unrelenting urge to lose myself in the pain of slicing my arm. I had forgotten that urge until our last night in the darkroom, that out of control sensation, like I was spinning out of orbit with no way to stop the momentum. The cutting grounded me; it focused me. Now that I'm back here with Taylor, I don't need it anymore. He grounds me.

CHAPTER EIGHT

Since there are some visible markings on my arms, I opt for a long-sleeved emerald green chiffon blouse buttoned to the top, tucked into a pair of tailored cropped black pants with tan ballet flats. I put my hair up in a topknot, add just a little bit of watermelon-colored blush and matching lipgloss with mascara. Just a few minutes before three o'clock, there is a ring at the doorbell. My heart skips a beat instinctually. Being alone in such a big house, especially after the recent events, even with Harrison on the premises, makes me react to every small sound, every creak, as though it were a loud crash. A portly middle-aged woman with a white chef's jacket is visible through the glass panel to the side of the front door.

"Hello! I'm Betty, the chef for your dinner party." Her voice is rich like a heavy sauce, but cheerful.

"Yes, please, come in. I'm Shyla."

"Pleased to meet you! I just wanted to say hello, but I am going to bring in the ingredients for tonight."

"Do you need help?"

"No, it's all in a rolling cart. If you could leave this door unlocked or opened, that would be great."

Less than a minute later she reappears at the door and I guide her to the kitchen. I offer her some wine, but she politely declines, reminding me she's on the job.

"So what's on the menu? Taylor surprised me with this dinner party."

"How nice of him! He asked for an Asian theme tonight. So we are going to start with steamed vegetable dumplings in a plum-soy glaze and chicken satay. Next will be seared ahi tuna with edamame and cucumber salad a top a bed of sticky white rice. Then I have a Dirty Thai Iced Tea, a special cocktail of mine. Finally, an assortment of various ice creams."

"Woah. I was just expecting some chicken-fried rice."

She laughs a hearty laugh from deep within her gut. "I don't think Mr. Holden brings me in to slap together some fried rice!"

Normally, I would leave her to do her thing, but it is nice to have company in the house and her presence is warm like a hug.

"Do you mind if I watch? I don't want to hover, I am just fascinated by your talents."

"Not at all! I teach classes as well, you should come to one."

"I would love to."

I stare intently as she masterfully chops carrots, cucumbers and whatever other vegetables she has on the chopping board. She must notice how intently I am staring, because she pauses and asks: "Do you want to join in?"

"Me? Really? I don't want to slow you down..."

"Any assistance can only help." She sets me up with some vegetables and shows me how to do that speed-chopping thing chefs do. Although, when I do it, it's still clumsy and slow compared to her near super-human speed.

Minutes later, I hear the clinking of keys in the front door. Taylor saunters into the great room, throwing his jacket and leather messenger bag on a sofa.

"Betty, I wouldn't let her touch that food if I was you. You should see the stuff she makes," he says as he loosens his tie.

I scrunch my nose at him.

"Oh, Mr. Holden, this lovely lady is doing an excellent job," Betty assures him.

Taylor walks over to me and kisses the top of my head. I feel a warm tingle from his breath blowing along my hairline. It's not the electric, sexual type, but one of tenderness and the security of being loved. He helps himself to my wine.

"It seems like you never pour your own wine these days," I tease.

"It's just that it tastes so much better when it's touched your lips," he whispers in my ear. "Betty, do you mind if I take my girl for a second?"

"Of course not. She's all yours."

"I'm not finished!" I insist.

"I think she'll be fine without you," Taylor winks at me.

He grabs my wine with one hand and my hand with the other and pulls me into the bedroom.

"Have a seat doll."

I plop on the bed. "How was the rest of your day?"

"It was great, especially since a gorgeous woman stopped by today and gave me a nice boost of energy."

I smirk.

"When are Henry and Lizzy coming over?"

"Around five-ish. You know, you're welcome to invite Kristin and Chad if you want. There will be plenty of food."

"Are you nuts?"

"What?"

"*Hello?* Henry and Kristin?"

"Oh, please. We're all adults here, it's not like we'll be kicking them under the table or elbow-nudging them."

"I know…but it'll be awkward for them."

"I can guarantee you Henry will be fine. He's slept with half of the United States, if he felt awkward for every ex-fuck he's ever had, he wouldn't leave his house."

"Oh, you should talk!" I pause for a second, realizing that comment could be taken as an insult, but instead he takes it in stride.

"Touché. I have to clarify: it's no secret to you I've had my share, but to put it into perspective, Henry runs circles around me in quantity."

"You sluts!"

"How about you?"

"Me? What do you mean?"

"How many?"

"Well it's not 35, that I can tell you."

"That I know," he says presumptuously.

"Well, excuse me!"

"Oh I didn't mean it like that. Touchy, touchy."

"Four, well, five. *Ugh.*"

"Including me?"

"Yes."

"Including…?"

I nod.

"Don't worry, I'm not gonna let that fuck with our night. Tell me about the others."

"Really?"

"Yeah."

"Well, I lost my virginity to a kid named Dave Sanders."

"Dave Sanders? Did he wear suspenders?"

"Oh stop it! He was my neighbor for years. One night, when my mom was passed out drunk, and his parents were out of town, I went next door to his place. We got high, and we did it."

"You were a naughty girl."

"I had my moments."

"Your mom, you said she was passed out?"

"Yeah, she started drinking a lot when I was in high school, it was bad for a while, but she's been sober for years. She helps other addicts for a living now. It was a pretty lonely time when she was at her worst. That's when I started all this." I motion to my arms.

"I see. Was it awkward?"

"Yup. He lasted like 2 minutes. But I don't regret it. We had known each other for years and he was a nice kid. It was his first time too."

"Where is he now?"

"I don't know. We moved out of the building eventually and we lost touch."

"Who was the next guy?"

The summer before college, I dated some guy. Meh."

"Then Rick?"

"Yes."

"Was he any good?"

"Taylor!"

"Oh don't be such a prude."

"Doesn't this make you jealous?"

"Of course it does, but I like getting jealous as long as I win. It makes me wanna teach you a lesson."

"Oh does it?"

"So was he?"

"Yes, he was if you must know, I mean for a normal person…but, then things fizzled. We just lost it."

"A normal person?"

"I mean not a natural-born sex machine like you." Taylor laughs and reveals his pristine crooked smile.

117

"I'll have you know, this is not all natural talent, but a finely cultivated gift."

"No, something about you, they way you are, that can't be taught."

"Are you trying to turn me on? Because it's working."

"I don't think I have to try very hard."

"I don't know how I feel about your sass."

"So you're the only one who gets to be sassy?"

"Yes. Well, you can act sassy all you want, but I'll make you pay," he says in suggestive manner.

"Poor me," I say, stretching out on the bed.

Taylor sits next to me and pulls me onto his lap. He slowly unbuttons my blouse and pulls it down past my shoulders, revealing my décolletage. Tenderly, he kisses my neck; all the fine hairs stand at attention. I lean my head back to invite more kisses, and he responds by lightly biting and sucking. He slides his left hand into the cup of one of my bras and massages my breast. The other hand slides down in between my thighs, over the fabric of my pants. He applies firm, even pressure with his palm and massages me, each wave of pressure building me up. His lips and hands all over me brew a heady sexual sensory overload. I moan, signaling him that I am ready to come soon. Each moan becomes louder, my voice quivers, and just as I am about to explode, he stops.

"Wha— huh?"

"I told you I would teach you a lesson."

"Are you fucking kidding me?"

He cocks an eyebrow to confirm I already know the answer.

I stand up to face him. "This is so unfair! You asked me to tell you. And now you're going to give me blue clit?"

"Blue clit?"

"Yes, like blue balls, but with a clit."

"Yeah, I got it."

"You played me."

"I did ask you. I did want to know. And I want you to sit at the dinner table tonight with your pussy hot and wet, begging for me to fuck it because no one can fuck you like me. And you would beg for my cock, even if it meant getting on your knees and groveling, but you would never do that for them."

He's right. I am dickmatized. "Sure Taylor, whatever you think." I say in a mocking tone, my bottom half still tingling, waiting for the fireworks show that was just seconds from happening. He grabs my arm.

"I'm right and you know I am. Tell me your pussy isn't throbbing right now." I remain silent. "I thought so. Now, maybe later, I'll relieve her if you ask nicely." I remain quiet, stewing in a mix of anger, sexual frustration, and desire for him to finish. "I'd like you to pick out my outfit tonight."

"Really?" I am surprisingly touched by the invitation. Taylor is so independent and particular about his things. His closet screams control-obsessed freak. In fact, I laughed to myself a few weeks ago when my designated area in the closet seemed to get a visit from the closet-organization fairy during one of Taylor's sleepless nights.

"Okay, this is exciting. It's like dressing a Ken doll with genitals!"

"On that note, I'm gonna hop in the shower."

"Will you keep the door open, so we can talk?"

"Yup."

As Taylor heads into the bathroom, I peruse the closet, eventually passing the hidden door to the darkroom. *When will we go in there again? Am I ready?* There is only one way to know for sure, but dinner plans are imminent. I shift my focus back to my

119

immediate task, picking out a thin sand-colored merino wool sweater to wear atop a navy blue and white checkered shirt with a pair of dark structured jeans. I tie it all up with a maroon pair of unworn Vans slip-on leather sneakers.

As I lay the clothes out on the bed, I turn to seek his approval on my selection and catch myself off guard with how fucking sexy he looks. The details of body are only slightly diffused by the fog on the shower door as he tilts his head back to rinse out his hair. Beads of water roll down every muscular curve of his body. His penis, even in a flaccid state, tempts me to awaken it. I just want to jump in and bone him. *He's right, I'm going to be hot for him all throughout this dinner.*

He walks out of the shower with his wet hair slicked back and a white towel wrapped around his waist. "So, what have you got for me?"

I point to the clothing laid out on the bed.

"Not bad. Comfortable, dare I say a bit preppy?"

"I don't know about preppy, I would say stylish yet casual. You wear suits all the time, since we are amongst friends I wanted you to be comfortable."

"Thank you."

"My pleasure."

"What about you?"

"What about me?"

"What are you wearing?"

"Well, I was wearing this. Why? Is it bad?"

"No, it's nice. Just wondering how I'm gonna get my hands in those pants under the dinner table."

I shove him playfully. "You would look hot with your hair a little longer. Like David Beckham used to have."

"Well thanks, but we already have one ponytail in the office," he says, referring to Henry.

"I guess, and knowing him, he'll claim you're trying to steal his vibe."

Taylor nods in agreement. I reassemble my shirt and pants as Taylor gets ready. "Hey Taylor, can you do your hair the way you did that night at the gala? You looked so handsome."

"You don't think it's a little formal?"

"I don't care. I like it."

"Well that's all that matters then. Why don't you do it?"

He sits in the bathroom as I grab a comb and some styling cream from the vanity drawer.

"I've never really done a guy's hair before. Rick always liked his hair scruffy and I assume girls first do that with their dad, and well, you know."

"I trust you."

"Okay…" I take a deep breath and make the part where I recall he had it previously. Then I pull out the hair lotion and scoop out a dollop.

"Wait." He gently grasps my wrist. "Just a little less, unless you're aiming to protect my skull from shrapnel," and he scoops a little bit of the cream out of my hand and puts it back into the jar.

I distribute the product by rubbing my palms together and deliberately raking it through his hair. He closes his eyes so I take that as a cue to massage his scalp. His body language softens. I don't ruin the moment by asking, but I doubt he ever gets massaged due to his condition; these small, seemingly mundane moments between us must be a great luxury to him.

After a few minutes, I notice it's close to five. "Mr. Sexypants. You're going to fall asleep."

He smiles and slowly rouses himself out of his relaxed state. "Do me a favor and never call me that outside of this bathroom."

"I think I'll call H.I. and ask for you by that moniker."

"I have the phone system set to self-destruct if you do. Come on." He stands up, taking my hand, and looks in the mirror. "What's this thing?" He refers to a bit of a lick I styled in at the front.

"I thought I would modernize it."

"Christ Shyla, I look like a massive tool."

"I think it's cute!" I pout.

"Only because we aren't leaving the house." And we head back out to the kitchen to await our guests.

Minutes, later the doorbell rings. Lizzy and Henry arrive together.

"What's with the hair?" is the first thing Lizzy asks. Taylor gives me a look out of the corner of his eye.

We vote to eat in the outdoor dining area to take advantage of the cool breeze. Just before we are about to sit, my phone rings with a call from Kristin. I debate whether or not to pick it up and invite her, but both Kristin and Henry are important parts of our lives and I can't keep them separated forever.

"Hello?"

"Hey!"

"Hey! How's it going?"

"Okay. I just wanted to see what you were up to tonight."

"Well, it's perfect that you called. Taylor surprised me with a dinner party. We are just getting started, you want to come over? Chad is welcome."

"He's at a dudes-only poker game, but I can stop by. Who's all there?"

"Taylor, me, Lizzy...and Henry."

"Oh lord."

"It'll be cool."

"I know, I might as well bite the bullet and get over the awkwardness."

"So, you down?"

"Sure. I just need to finish up getting ready. I can be there in 30 minutes."

We are well into the appetizers when the doorbell rings. I motion to rise out of my chair, but Taylor insists that he get the door. Moments later, Taylor and Kristin approach the table. Kristin looks especially vibrant in a one-armed black mini kaftan dress with sparkly flat sandals. Her normally puffy hair is slicked back into a low bun and her brown skin shimmers with some sort of gold highlighter and as always she has on lipstick; this time it's coral. I wonder if she's trying to impress Henry and it concerns me.

Everyone stands up to greet her. She met Lizzy at karaoke night, so they are well-acquainted. I do my best to observe the interaction between Henry and Kristin, to see if there is any awkwardness or even worse, some remaining attraction. Admittedly, Henry looks good today as well. His dirty-blond hair is tied back into a loose ponytail, and he's wearing a dark-gray vest over a striped button-down shirt with the sleeves rolled up and a pair of navy blue pants. Kristin sits next to Henry, and I can only assume this is to *pull off the bandaid*, so the speak. The conversation is lively, sometimes splitting off into mini conversations between just the ladies and the guys.

"Thanks! I love gel manicures. They last forever," Lizzy states after Kristin compliments her nails.

"I dunno, I'm just too lazy and impatient to get my nails done. I just trim them and paint them at home," I add.

"You have like no cuticles though, so you can get away with that." Just as Kristin adds her two cents, Taylor's hand slides on my thigh. I glance over at him, but he's not looking at me, instead, he is staring directly at Henry, nodding at whatever he is saying. I take it as a gesture of affection, and I place my hand on top of his. Instead of leaving it there, however, he runs his hand up my thigh and in between my legs, causing me to sit erect.

Just wondering how I'm gonna get my hands in those pants under the dinner table...Omg he was serious!

I look at him again and try to give him the "what are you doing" eye and he turns to me and nonchalantly says: "What's up Shy?" *You know damned well what's up you kinky SOB.*

"Nothing, just wondering what you guys were talking about," I fib.

"Actually Henry we thinks we should go on a vacation together. I agree."

"Where to?"

"That's what we were discussing. Somewhere tropical perhaps?"

"That would be nice, but I can't do anything longer than a few days."

"We were thinking Labor Day weekend," Henry chimes in.

"Ooooh, are you guys talking about going on a group vacation?" Lizzy asks.

Taylor begins to rub. I fidget in my seat, certain what is happening is written all over my face.

"You guys are so lucky. I am so broke," Kristin mopes.

"You wouldn't have to worry about much. Taylor and I were just talking about it. Taylor would fly us all in the jet and we'd get a house. You don't need to worry about those expenses." *Henry, leave my hot friend alone!*

"I say let's do it." Taylor declares. Taylor is literally the boss of two (well three if you include sexcapades) people at the table. What he says, goes.

"Where?" Lizzy asks with an almost child-like enthusiasm.

Taylor artfully unbuttons my pants with one hand and slides his hand down. I take a nervous gulp. He glides his fingers underneath my lace panties and massages my labia. I can barely keep up with the conversation, my heart is pounding with excitement and fear that someone else at the table may notice. I purposely stay out of the conversation since I am not sure my sentences will even be coherent at this point.

"I think we should go to Costa Rica," Henry suggests.

"No!" I blurt out. Everyone at the table stops talking and looks at me. "I mean, I don't want to go to South America just for a long weekend. Maybe we should stick to the Caribbean." I can't tell them the real reason I don't want to be on that continent.

"It's more like Central America, and with the direct flight on the jet, it won't be a problem." *Fucking Henry.*

"I'm sure it'll be fine Shy." Taylor knows my real concern, so his opinion holds real weight.

"Well, okay then," is all I can muster to the man who has his hand down my pants.

He resumes playing with me as Henry, Lizzy, and Kristin take over the conversation. His fingers tease, occasionally slipping inside of me. He knows exactly how much he needs to do, to tantalize me, to make me wet and nervous, without embarrassing myself.

Betty and a server arrive with plates of ahi tuna. Taylor slips his hand out of my pants as they walk towards the table. I breathe a sigh of relief mixed with disappointment. The tension was torturous, but so hot at the same time. I lose track of the conversation at the table as everyone goes back and forth about what town to stay in and other travel arrangements. I then I look over at Taylor who crosses one arm under his chest and rests the other elbow on it, raising the hand that was just in my pants and resting it over his mouth.

"Smells delicious." Everyone thinks he's talking about dinner, but from the look he gives me out of the corner of his eye, I know it's something else.

"Excuse me, I'll be right back." Taylor stands up and walks back into the house. I wonder if I should follow, but don't want to draw attention to us by leaving at the same time.

"Alright," Henry says, "I'll look into accommodations in the area."

"This is so exciting!" Kristin exclaims.

"Where did Taylor go?" Lizzy asks after a couple of minutes.

"Not sure. Let me go check on him. You three keep enjoying the meal."

"*Mmm hmm…*" Lizzy says suspiciously as she winks at me.

"Oh please!" I shake my head and roll my eyes at her, knowing full well she's onto me.

Betty informs me that Taylor went down the hallway that holds his bedroom and office. I gingerly approach his bedroom which is locked. There is no response after tapping on the door. Next, I make my way to the office. As I near it, the light flowing into the hallway from the threshold signals he is likely in there. When I peak my head into the doorway, I find him, leaning back with his arms crossed on his desk as if awaiting my arrival.

"Hey," I whisper.

"Hey."

"What's going on? I wasn't sure if I should follow you, having guests and all."

"It's good you came. I just wanted some alone time with you. Come here." I walk to him and he pulls me on top of him. "I was watching you talk tonight. I love to watch you laugh. Your smile is one of the few things that makes me feel…happy." The unusually romantic tone of his compliment makes my cheeks burn red.

"Thank you." He kisses me softly and I feel him harden. "You've been teasing me all night," I say.

"I know and I didn't lure you here to relieve you. That's for later."

"Oh."

"I just wanted to be alone with you for a bit, in this quiet."

"Okay."

"I'm sorry for everything that has happened to you."

"You don't need to apologize. I'm fine, I'll be fine. I am so happy I met you. You rock my world," I say with a smile as I bury my head into his chest.

"You rock mine too," he says under a grin. "Hey, look at me." He tilts my chin up. "I want to say something to you because I think you deserve to hear it from me in a quiet moment. Not during sex, or in a time of pain or chaos, or out of desperation." I nod, not breaking my gaze into his piercing luminous eyes. "Remember when I asked you what it was like to love someone?"

"Yes."

"Remember what you said to me?"

"Yes…and…"

"Tell me," Taylor insists.

"Well, I was just a little sad. Because I thought you might never be able to feel that way about me, because I have always felt that way about you. Even in the car when we first met, you took my breath away. I didn't know it then, but I was falling for you right there."

"I love you," he says as he stares into my eyes; I fight not to look away. "You may not hear me say this much, and you might even question it because of the way I am, or the things I do, but when you do, think back to this moment and know that it will never change."

I smile at him, wishing I could freeze time and be here with him in this still place forever. And I will do my best to never forget it, just as he asked.

"Come on," he says, taking my hand, "let's go back out there before we have to deal with quickie jokes from Lizzy all night," Taylor says.

CHAPTER NINE

It's about midnight when we bid everyone goodnight, including Betty.

"That was so much fun," I say to Taylor as we head into the bedroom. "Thank you for putting this together. The food was fantastic, by the way."

"Yes, I've known Betty nearly all my life. She was the family chef and I always use her for events or dinners."

"I wondered about that. I know how private you are…"

"Yeah, I trust her. The year I first moved into the house, when I wouldn't speak, I used to sneak out of my bedroom at night and wander aimlessly around the house. One night, I walked into the kitchen and she was there. I thought I would be in big trouble, maybe even beaten because that's all I knew. She looked at me and put her fingers over her lips to shush me, which in retrospect was strange because everyone knew I didn't speak. But from that night on, whenever I would sneak out of my bedroom, I would find a chocolate chip cookie and a glass of milk waiting for me in the prep kitchen."

"Oh my god, that is so sweet! Can I just tell you something?"

"Of course."

"You are so blessed."

"What do you mean?"

"I know you have been through terrible things, but it seems all along the way, there were people who cared enough to help you. From the lady who found you, to Betty's cookies in the kitchen, to Lizzy and Henry —"

"And you?"

"If you say so…"

I stand in front of the bathroom mirror to take down my hair, and just as I begin to remove my earrings, Taylor comes up behind me.

"I guess I always focused on the people who did me wrong, and I thought I was damaged irreparably, but you make me feel…normal."

"Thank you for being who you are despite the people who have hurt you."

Taylor nods and exits the bathroom. Having a moment to think about how he teased me all night makes me hot again. I expected him to pounce me once everyone left, but he hasn't. There was something about tonight, a tenderness about him that made me feel so full, so warm and secure in his presence. And strangely, because of that I feel the need to make this night complete by having the other side of Taylor: the full spectrum experience. I strip down to my emerald green lace demi bra and thong and slide open the door that connects the bathroom to the walk-in closet so Taylor won't see me grab a pair of black platform strappy heels. I bring them back into the bathroom, shake my hair out to make it full and luscious and refresh my lipstick with a dark blood-red shade. I take a deep breath and slowly open the bathroom door to combat my shyness.

Taylor is shirtless and barefoot, but still in his jeans looking down at his phone when the sound of door opening catches his attention.

"Woah," he says when he looks up. He throws his phone on the bed and slowly walks over to me taking me in with his eyes, studying my body. "You don't look like a good girl at all right now. You were hiding this under your little conservative outfit tonight?"

I nod. "Taylor, don't tease me anymore." He stands over me, as I lean back on the door frame, resting his hand on it above my head so that his body shrouds mine.

"You've just made me way too fucking hard just to tease you. Feel it," he says as he guides my hands over his jeans and I feel the length of his hardness resting against his thigh. "Do you want this?"

"You know I do."

"Tell me."

"I want it."

"Beg me."

"Please. Fuck me. Make me come."

"More."

"Please Taylor, just fuck me for fuck's sake. Take me to the darkroom. Do whatever you want to me in there." He thrusts his pelvis against mine, the force slamming my hips against the doorframe. He picks me up by my ass; I wrap my legs around his torso, my long brown hair engulfs his face, and he carries me into the darkroom.

"Anything I want?"

I nod, biting my lip in anticipation. He lets me down.

"Get on all fours." I do it without hesitation on the lambskin rug. I want nothing more than to please him at this very moment. "Reach underneath and play with yourself. Suck on your fingers first, make them wet." I follow his instructions. He walks around so that he is facing my backside and he can watch me play with myself. "How does that feel baby?"

"It's good, but not as good as you."

"You're gonna have to wait for that."

I'm so charged I have to slow down in order not to come; I want to come with him tonight. He goes into one of his drawers and pulls something out. "What I

131

really want is to fuck you in the ass, but you wouldn't be able to handle that."

"Do whatever you want."

"Shhh...trust me, you want to ease into that. But I am going to play with your ass." My stomach knots up. I am officially ass virgin. Well sort of. Rick clumsily tried it once and before he was even an eighth of the way in it hurt so much, I made him stop.

He pulls my thong to the side. "Fuck, even your asshole is cute," he says before he glides his tongue over it. "I'm going to put these inside of you, nice and slowly. I need you to relax, okay? Take deep breaths." He gently caresses my back as I feel the pressure of the slickly lubed tiny beads sliding inside of me. I try to contain my moans, but am unable to. The feeling is foreign and tight. "How does it feel?" he asks calmly.

"There's a lot of pressure."

"I know. Your little ass is really tight. Just relax." I take a few more deep breathes and the pressure subsides. "Your little moans are making it hard for me to hold out on fucking you. Stand up." I do so gingerly and he slides my bra off. I take him in as he stands in front of me, his erection begging for me to free it from his jeans. "Those heels, fuck they make your legs and ass look even more amazing." He walks up to me and squats down, kissing me in between my legs over my lace panties. "Oh, your clit," he says as he rubs it with his thumb, "you are really horny, aren't you?"

"Yes."

He stands up and takes the very tips of his tongue to one of my nipples. "I love your breasts. Do you want me to take out my cock?"

"Fuck me with it already!"

"Woah...now wait a minute. I decide when you get fucked," he says with the kind of smirk that tells me he liked my sass. Taylor pulls my thong down to the floor, so that I am naked besides my heels. He guides me by my hand to a spot in front on a huge mirror, likely 8x8 feet. He makes me face it as I stand behind him. "Do you see what I see? Do you understand why I want to fuck you all the time?" I am too modest to answer. His hands invade my body, gliding over and fondling my breasts, his erection firmly against my backside as he slides one hand between my legs, forcing them apart. "I want to be a good guy, Shy, but you make me want to do bad things. Now bend over for me."

To my left is the bed, so I place my hands on it and give him my backside. "Keep your eyes on the mirror. I want you to watch me fuck you. I want you to see your face when I make you come." Finally, he unbuttons his pants and pulls off his underwear. His thick, firm erection stands at attention. "I'm going to put this in your pussy, nice and easy."

We both let out a long moan when he slides inside of me. "You are so wet. Fuck."

I watch him in the mirror, but he never looks at it. Instead, he admires me, rubbing my backside, squeezing it firmly, smacking it, to the point of making me yell out in painful ecstasy. Every time he thrusts deep inside of me, the weight of his pelvis on my backside makes me aware of the beads still inside of me. Taylor keeps the pace, rhythmic and slow. I can tell he is so hard, that if he goes any faster, neither one of us will be able to hold out. He slowly pulls out, almost all the way, and makes it disappear inside of me over and over. Being a spectator to our beautiful bodies intertwined in these lustful acts make me too hot to hold out any longer and I tighten around him. My moans become louder with each thrust.

"Tell me when you're coming, Shy," he says in a breathy voice.

"I am! I'm coming!" Taylor does not change his pace, instead he very slowly pulls out the beads so that there is a total feeling of release combined with the explosion. I can't even look at the mirror, as I tilt my head back, crying out his name in a shaky voice, clenching onto the bed as if I would float away if I were to let go. My legs shake so much that I think might collapse, but Taylor holds onto me. He then lets out a deep moan, squeezing the flesh of my waist as he releases into me.

I collapse on the bed and he on top of me, our sweaty bodies panting in unison. "You rock my world," I say to him.

"You…you…Christ…" he says in between breathes and for once, I believe Taylor is completely lost for words.

❖❖❖

As I pack my bags, I am bursting with excitement to go on vacation with the most interesting people I know. We settled on Labor Day weekend to take advantage of the extra day off. Kristin invited Chad, so he managed not only go get both of us the day off on Friday, but also an early Thursday departure.

"Taylor, this is a little ridiculous for four days," I say as I sit on top of my suitcase trying to cram in the last bit of clothes. He insisted Mona, his (*our?*) stylist, take me shopping, so I have a huge travel wardrobe with no baggage limits since we are using the jet.

"It is, but who cares? You don't have to lug it through an airport or anything. If you don't want to bring all this stuff, take some stuff out."

"But I like it all!"

Taylor throws a pair of balled up socks at me.

Since the incident with Eric, I have spent every night at Taylor's place. I still have intentions of going back to live in the condo, I just haven't gotten around to confronting it. Plus, staying with Taylor has been great. In the morning he either sees me off if he's working from home, or we drive in together if he's going to headquarters. We have slowly been trying to move forward from Eric's betrayal, and deep down inside, I fear being forced to confront the last place I saw him will revive the many mixed feelings I have about him and what he did. I think it helps Taylor to see that I am doing okay, and if I begin to show signs that I am not, I will take him down with me.

"Do you think I should bring a sweater?" I ask.

"Maybe something light, you always get cold."

My favorite cardigan is in the box Marsha gave to me weeks ago that I have yet to unload. It's in a storage closet near the foyer and I lug it into the bedroom, resting it on a chair. Out of the box comes the cardigan, various books, a couple of photos, some used notepads, and a small unmarked envelope. Inside the envelope is a piece of gold jewelry. I tilt the envelope so that it spills onto my palm. On a thin yellow-gold chain is an angel wing charm and, separately, what appears to be a solitaire ruby. It is puzzling to find this in the box because it does not belong to me. I assume it's Marsha's, maybe she accidentally put it in there, but a quick text to her informs me that she found it in my old office caught in the back of one of the file drawers. She tells me to hold onto it since no one has asked about it (that file cabinet hadn't been used for over a year before becoming mine) and she's almost certain it may never be claimed. It's a pretty, charming piece and I slip it into my travel case to bring with me on the trip.

As I continue to pack, I receive a call from Mr. MacAllister, but ignore it, resolving to call him when I can find some private time to speak with him. Eventually, Taylor retreats to his office for an overseas conference call late into the night, and I sneak off to the small office upstairs to call him.

"Hi, Mr. MacAllister."

"Hi Shyla. How are you?"

"I'm well. Any news?"

"I'm afraid to say, I may be at an impasse."

"How so?"

"Everyone I can find who was in C.O.S who knew Lyla says they believe she is dead. As far as they all know Alan Peters was obsessed with her and she rarely ever left his sight. The common belief is the reason her body was not at the scene is because she was killed and disposed of before then. They don't believe Alan would have let her out alive."

"Do you think that's true?"

"I have to tell you, my gut says something is off. I have no evidence to go either way, but I just don't believe she was killed. It makes no sense that her son would be left alive in that case. I believe she had to have protected him in some way. The problem is, she seems to have literally vanished off of the face of the earth. She may be in another country with a new identity and has had many years to cover her tracks. I want to keep digging, but I have to let you know I don't think I can find her without a break."

"I understand, but I want you to keep digging. Let's keep going until we have exhausted every possible lead. Spoken to every person who ever knew her."

"I agree, I know there is a break out there, and I will keep searching as long as you want me to, but I have to ask you something."

"Okay."

"I assume you're not investing into this as a hobby, that there is a personal reason behind this…"

"Yes," I say hesitantly.

"Do you know someone who knew her? Knew about her?"

"I can't. I can't bring them into this."

"They may be the key."

He's right, Taylor may not be of any help, but Taylor's father had to have known her body was never found and he intentionally kept that information from his son. But I don't have the nerve to send a P.I. to Taylor's father, that would really be overstepping my bounds.

"That has to be an absolute last resort. I can't bring this back without knowing she is alive first. It would be too painful, dealing with her death all over again."

"Well my next step is to find out the identity of the child's father. Even though he was not part of the cult, he may know something."

"No, you can't go there."

"You're really narrowing my field here."

"Please trust me here, we need fresh information."

"Just because he's old news doesn't mean he doesn't have fresh information."

"He is on that list of people we don't touch until we have exhausted every other person who was in C.O.S. I know it's difficult with all the name changing and the moving around the country, but there are people out there that have to know something."

"Okay. We'll do it your way, but this could be a long haul."

"I understand, and thank you." As we are about to hang up, I remember a clue.

"Wait, there is something I can tell you. The person who saved the child, she was a close friend of Lyla's it seems. She had long brown hair. Maybe you can ask if anyone knows who she was."

"Yes, that's helpful. I did find reports about a woman discovering the scene, her name was Marie Portero. It looks like her whereabouts are unknown at this point too. She definitely left the state, so I am trying to track her down as well. These survivors are a close-knit group and I am beginning to think they helped both of these women disappear, but again, this is all a hunch."

I make my way downstairs feeling uneasy about this whole C.O.S investigation. Maybe some questions are better left unanswered, but I feel in my gut that unraveling this mystery can help Taylor. If his mother went through great lengths to protect him, he needs to know. But what if after all this, Taylor doesn't care or loses his trust in me? Am I trying to help him resolve the pain of his past, or trying to satisfy a morbid curiosity? At this point, I am too deep in this investigation to let it go. I need to know what happened to Lyla and I sincerely feel Taylor does too.

CHAPTER TEN

Giddiness and excitement permeates in the air as we all wheel our luggage to the jet. Lizzy insisted that we all wear giant sun hats, so Kristin and I comply. I match mine up with a black sundress with big bright flowers of various colors, a pair of wedge espadrilles, and a large pair of black sunglasses.

"Don't you look glamorous," Taylor said when he saw me emerge from the bedroom dressed and ready to go.

He is quiet during the ride to the airport, but when we emerge from the SUV and he sees both Lizzy and Kristin wearing enormous hats as well, he turns to me and asks: "Let me guess, Lizzy's idea?"

"How did you know?" I asked.

"Because I do," he says with a cocked eyebrow.

Chad and Kristin look happy and comfortable together. This is the first time Chad and Henry will meet each other and I wondered if there would be any tension, but Henry uses his gregarious nature to make Chad comfortable and so he seems to be none the wiser about Kristin and Henry's one night stand.

Before taking off, I text my mother, just to let her know I'll be out of town.

Me:
Just an FYI. I will be out of town for a few days. Going on vacation to Costa Rica.

Mom:
With Taylor?

Me:
Yes. Kristin and a bunch of others too.

Mom:
Okay, well have fun and stay safe.

Something is off about her. I can't put my finger on it, but she hasn't been herself since I last saw her. I think it's because she saw the cuts, but her usual tactic would be to flood me with concern. Instead, she has been short and dare I say, avoidant. It's usually me dodging the phone calls or concerns.

Chad and I devote most of our plane ride to working. In fact, almost all of us do. Once we land, we are driven to the Arenal area where we will be staying. We arrive at an opulent mansion on the hillside with beautiful views of the volcano. Even having been exposed to so much luxury since I met Taylor, it's hard not to be in awe of this palatial home. The ceilings must be thirty feet high, with marble floors and colossal white columns that lead to a seemingly endless infinity pool overlooking the mountainside and volcano.

We all agree to immediately change into swimsuits and take advantage of the beautiful pool and deck.

I pull the tags off of my new royal-blue bandeau bikini. "You're gonna give Henry a seizure," Taylor says when he gives me the once over.

"That is such old news," I say, checking out my butt in the mirror.

"No, he still thinks you're hot and he's a perv. I don't blame him though."

"It's not like we all didn't go skinny dipping together."

"Yeah, but it was dark."

"You're not jealous are you?"

"I don't mind people looking, I was just making an observation. Besides, you know I like to get a little jealous, it gets me fired up."

I grab my sun hat and sunglasses and walk out to the pool. Taylor stays out of the fray, sitting quietly on a lounge chair with his laptop. I understand the perks of his life come with huge challenges such as always needing to be connected, but something about him seems off today. Besides a few comments about my hat and bikini, he hasn't said much to me all morning. Instead of pestering him, I give him space and instead hang out with the people who want to have some fun instead. Henry, Kristin and Chad are already at the pool so I join them. The butler — cabana-man — I am not sure what to call him -- brings us drinks as we discuss our plans for what to do during our stay. As I chat with the gang, Lizzy comes out and sits next to Taylor. She leans in to talk to him and he puts his laptop aside and has a very engaged conversation with her. I attempt to eavesdrop, but promptly notice they are speaking in French. Taylor and Lizzy have never done that before, exclusively spoken French in the presence of the rest of us, and while we are not in the same conversation, it irks me.

He's been quiet all morning, not saying a word since we have arrived except to point out that his friend thinks I am hot, but here he is engaging with Lizzy to the point of excluding the rest of us by speaking another language. They then both stand up and enter the house. I refuse to act jealous by following them, and I know they don't see each other that way, but I am so used to Taylor's attentiveness that seeing him place it on any other woman makes me uneasy. I turn my attention back the conversation at the pool and another hour passes, then another half hour and they are nowhere to be seen.

We all agree to shower and head out to a restaurant together, emerging from the pool and entering the house all at once. Taylor and Lizzy are in a deep conversation and abruptly stop and disengage when we all enter. I begin to seethe. This is our first vacation together as a couple and he seems to be more interested in spending time with Lizzy than me. I walk directly to our bedroom without saying a word to him.

He follows a few minutes later. "It looks like we will be leaving in an hour," he says.

"I know," I respond in a short tone.

"Something wrong?"

"Nope," but my tone says it all.

"Okay, so something is wrong. Are you going to tell me, or are you going to beat around the bush about it?"

"I would just like to get ready for dinner if that's okay with you."

"So are you going to be short with me all night?"

I grab my things and go directly into the bathroom without responding, but he follows me.

"This isn't fair, you need to tell me what I've done if you're upset with me."

"I don't need to do anything." I am sort of enjoying pulling his strings to get his attention even if it's in a childish manner.

"How much have you had to drink?" His question only fuels my anger.

"Of course that could be the only reason I could be upset with you, Mr. Perfect."

"Wow Shyla, I am not sure what I did to make you this upset..."

"That's the problem!"

"So I am supposed to be a mind-reader?"

"Why don't you go talk to Lizzy, maybe she can help you figure it out!"

I watch his face as my comment registers. It changes from despondent, to a grin, to all out keeled over laughter. Between laughs he gets out a response. "Wait, so you're jealous of me and Lizzy?" He laughs some more, as my cheeks flush red with embarrassment at how silly he is making me feel.

"It's not funny."

"I'm sorry. Yes, it is."

"Well I am so glad I could humor you," I say trying to hold back a smile, his unusual laughter is contagious and is flushing out my anger against my will.

"You've been quiet all day, and then right when we get here, you two go off and have Francophone quality time. Sorry that I was hoping to have some time with you."

"It has nothing to do with us. Lizzy just wanted to bounce some things off of me." I don't say a word back. "You know, I have to get you jealous more often, you get really cute when you're angry," he says walking out of the bathroom.

"Just let me borrow your creepy journal of sluts, that'll give me tons of fuel." *Oops, that wasn't very nice.*

Taylor's eyes widen and his smile disappears. "Low blow," he says in a firm tone, closing the door behind him. Well fuck, now *he's pissed*. When I exit the bathroom, Taylor passes me without saying a word; *now this is the silent treatment*. Man can he get icy, I mean I feel an actual drop in temperature as he passes me. We both quietly ride to the restaurant, avoiding conversation with one another, while engaging in conversation with others. Usually when Taylor gets quiet, he is universally so. Everyone just chalks it up to Taylor being Taylor, but tonight the fact that he is not off by himself having some quiet time is a clear signal that he is sending me a message. Surprisingly, Lizzy is pretty quiet too. She didn't spend any time with us in the pool and has been quietly downing wine in the car.

We arrive at an open air steakhouse in La Fortuna and promptly place our orders. As soon as the waiter walks away, a giant toad hops its way into the restaurant and over to us as some of the group tries to snap pictures on their phones.

"Okay guys, I'm sorry, but I have to get this out," Lizzy blurts. Everyone at the table turns to her and goes silent. "Kristin, Chad, I'm sorry if you feel weird about this, but I didn't want to exclude you from this dinner even though we just started getting to know each other."

I look at Taylor to get some sort of reaction from him, wondering what it is that Lizzy wants to tell us. He keeps his eyes on her.

Henry looks clueless and just as confused as I feel.

Lizzy takes a deep breath, her eyes water.

"Lizzy, please tell us, you're making me nervous," I plead, fearing some terrible news.

She takes a big dramatic gulp and looks up before saying: "Guys, I am going to have a baby!"

Henry almost spits out his beer.

We all look around at one another, bewildered, except for Taylor, of course.

"Are you pregnant?" I ask.

"Not yet. I have been planning this, Taylor already knows because I'll eventually have to take some time off." And now I feel like a giant raging hemorrhoid for giving him a hard time about spending the afternoon talking to Lizzy.

"Planning?" I ask.

"Yes, I am almost 36. I'm not getting any younger, and I don't think I'll ever find that guy, you know. I like being on my own. And even If I do, it might be too late.

I have always wanted to be a mother and I have accomplished all the other things I wanted with my life. This is the one thing that has been missing. I don't need a man to be a mother because I have an amazing network of friends and family and I include you all in that group. I know I won't be alone in this. That's why I wanted to share this with you. I'll be getting a donor and going through hormones and stuff and I wanted you all to know if I start acting like a hormonal psycho bitch."

"Well, I am happy for you, and I am so looking forward to becoming an auntie," I say, getting up to give her a hug. Henry is suspiciously quiet and I can only think he is taking some time to digest everything. They have always been partners in crime together, but when she has a baby, things will change big-time.

We all toast to her announcement; Henry seems to do so begrudgingly.

"Since I won't be able to have wild fun anymore… we need to live it up on this vacation!" Lizzy proclaims. We barrage Lizzy with curious questions about her plans, when about halfway through the meal, Henry excuses himself from the table. Everyone goes silent, as the sound of his chair sliding against the floor is like a nonverbal protest. We all give befuddled looks to one another, unsure if anyone should follow him.

After a few minutes, Lizzy, who is visibly distracted by Henry's absence, excuses herself from the table to talk to him. Shortly after we all head back to the house. The mood in the car is different on the way back since there is now more than one silent treatment being dosed out in the car. Kristin and Chad, innocent bystanders caught up in the awkwardness, also sit in silence. When we return to the house, Kristin and Chad announce they are going to the hot tub while the rest of us retreat to our bedrooms.

Taylor is unbuttoning his shirt when I enter. I close the door behind me.

"So let me guess. You knew all along?"

"Yup," he says not looking in my direction.

"And you were quiet because you wanted to tell me but couldn't."

"Uh huh," he says pulling off his shirt.

I walk closely to him with my head down. "I'm sorry," I say as cutely as possible, turning on the baby-faced look.

"You don't trust me and I'm not sure you ever will."

"Of course I do. Just because someone expresses that they are feeling upset about something, doesn't mean they don't trust you."

"Well, you pretty much tried to blame me for Em's death. Then you thought, I don't know, that Lizzy and I were, what? Fucking around?"

"No! I was just jealous. I was being needy. I like having all of your attention. It's greedy, I know."

"I was trying to be a good friend and boss. She wanted to be the one to tell you. You're the one who has told me I should be available to the people who care about me."

"I know."

"But you throw stuff in my face. Stuff that is important to me, stuff that I only share with you. You use it as a way to push my buttons. I know the game Shy. I can play the game, and the reason it pushes my buttons is because you are the only person who can do that. Otherwise, I would not give a half a shit. There is a reason the list of people before you is long. What you pulled in there would've gotten any other girl her own personal hotel room away from me during this trip and she would have never seen me again. That right there should remove any insecurities you have about whatever scenarios you have built up in your head."

"I can't help it. You make me a little crazy."

"Likewise."

"Well, I'm happy for Lizzy."

"If that's what she wants to do, I told her she has my full support."

"What's the deal with Henry?"

"Henry? Oh, he's madly in love with her. You didn't know that?"

"What?" I ask in disbelief. "Um, no, I didn't. I asked you if they ever did anything and you said you weren't sure."

"You asked if they fucked. And no, I haven't asked them, but I would guess yes. That is not the same as asking if Henry is in love with her."

"Has he told you?"

"Not in those words, but he doesn't have to."

"Why doesn't he just tell her?"

"He knows it wouldn't work out," he says a matter of factly as he removes his pants, revealing his tanned physique in a pair of boxer briefs. "They're too much alike. He can't keep faithful and she's a lot to handle. Just because you love someone, doesn't mean it's meant to be."

"Does Lizzy know?"

"I don't know. I can't imagine she'd be so clueless."

"Well color me clueless because I had no idea."

"Sometimes it's better. I suffer from the ability to read people all too well. I wish I didn't."

"I guess. Do you think he wants to be the dad?"

"I'm not even going to touch the idea of those two creating a spawn," Taylor jokes.

"What about you?" I ask.

"What about me?"

"Do you imagine yourself being a dad one day?"

"I had a feeling this would be coming."

"Sorry. I was just asking," I shrug.

"No, it's fine. I was also thinking about that a lot today. I knew her bringing up that news would raise some important questions and I wanted to see how I felt about the whole thing. Which is also why I was feeling contemplative."

"Oh."

He squares up to me. "Listen, I've never imagined myself being a father. I never entertained the thought previously, because well, I never imagined being in a real relationship with those possibilities. Hell, I never thought of even being in any long term relationship. And now it is something I have to think about, because if there is anyone I would want those things with, that person would be you…"

"But?"

Taylor takes a deep sigh. "But, right now, I still don't see myself ever being a father. I don't think I am equipped. I don't think I can love something just because I helped create it. You know how they say your child comes into the world and suddenly you fall in love? I know it's a very big possibility I will feel nothing, and then what? I can't gamble on bringing a child into this world that won't be loved by its father."

"But if it was a person we made together? A person we created out of our mutual love, don't you think that you would love it?"

"I don't know. I just don't know. Let's say we have a kid, and I don't love it, that will change the way you feel about me. Won't it?"

"I don't know."

"It will. Because you will expect what anybody expects, except you won't get it. I know what it's like to feel uncared for and I don't want to continue the cycle. Look at my brother and me -- what if this is not all environmental, what if we're defective?"

"You're not defective."

"We'll never know."

"Don't you want to have children to make it right? To make right the things your parents did wrong? I always wanted my kids to have a dad...not even an amazing one, just have one." My face sinks, it's something I try not to think about often, but like Taylor, I feel as though I missed out on certain things in my childhood.

"You can't have children to make up for other people's mistakes. That's not how it works."

I guess he's right, but I can't say I'm not devastated. It's not that my ultimate fantasy in life is to have a child. I don't think I would do what Lizzy is doing. But I always imagined if I found the right guy, and if we loved each other, we could make the family I never had. To have the possibility eliminated just like that, to not see the beautiful dark-haired babies we would have, breaks my heart in a way I never expected. If he and I were never married, I could live with that, but to know the option of a child is off the table kills so many of the dreams I had begun to imagine for us. This vacation has gotten a lot heavier than I expected. Part of me wonders if it's not only that he can't love his own child, but if he fears my love and attention for him will be diluted if I spread it to someone else. After all, I felt that way when he gave Lizzy a few hours of his time to discuss a life-changing announcement with her.

"It could change, I don't know. Other people have had a lifetime to think about this stuff, I've only had a few months." He doesn't even bring up the idea of marriage, not that I was even expecting it, but these discussions do come up eventually in relationships.

"I understand," I say. I'm at a loss with what to do with this information other than mourn the children we will likely never have. I don't know if it's a deal breaker, and even if it was, I know I wouldn't leave him over it.

Deal breakers don't exist for me with Taylor. I can only hope his mind will change over time.

"Well this vacation has turned out to be contentious," Taylor says to lighten the mood.

"I'm going to look for Lizzy, see how she is doing." I need to talk to someone else, get my mind off of Taylor's confession.

Kristin and Chad are alone on the pool deck, and Lizzy is in the shower. Eventually, I stumble on Henry, who is sitting alone in front of the house, smoking a cigarette.

"I didn't know you smoked."

"I don't, I bummed it off of *Cristobal*," he says in a Spanish accent, taking a drag. "Want a puff?"

"What the hell," I say as I sit on the step next to him. It seems like we have both have had a rough night.

"So, are you as shocked about Lizzy as I am?" I ask.

"Oh yeah."

"I am really happy for her. I just never knew she wanted to be a mommy."

"She and I had talked about it before. Her wanting a family. I guess I just thought that one day it would just happen with us." His forthrightness with this information takes me aback. "But, it would never work out, her and me." His mirroring of Taylor's analysis freaks me out a bit.

"Have you ever told her?"

"Oh she knows. We've always joked that we were soulmates, two birds of a feather, and it's because of that we could never pull the trigger."

"Do you want to be the father? Has she asked?"

"We talked tonight. The possibility was tossed out, but I can't just give my sperm to her and forget about the kid. I would want to be a dad to him or her and that could complicate things. I'll love the kid because it would be mine too. It's not like giving up sperm to a sperm bank. I don't know if I am ready, and she's not going to wait around for me to become husband or dad material. I don't blame her because that time may never come. She's a smart gal."

"I get it. It's pretty heavy."

"She thinks I have great genes though, so there's that," he says, nudging me with his elbow. *Tooting his own horn, how typical.*

"Well, hold onto your knickers, because I am about to compliment you and I am not rolling on E, but I think you would have some pretty cute kiddos."

"How about you? You know Taylor is crazy about you." I shrug. "Seriously, he was a player. Well, that's the wrong word, he didn't parade women around or brag, but I knew he had his pieces on the side. He never introduced any girls he was with to us and he would have never brought them on vacation. Plus, I see the way you touch him. I know how he is about that. At the gala, in Russia, he was the most relaxed I had ever seen. You didn't know the pre-Shyla Taylor."

"There's a 'pre-Shyla Taylor?' What was he like?"

"Well, he was cool with me and Lizzy, but that's because we get him. Probably not as well as you do, but we could get him out of his shell. We know he needs his space, we get that his moods are his and that doesn't mean shit about our friendship. But he was way more secluded and isolated. He would be around for a few weeks and then we wouldn't see him for months. He would just hole up in his house, use couriers and conference calls. He would rarely come to meetings unless his presence was necessary. This is the longest I have seen him be so happy. Even when he used to be around, that didn't guarantee he would be the Taylor we see so often now."

"Really? Sometimes I feel like I can't get through."

"Woman, you have no idea," he says, passing me the cigarette. "He's not the kind of guy that will scream for the hills about how great he feels, but you've had more of an impact than you might ever know." Henry doesn't know it, but he has pieced my heart back together from hearing the news that Taylor may never want a child.

"Well, not that it means anything, but I think you would make a really cool dad."

"Oh, it means something," he says, as he puts out the cigarette and heads back into the house.

*** *

The next morning we wake up to beautiful Costa Rican weather and plan on renting some ATVs to take along the various nature trails. Due to the excitement, I have a hard time sleeping in on vacation, so I wake up before Taylor. I slip out of the room hoping to make coffee for the group, but find people preparing breakfast in the kitchen. This must be a surprise from Taylor or Henry. I slip back into the bedroom and onto the bed unnoticed since Taylor's meds make him a heavier sleeper than normal. He is sprawled out in a pair of boxers with no shirt on. I admire him in this moment of peace and quiet, following the outline of his full lips and angular jawline. I admire his long, dark eyelashes that beautifully frame his greenish-blue eyes. He rustles for a moment, but doesn't wake, so I continue to watch him sleep peacefully. A few minutes later he opens his eyes.

"Have you been watching me sleep?"

"Yeah, there's a whole crew of people in the kitchen, but I am too excited to go back to sleep. You're fun to look at."

"Well, you're sweet, but maybe we need to get you some hobbies," he says, sitting up.

"My plate's pretty full, but thanks. It's a full time job, checking you out."

"I know, I can't stop looking at me either."

I shove him and he grabs my wrists, toppling me over and pinning me down.

"You really think you are going to overpower me?"

"Where there's a will, there's a way!" I say as I take one leg and attempt to reach it over his head.

"Oooh, you're scrappy," he says, pinning it back down. "If you keep fighting me, you're gonna get fucked. Literally."

"You're not as strong as you look," I say as I thrust my hips up enough to elevate him and squirm out from under him. I get on my knees and dive towards him, getting him on his back. "I think it's time for me to be boss."

"That'll never happen. You know this is only happening because I'm letting you win."

"Oh shut up," I say as I mount him, pin his hands down and ride him.

***

We emerge from the bedroom, all smiles, raring and ready to go and join everyone else for breakfast. The spread is delectable, including *el tipico* Costa Rican breakfast. After a long day of exploring the lush, tropical countryside, we get back to the house utterly exhausted.

"Come on ladies, let's put Cristobal to work," Lizzy says with her arms around Kristin and me as we walk back into the house. We all congregate on the poolside, music blaring, tropical drinks in hand.

Taylor refrains from the alcoholic part of the festivities. "I'll pass, but please enjoy yourself. I don't mind a horny drunk girl in my bed," he says winking at me. After a couple of drinks, I feel loosey-goosey and I pull Taylor out of his seat and insist he dance with me since Henry is dancing with Lizzy (things seem to be better between them) and Chad and Kristin are dancing. He very hesitantly allows me to drag him to his feet, wearing a pained look on his face. Cristobal throws on some salsa music and I figure there is finally something I know that Taylor doesn't.

"I'm going to teach you salsa."

"Oh no."

"Put your hand here and your other hand here. Now you have to lead me like this." I show him his footwork. "Now do what I did." Taylor takes a few steps and does a pretty good job for his first time.

"Here lemme help ju," Cristobal says in a thick Spanish accent. Taylor doesn't seem fazed that this man is stealing me from his arms. Let's just say that between Taylor and me, I wouldn't be the person Cris would be interested in. Cristobal goes nuts with me, his salsa literacy is way better than mine and he sends me twirling and gliding all over the place. Taylor watches intently with a big smile on his face, his chin resting on his hand.

"Pass me the lady," Taylor says, "I think I got this." Cristobal pulls me in close, then twirls me away from his body so that I spin into Taylor's arms.

"Asi?" Taylor asks Cristobal as he leads me in some basic moves.

"Hablas español?"

"Claro que si!" Taylor replies.

"Ay, pues dale, lo estas haciendo bien, mi hermano!" Cristobal claps with excitement.

"Show off," I say as Taylor dips me.

"You know Spanish too."

"I can order an enchilada. You know like a gazillion languages."

He pulls me close, a la Dirty Dancing, and we start grinding on each other. Taylor nuzzles my neck as I notice that Chad, Kristin and Henry are gone. Lizzy is talking it up with Cristobal at the bar. The song ends just as Taylor's phone starts lighting up and buzzing on his lounge chair. "Shit. Shy, I gotta take this."

"It's fine," I say as Taylor grabs his phone and walks to the other side of the house for some quiet. I meander back into the living room and find Chad crashed on the sofa. *Lightweight.* I wander through the rest of the house looking for the others, making it to a spare bedroom with the door closed. After giving two good warning knocks, I open the door.

Henry jumps away from Kristin, her trademarked lipstick is smudged on his mouth.

"Really?" I exclaim, shutting the door and marching off back to my room. I hear Kristin's footsteps pattering behind me.

"Shyla," she whispers. "Shyla!"

"You're nuts."

"Come here," she drags me by the arm into her room and closes the door. "It's not what it looks like. Henry kissed me."

"You know normally I wouldn't care. You are your own person and make your own decisions, but this is my boss you're dating. And you know what? I like him and he doesn't deserve to be played."

"I like him too! I swear, we were only flirting, but then he pounced me right before you opened the door."

"You were in a spare room with the door closed."

"I got carried away for a second, but I realized I was being stupid before he kissed me."

"You know the only reason I believe you? Because he did the same thing to me, before I started seeing Taylor."

"He did?"

"Yes, he's a huge whore. Maybe borderline sex addict; I don't know."

"Why didn't you tell me he hit on you?"

"Because I didn't think it mattered. Because you're with Chad, and you two just did your thing because you were both available to each other that night. If I had thought you really liked him, I would have warned you more thoroughly."

"Now you have to tell me what you know about him."

"Guys like Henry don't change. They never do. He'll be the first one to tell you."

"I know, I know, but he's so hot. I really was just flirting and I'm tipsy..."

"You can't just flirt with Henry. He doesn't just flirt. What if I was Chad? You would've really hurt him and caused a big riff here."

"I know, I know. Chad's passed out though. I would never put him in a position to see that."

I palm my forehead. "I just don't want to see you mess things up with Chad because you and Henry get all grabby and kissy when you've had too much to drink. I know he's good looking, and fun, and rich, but he'll be just like the other guys you've dated."

"Well minus the rich thing, but I get your point. So, you really think he's that bad?"

"Not bad, just not right." I pause for a moment and whisper: "You can't say anything...but do you know he's in love with Lizzy? Like seriously in love, and he can't commit to her? I think he's going after you because he's confused. No offense, you're hot and fabulous, but I spoke to him last night and there is a lot going on in his head. I know he has no shame, but he respects relationships. I don't think under normal circumstances he would try to go after you with Chad in the house. I think he drank too much and he's acting out because he is incapable of committing to the person who he is in love with and she's moving on without him."

"So that's why he was pouting during dinner."

"Yes. Honestly, I didn't know until Taylor told me. So please, do not risk losing Chad over playing around with Henry. He is a dead end. You need to stop trying to go after the guys who you think you can save."

"I won't, I won't. And I would make sure that no matter what happens with me and Chad, it doesn't affect your job. You know Chad's not like that."

"I do, but hurt feelings make people do crazy things. And I am telling you this because I love you. If you don't want to be with Chad, don't, but don't hurt him. Do it the right way."

"No, I want to be with him. I really do. I guess I'm freaking out because this feels really permanent. I mean, I really, really like him. I am so used to getting burned and sometimes I feel like I have to do it before he hurts me first."

"Please stop trying to sabotage yourself. Chad is not a jerk, he will not intentionally hurt you. You know that. Your relationship with him is not a competition."

"Thank you for talking some sense into me. You need to have your own column or TV show about relationships. You always have your shit together." *If she only knew.*

CHAPTER ELEVEN

During our final full day in Arenal, we spend an afternoon in our own private hot springs. Taylor packs his phone away and promises to give me one full afternoon of his attention. Something I only notice on this final day is that Eric has not crossed my mind since we arrived in Costa Rica. I thought I would be scared and paranoid from the thought of possibly being geographically closer to him, but the security of my friends and Taylor make me forget for a while that there is someone out there who may want to hurt us. That feeling might return when we are back home, no longer tucked away in the jungle, but for now, I am happy to be truly relaxed for the first time in weeks.

Kristin is all over Chad today; my gut tells me it's to make it clear to Henry that she is now off limits. Learning what I have about Henry gives me an entirely new view on his behavior. It's as if he torturing himself. But why? Why would someone want to do that? I know it seems almost hypocritical for me to ask that, but I'm not referring to the flesh. Physical pain is fleeting, and it can even feel good under the proper circumstances, but emotional torture, a life full of what-ifs, is far more painful than a slap or a cut. Maybe he genuinely wants two opposing things, and so, his needs will never be reconciled. One will have to give in to the other. For a moment that night when we shared the cigarette, I was certain he would choose to convince Lizzy that he should be the father of her child, that even though they might not be together, they could still share a life together. But less than 24 hours later, I stumble upon him trying to make out with my friend while her boyfriend is passed out in the next room. Now I see how helpless he really is.

Upon our return to the house Taylor informs me that he has made surprise dinner plans just for the two of us. It's very humid, so I put my hair back into a high bun and finally get to sport a white, billowy, off-the-shoulder mini dress I bought for the trip. I pair it with strappy gold heels and remember the necklace that Marsha slipped into my box.

"You look so glamorous!" Lizzy says as I enter the living room. Taylor looks striking as usual, wearing a pair of pale chinos and a white linen shirt with the sleeves rolled up. He tans well and his eyes pop now more than ever against the olive glow.

"Ready?" he asks.

"Sure. Where are we going?"

"You'll find out soon enough." Our driver is a local, but I can't help but feel really nervous as he navigates the twists and turns on the very dark country roads. "You're scared."

"No…Okay, yes. It's so dark, it feels like we are going to career off the road," I whisper.

"We'll be fine. If we are gonna go out, something tells me the circumstances would be far more dramatic than this."

"Well, isn't that comforting?"

Eventually, we arrive to a very isolated side of the mountain. It is pitch black, so dark that the driver needs to use an industrial flashlight to guide us down the path.

"If I didn't know any better, I would think you are trying to lead me to my imminent death," I whisper to

Taylor as I struggle to walk in my heels. "I wish you had told me not to wear these things."

"There's a simple solution to that." Taylor swoops me up in his arms as I let out a yelp. I wrap my arms around his neck as he carries me through the dark mountainside. It is eerily silent, yet alive with countless exotic animal noises surrounding us. Minutes later, I see a light in the distance and once we arrive, a picnic area surrounded by tiki torches and completely canopied by sheer fabric. The torches cast a soft yellow glow that make the mosquito nets look like delicate chiffon. Taylor puts me down and raises the netting for me to pass through. The lavishly decorated picnic area is lush with pillows and fabrics and looks like an ancient king's harem.

"Make yourself comfortable."

"Taylor, this is crazy. I love it."

"Turn around." And behind me in the distance are gorgeous nighttime views of the volcano; bright orange glowing lava splitting the black night-sky.

"Oh my god, that's beautiful! When did you think of this? Is it because I was upset we couldn't see it the other day?" We had tried to observe the lava-side of the volcano, but intense fog had made it impossible.

He simply smiles at me.

"I thought we could just chill out here for a while. It's been fun, but I need a break from everyone. Being around people non-stop. It gets me on edge."

"I think you've been great. And if you want to spend some time unwinding in the middle of the Costa Rican wilderness with views of a glowing volcano, who am I to protest?

We dine on cheese, crackers, and wine. I lay my head on his lap and we sit in silence for a long while.

"You know, I spoke to Henry the other night."

"Did you?"

"Yeah, he told me he was in love with Lizzy. You were right."

"I know."

"I just don't get him. He has a heart to heart with me about how he is afraid that if he doesn't step up, he'll never have the chance to have a life with Lizzy and then the next day, I catch him trying to make out with Kristin. It makes no sense."

"People are who they are. There is no point in trying to figure it out. We're all full of contradictions, some just wear them more obviously than others. I assume that's why he's in love with Lizzy, she doesn't try to change him, or insist he becomes someone else. And yet it's the very same reason why they'll never be together."

"Isn't it tragic?"

"I don't know. Would an ultimatum that forced him to resent her be any less tragic?"

"I guess not."

"They're caught in a paradox. He loves her because she won't be with him because she loves him the way he is."

"You just made my brain hurt," I say as I fiddle with the charm on my neck.

"Let me see that," Taylor says, sliding the charm out of my fingers. His tone shifts from relaxed to interrogative. "Shy, where did you get this?" I sit up quickly, and look down at it wondering how this innocent little necklace could cause such a reaction.

"Marsha put it in the box she gave to me. She found it in my old office and thought it was mine. I told her it wasn't, but she told me to hold onto it. Why? Do you know whose it is?" He leans in and places it in his fingers again, closely observing it, twirling it as he shakes his head and moves his lips silently. He is obviously in disbelief. "Taylor." He quickly yanks it off of my neck and takes a closer look. "You broke it!"

"You can't wear this. This is *Em's* necklace."

"What?"

"Yeah. She swore she lost it at my place. She went nuts that week, apparently it had a lot of sentimental value. Her mother had given it to her for her 16th birthday. She thought she took it off at my place and that the cleaning lady had stolen it. It was a mess. She was crying about it that whole week and she was upset because I wouldn't fire Irma. Then I broke up with her the next week."

"Over the necklace?"

"Well, partly. I didn't like how she accused Irma. But, like I told you, our time together had run its course."

"Woah. I had no idea. I would have never have worn this if I had known."

"I know. We should just get it back to her mom."

"Absolutely. Listen, I'll send it back to Marsha and have her send it to Emily's family. I'll keep it safe in the case that I brought it in," I say as I take the chain from him and slip it in my purse.

"You sure? I can do it."

"Marsha told me how many times she reminded you to get me the box and we saw how that went. You're too busy to be bothered with these trivial things."

The beautiful dark jungle that was once a relaxing retreat turns ominous. I was wearing the necklace of a dead girl. A necklace that was very important to her and preceded the demise of her relationship with Taylor. My earlier doubts begin to creep in. Henry told me I didn't know the pre-Shyla Taylor, the man who would spend months holed up in his house, who had sex slaves at his beck and call and who would then discard them on a whim. I often forget who he was when we first met: his cold, calculated demeanor even when he thought I was special. I can only imagine how cold he could have been to her. After Taylor told me about her death, and our ensuing argument, I tried to bury it deep in my thoughts, to move on past their relationship, but I can't help but feel as though this is a sign. My dangerous curiosity, the one that blew the case of Taylor's mother's death wide open, the one that unlocked Taylor's bedroom door, begins to rear its ugly face again. I must learn more about Emily, if only to learn more about Taylor.

❈ ❈ ❈

The Monday afternoon on the day of our return is spent quietly in Taylor's house. He retreats to his office to do some catching up, which gives me an opportunity to feed my hunger for knowledge about Emily. Unfortunately simply googling "Emily Brown" yields about *234,000,000* indistinct results. I narrow it down to "Emily Brown car accident," then "Emily Brown drunk driving accident." Finally, I find a handful of small articles discussing her death. Most are just a brief paragraph along the lines of: "A young woman's body was retrieved from a river after her car careened off of a bridge. Autopsy results show she was at 2.5 times the legal alcohol limit." Taylor never mentioned how horrific the accident was. The thought of her drowning in her car is unimaginable. Strangely, I have thought about dying that way before. There is something especially terrifying about it; while it's sudden and jarring, if you are conscious, there is still time to contemplate your imminent death. Was she unfortunate enough to know her death was coming? Did she think of Taylor in her last moments?

Finally, I come across an article with a little more detail. In it, her mother is mentioned. Needless to say, she was devastated by the loss of her young daughter. There is a picture of Emily. She looks exactly how I had pictured her: long auburn hair, green eyes, and pale with rosy cheeks and small lips. She looks thicker than me, not chunky or anything, just a larger frame with an ample bust, at least large enough for me to notice it through a sweater. *Ugh.* She was pretty, but not in a threatening way; the kind of sweet-looking girl that you could bring home to your mother. Getting visual confirmation of Emily makes me wonder what Taylor's other subs looked like. There are no distinct similarities between us, other than the fact that I appear young for my age, which can also be interpreted as sweet-looking. That's really grasping for straws; she and I look nothing alike. The article also contains the first mention of a fiancé, which catches me off guard since I am certain both Marsha and Taylor said she was already married. Maybe she never got that far. The article simply states that Evan Sumner, her fiancé, called the police hours after she left their home the night before. My heart breaks for this Evan guy, I can only imagine how panicked he must have felt, hoping for her safe return, only to then lose her forever. *Maybe I should drive up to the small town her family lives in, just two hours north, and deliver the necklace myself.* I feel an odd sisterhood with this girl, as jealous as I may be of the fact that Taylor was with her. I shelve the thought for now as there would be no way for me to do so without Taylor finding out.

As I peruse the articles, my phone rings with a call from my mother. We haven't communicated since we texted just before the vacation to Costa Rica. Even before that text, we hadn't spoken in weeks. Whenever I asked her if something was wrong, she would say she was just stressed out by her job, and it makes me worry about a relapse. However, she has sounded sober when we have spoken, and so, I can only take her word that she is fine.

"Hi mom."

"Hey Shyla."

"What's going on?"

"Actually, I wanted to let you know I am flying in tomorrow. I was hoping you and I could have a couple of hours alone tomorrow night."

"Uh…of course mom. What's going on? Is something wrong?"

"Oh nothing. I just missed you. You were so sick when you visited and I wanted to spend some more time with you."

"Well of course you are welcome to come visit. You just sound funny, like you're upset."

"No sweetie. I'm fine."

"Okay. Maybe Taylor will want to come."

"I'm only staying for a day or so. Let's not plan anything okay? Let's just plan on meeting at your place, just the two of us. My flight arrives at five, don't worry about picking me up."

"Uhhh…okay?"

"Alright, I love you and I'll see you tomorrow."

I wander out of my bedroom in a stupor. My mother sounded like a complete stranger on the phone. Her poor planning, her tone, her lack of any desire to meet Taylor, even the fact that she didn't ask for me to pick her up from the airport — none of that sounds like her. A terrible premonition stirs deep inside my belly.

"Come in." I enter Taylor's office, visibly puzzled, my phone still perched in my hand, and sit in the very chair in which he first interviewed me. "What's going on? You look like you just saw a ghost."

"I think something is wrong with my mother. Like really wrong."

"Why?"

"She's been acting strangely since I last saw her. She saw the cuts, but I think it's more than that. I was worried maybe she relapsed, but I don't think that's it."

"Did you ask?"

"That's the thing. She just called me to tell me she's flying in tomorrow and wants to speak with me alone. It was so bizarre, Taylor."

"Maybe she just misses you."

"No, that wasn't it. It feels bad. Really, really bad. I think she might be sick or something."

"Don't think the worst. You'll know tomorrow and building something in your head will only drive you crazy."

"Taylor. I know something isn't right. My mom, she's the type to keep something like that for as long as possible because she wouldn't want to worry me," I say, burying my head in my hands.

"It'll be fine. Whatever it is."

"God, I hope so. But she has never acted like this before. Mom is usually so open about everything. I'm the one who's all closed up and private."

The next day, work seems to never end; the clock moves so slowly, it seems to be moving backwards as I run through all the possible scenarios in my head. Cancer? Liver disease? As soon as the clock strikes five, I grab my purse and dart out of the office. Harrison drives me to my apartment. This was not how I planned being reintroduced to the loft, but it is the best place to meet her. I manically add new sheets to my bed, and clean up any other traces of the last unexpected visitor. She buzzes the intercom at around 6:15. Harrison, who is parked in front of the building, spots her and helps her bring her luggage into my apartment.

"Wow, Shyla, this place is very nice," she says. Her affect is much flatter than usual, as if she is distracted. I give her a big hug and invite her to get comfortable on the couch.

"Do you want a drink?"

"Whatever you're having. Was this a gift?"

I wish she hadn't asked, but she's not stupid, she knows I can't afford this place. "It's Taylor's. He has a house and he is letting me stay here rent-free." I can't tell her the full truth, she'll get all preachy about accepting gifts from men as if I didn't already know that's frowned upon.

I prepare a pot of tea. Like everything else today, it boils in slow motion. I arrive at the couch where my mother is sitting with two cups of piping hot tea and rest them on the coffee table. I settle in to face her and my gut swirls with intuition. The last big news I heard on the couch was from Taylor, the night he first told me about Eric. Maybe I should throw this godforsaken thing away, it could be cursed. The tension in the air is so thick, my stomach feels like a jumbled mess.

"Mom, tell me what's going on. I know you're not here just to say hi. I'm not stupid."

The look on her face, the way it almost melts when she sees that I know something is not right confirms my suspicions. She fights the frown, trying to hold back tears, and grabs her cup of tea. She blows on it a few times, the curvy strands of steam lilting to her breath, and takes a tiny sip, setting it back down on the coaster. She then silently reaches into a large tote bag she has resting by her feet and pulls out a shoebox, placing it between us.

"Go ahead and look inside," she says from the back of her throat.

I peer at her suspiciously while slowly sliding the lid off of the shoebox. Inside, there are what appears to be dozens of pictures and mementos. I grab the stack of photographs, many of which are yellowed with age. The top one is a picture of a young, pretty brunette wearing a pale yellow sleeveless A-line dress with a boatneck collar. Her hair is long, puffy, and brown as was the style in the late 70s-early 80s. She is small-framed, but taller than me, with large hazel eyes and a full pout. Besides the eye color, we look very much alike.

"That's you?" I ask.

"Yes."

I move to the next picture. There is my young mother is again, with a plump, bald baby on her lap. Sitting next to her is a man with wavy shoulder-length light brown hair and a thick beard. His irises are very large and brown, giving him the same sympathetic eyes of a baby deer underneath all the manly scruff.

"Is that...me? Is that...dad?" I choke through the latter question.

She nods.

I thought all these pictures were gone. As far as I could remember, whenever I asked my mother for pictures of my dad or her when she was young, she told me someone had stolen them all in a burglary when I was very little. In fact, I only have one picture of my infancy.

"I thought they were stolen."

She shakes her head. "No honey. I kept them from you, and for that I am sorry."

"But, why?"

"Because I was trying to protect you."

"I don't understand. Mom, you're freaking me out."

"I haven't been completely honest with you about your father. He did die, but it wasn't under the circumstances that I told you."

"So then what happened?"

"He was poisoned."

"What? He was murdered? By who?"

"No, he committed suicide."

"What? I don't understand. Why would you lie about that? Why would you lie about the pictures?"

"Because I hoped you would never learn who he really was. I thought you could go your whole life not knowing, but I was foolish and I was wrong. It's time you knew."

"Knew what?"

"Your father's name was not Desmond Ball."

"Well then what was it?"

"His name was Alan Peters."

CHAPTER TWELVE

I stare at her, frozen, trying to make sense of the words she has just uttered.

"Alan Peters? Who is…" And like a tsunami, the realization nearly knocks me off of the couch. I know exactly who Alan Peters is. I know why he poisoned himself and hundreds of other people. I know he is the man who held Lyla prisoner, who may have even murdered her.

He is the man who has damaged Taylor beyond repair.

It's too unbelievable to comprehend and for a fraction of a second, I think this all might be a prank. I whip my head around to see if Taylor is hiding somewhere, but just as quickly the reality encases me like cement.

"You mean Alan Peters of C.O.S?"

"So you know who he is?"

"Yes!" I stand up, with no intent to exit, but unable to contain myself on the couch. "This doesn't make any sense mom. How can I be his daughter? You weren't in the cult."

"Shyla, I was. I was in C.O.S for years. I just never told anyone once I escaped." My face turns hot and flushed, my breathing becomes heavy. My lungs won't fill; I am drowning out of water. "I am so sorry I lied to you, but I had to," she says through tears.

"What difference did it make, mom? Was telling me my father was a worthless drug addict any better?" I shout.

"Better than a murderer. I knew you would ask less about him if I just wrote him off. If I created some amazing character for you that story would be much harder to keep. We started over again. I couldn't risk telling you the truth."

"Why? You thought I would tell someone?"

"Maybe, at least when you were younger. It would have been a lot for you to keep to yourself. I was afraid knowing would damage you somehow."

"You are so backwards…Why did you hide? If he was already dead, why did it matter?"

"Honey, at the time, this thing was all over the press. We were demonized. People thought we were all child abusers, but we weren't. Many of the adults were also abused or brainwashed. We were made to believe that we would fail if we tried to leave or even worse, we would be killed or beaten. We all just wanted to go on with our lives and it was impossible with people threatening us, or the press calling us. I had you to think about. You were the daughter of a famous cult leader. I didn't want you to live with that cloud over you. I had a chance to start over and I took it."

I sit in silence for I don't know how long, my mind racing with so many questions, I don't know what to ask next.

"*Taylor*," I say pensively, "You felt you had to tell me because of Taylor."

"Yes. His mother was my best friend. I loved that boy like he was my son."

The look in her eyes when she says this, as if it is another confession, sends my thoughts into an irrational tail spin. "Wait. Taylor isn't my brother, is he?"

"No! No! Not at all. I didn't mean to imply that."

"Thank god. Oh my god…were you the one…were you the person who found him?"

I glance down at the picture of her, young and beautiful, in a pale yellow dress framed by a bright blue sky. She was the angel with the long brown hair. Her crying elevates from a subdued sob to uncontrolled weeping. The rotting bodies of her friends, the stench of death; the crying, starving boy she loved as a son who she would never see again: Taylor wasn't the only one who was damaged.

"That wasn't the way things were supposed to happen. They weren't supposed to even be there," she cries.

"What do you mean?"

"We ran away a couple of weeks before the incident. Lyla and Taylor were supposed to come with us, but she had to distract Alan at the last minute. She sacrificed herself so we could leave. She made me promise not to worry, and that she would run away with Taylor the next week. She said she would find a way to call me at the safe house where we all went. But then a week passed, and then another without hearing from her. Finally, I risked it all to go back and find her…and that's…that's when I realized they were all dead."

"Oh, mom."

"It was terrible. The building was so dark, and the smell…the smell." Her nose scrunches as if she could still sense it. "I was in shock, I tripped over some of the bodies and panicked. They were everywhere. My friends, people I had lived with for years, so many of them gone. I thought I was going to break. Then I heard him, a tiny whimper across the room. When I found him, I squeezed him so tight. He became my mission. It was a miracle. That was all Lyla ever wanted, was to get him out of there."

"If you loved him like a son, why didn't you stay in touch? Why did you disappear?"

"His father wanted nothing to do with us and I don't blame him. In his eyes, we were all Alan Peters. He wanted Taylor to start over just as I wanted you to start over. They told me to say my goodbyes right there in the hospital."

"Taylor believes his mother never loved him."

My mother wipes her tears on her sleeve and I begrudgingly pass her a box of tissues. "I feared that the most and I know she did too. There is so much he was far too young to understand. I tried to tell him that his mother loved him, I tried so hard to ingrain that in him when I said goodbye, but he was so young."

"Mom, he remembers you. He doesn't remember who you were, but he remembers you saving him. He remembers what you said."

She lets out a faint smile.

"When I saw the bruises and the cuts, and then you told me you were dating him…My soul was crushed. I thought we had saved him, my worst fear was that it was all for nothing. That he would become like the person who terrorized him and that you had become a victim like Lyla and me." I don't say a word. He's not like *my father* but he is not unscathed. "You know, I named you after her."

"Lyla?"

"Yes, a variation of her name."

I cup my hands to my face. *How have I been so oblivious?* I should be crying, but I feel numb. I'm not even sure if this is all real. Maybe this is like one of those vivid nightmares that Taylor has, where no matter how hard he kicks, or chokes, or screams, he can't seem to wake.

"Mom, I'm safe with him. He's not like Alan Peters."

"Are you sure?"

"Yes!" I say defensively.

She sits back a bit, knowing she is no position to ask for my trust or to insist upon anything at this moment. It is my world that is crumbling here in this room.

"Mom…I know what they did to the kids there. Did they…did they do that to me?" I can barely get the question out.

"No. I got you out of there before that could happen. I will never know if you would have been subject to it, but I couldn't take my chances. What you need to understand is that you were special in your father's eyes. It was a little known secret that he had trouble making children. He would take up women, and when they wouldn't conceive, he would cast them from his bedroom, saying they were unfit, but really, he was ashamed of his inability to produce. You were his only child and as a result, I was never banished. I, along with Lyla, were forced to stay close with him."

"So he was trying to impregnate Lyla?"

"I guess, but truly, he was obsessed with her. He just fixated on her. He didn't love me like he loved Lyla. I think he had always wished she had given him the child and not me. He's not someone you want loving you though. It's a dangerous love." I sit back in my original spot on the couch. I am very upset with my mother, but too curious to lash out at her. "You two would be too young to remember, especially you, but you and Taylor were once friends." I think back to the note with the Bradbury quote that he had slipped to me in St. Petersburg that I found in my closet months later: *"Why is it," he said, one time, at the subway entrance, "I feel I've known you for so many years?"*

"We were?"

She reaches for the pile of pictures and flips through them until she finds the one she is looking for and slowly hands it over to me. It is a picture of a beautiful boy with piercing eyes, wild, dark hair in a navy and white striped t-shirt and a pair of red shorts. Posed on his lap is a toddler with big brown eyes and a few straggly tendrils in a short purple sundress with a diaper peeking out from underneath.

"That's the two of you." Taylor and I felt as though we had always known each other, and it's because we have. I grip the picture so hard I might crush it; this one will stay with me forever. "Shyla, he was very protective of you. When Alan got angry or violent towards me or Lyla, he would take you and hide in the closet or wherever he could. When he would beat us, you would scream, just as any baby would, and Taylor would take you away. Despite it all, your father favored you, you were his little Shy. Alan never hit you, but he was very hard on Taylor. He was jealous of Taylor because of his obsession with Lyla and in a sick way he competed with that little boy. And then, when he saw Taylor getting attached to you, he was even harder on him. The only reason he allowed Taylor around at all was because he knew he could use him to control Lyla. If he took Taylor away from Lyla, there would be no chance she would ever love Alan back. There is so much Taylor doesn't know, so much he doesn't understand about what happened."

I stand in silence, slowly shaking my head in disbelief. There are no words. Taylor got the beatings, Taylor got the abuse, Taylor lost his mother. I was the favorite, the apple of Alan's eye. I was spared the horrors, I escaped while Taylor stayed behind and sacrificed everything. Taylor suffered more to protect me.

"I should have told you earlier. Not just to be honest with you, but for my health, for my sobriety. It was the one thing I didn't follow through AA. I couldn't call you then to tell you the real reason why I drank. The guilt for joining the cult, for allowing myself to be brainwashed, for leaving my friends to die, for having to hide the truth from my own daughter, for letting Lyla stay behind…"

"So that's why you drank?"

"Yes. I was so alone in my world of secrets. I didn't want to bury you with the burden. I didn't want you growing up with the guilt of what your father did."

All these years I had assumed her loneliness stemmed from an obligation to raise me on her own, her struggling to make ends meet to make a better life for me, for secretly resenting having me with my deadbeat father.

"I thought it was me."

"What?"

"All this time, I thought you drank because of me."

"What? No! I love you. I would do anything for you. I risked my life to spare you the terrible things that were happening there!"

"How was I to know, mom? How could I possibly know that?" The guilt, the cutting, the solitude I felt as I watched her passed out on the couch, thinking it was me who drove her to her alcoholism, thinking she only stayed with my druggie father as long as she did because of me, thinking that it would be better if I didn't exist. I felt like I was invisible, that the world had forgotten me. Sometimes I felt like I wasn't even real.

"I never blamed you, ever. Shyla, you were are my world. You still are."

"I know you never said anything mom, but that's what I thought! I saw how sad you were, and the only person standing in your way of starting over was me!" I stand up from the couch and grab my purse. "I have to go mom. I'll be back in a little bit."

"What? You're in no condition to go out," she grabs my arm.

"No," I say, pulling my arm away from her grip. "I need some time to process this. I want to be left alone."

"Then I'll go."

"No, we're not done. You don't even know the area. And I need some air. Please, just let me go. I'll be back, I promise," I say, storming to the elevator.

I jam the button frantically about a dozen times before impatiently running to the staircase, all the while feeling my mother's silent tearful gaze on me until I am out of her sight. My footsteps create a distracting rhythm as I wind down each flight of stairs. I erupt out of the lobby and keel over, resting my hands on my knees, gasping the cool night air. The weight of this knowledge is too much, it crushes my chest. Harrison runs over to me, his normally stoic face flooded with concern.

"Shyla? Shyla? Are you okay?"

I put up my hand to him and slowly rise. "I have to go. Alone. I need to be alone. Please don't follow me. I just have to go."

I make my way to Ladybug, good old Ladybug, who I haven't driven in a while. I kneel on the sidewalk, and spill the contents of my purse on the street, looking for the keys. When I find them, I only shove back in what I need and leave the random contents of my purse on the sidewalk. My hands shakily slide the keys into the ignition and I peel out onto the street checking in the rearview mirror to make sure I am not being followed.

Almost immediately, my cell phone lights up and buzzes. *It's Taylor.* I can't pick up. I don't know how to tell him. How do I tell him that the person who tortured him, the person who haunts his nightmares, is half of me?

All this time we thought Taylor had the darkness inside of him, but we were wrong. It was me. I am the spawn of evil.

He won't love me anymore.

I speed on the freeway heading North with no destination in mind. Then Eric's cautionary words pass through my thoughts: *"nothing around Taylor happens by choice."* Is it possible none of this is real? That this has all been planned? Does Taylor already know who I am? I don't know who to trust. My own mother has lied to me my entire life and in moments the entire foundation of my identity is shattered. In this flurry of thoughts, I can no longer decipher the rational possibilities from the paranoid ones.

Eventually I end up on a dark road in the middle of nowhere, unable to remember how I arrived, and pull over for a moment to collect my bearings. My phone has been ringing in intervals since I left, but I barely noticed in my fugue. I glance over: 15 missed calls from Taylor.

Ladybug sits on the side of the road on the dirt. I do not know where I am or how I am going to find my way back, but at this moment it seems like an unimportant detail. I think back to the family photo. Alan didn't look like the big, angry, menacing figure I had conjured in my head. He looked respectable, well-dressed, even kind. His brown eyes were warm, trustworthy. *Those eyes.* I look so much like my mother did, but I have his brown eyes. The sudden urge to claw at them consumes me. I want to tear myself in half, split myself at the cellular level, eliminate every trace of that man inside of me.

Now that my mind is no longer distracted by driving, the car feels cramped and suffocating. My face flushes with heat and I seek the crisp night air to cool my skin. I don't give a shit about my safety or if Eric is hiding behind the bushes somewhere. I am tired.

I am reaching my limit.

Time passes indefinitely until car lights emerge from a bend in the road a few hundred feet away. I don't move. I don't raise my head. I don't care.

"Shyla!" Taylor slams his car door behind him. He runs towards me, but his brown boots skid in the dirt to a complete stop when he sees me sitting on the side of the road with my arms wrapped around my knees. "Shyla..." he kneels down to my level. "What happened?"

"You'll never love me again. You'll hate me," I murmur inaudibly.

Taylor looks up to someone, and it's then I realize Harrison is there too. Taylor tilts his head at Harrison to signal he needs some alone time.

"How did you find me here?" I ask.

"Your phone, we can triangulate a singal...nevermind, don't worry about that." I nod. I worked at H.I. long enough to know Taylor has access to vast amounts of technology. He sits by my side. "Shyla, is your mother sick?"

I shake my head.

"You've got to talk to me here."

I pull out the picture of him and me from my back pocket and hand it over to him. *This is it. He'll hate me, who I am, who I come from.*

"What is this?"

"It's us."

He flashes his phone on the picture to get a better look. The genuine look of confusion on his face informs me my earlier theories in the car were just jumbled paranoia.

"What?"

"Taylor. My mother is not sick. She's fine. I just found out today she has been lying to me for my entire life." Taylor doesn't say anything. He just observes the picture, as if it will hold all of the answers, but it doesn't even begin to tell the story. Taylor doesn't beg me to tell him, or insist I spill everything. Instead, he waits quietly for me to continue or maybe say nothing at all. "Taylor, I don't know anymore. I don't know which way is up." I pause again. How do I even begin to say the words? He may never again see me as the pure Shyla, his savior; the person who could lay a hand on him without making him shudder. He may finally look into my brown eyes and recognize the familiar devil that haunts his nightmares.

"Taylor, that's us in the pictures because my mother was in C.O.S. I was born into C.O.S." He doesn't say a word. He just stares at me quietly, not revealing a single emotion. "She lied to me about who my father was. It's Alan, Taylor. He's my father."

The look of concentration melts from his face, and he tilts his head back slowly releasing air from his lungs. He looks at the photo again. His silence is haunting.

"How can this be possible?"

"We've always known each other. My mother said you protected me," I say as I reach out to touch his hand. He doesn't respond. *It's happening.*

"I don't remember," he says coldly.

"Me neither."

"So your mother was one of those sick fucks too?"

"Excuse me?"

"So that's it? That's why you ran out here to the middle of nowhere like a mad woman?" he says.

"What do you mean 'that's it?'" I know what he's doing. He's shutting down on me.

"What fucking difference does it make Shyla? You're sitting on the side of the road, about to become roadkill over something that changes nothing. You could have just come to me instead of running out like that."

"Why are you being like this?"

"What do you want me to do? It's done. Your parents fucked and they made you. You thought he was a drug addict, and now you know was a homicidal cult leader," he says standing up.

"You're being cruel. You know this means more than that." He looks up indignantly, biting his lip. "Taylor, my mother and your mother were best friends. My mother was the lady with the brown hair, the one who saved you." He looks down at me, and for the first time I sense an emotional reaction. "In the pictures, she looked just like me."

He smirks mockingly, nodding his head. "So let me guess, your psychological theory is that I let you touch me because you look like her?"

"Well, that, or because we were close friends a long time ago. I don't know, but it's definitely something along those lines." He condescendingly laughs to himself, pacing away from me. "Taylor, there's something else you need to know that is important. My mother says that your mother loved you very much, and she was doing everything in her —"

"No! No!" He turns and yells, pointing a finger at me. "That's enough!"

The rage in his voice silences me for several minutes, but eventually I have to say something.

"Don't you want to meet her? You told me how much she meant to you, what she did. And she said she loved you dearly, like a son."

"Shyla, that was a story, an idealization. People are never as perfect as we remember them."

"They're hardly ever as bad either."

"That's where you're mistaken. I'll take you back to your place so you can be with your mother. I don't care if Eric is in fucking Africa, no woman should ever be sitting on the side of a deserted road." he says.

He'll never love me like he did before.

He drives me back in the SUV while Harrison follows with Ladybug. We sit in dark silence for the duration of the drive. I expected sympathy, shock, tears, disbelief, anything but his cold dismissal. Sometimes that's too much to ask of Taylor. I've been spoiled. Things have been so good lately, I almost forgot who I was dealing with, but tonight he made sure I remembered. *He won't let her hurt him again.* Throughout his entire life he has learned that when he cares, when he shows love, it will backfire with greater pain. Even falling in love with me has caused him hurt and devastation. I try my best to recall that night in the study, when we stole away for some quiet time. He asked me to remember that he loves me and always will, but that seems so distant, so hard for me to hold onto. What is here now is the pain of knowing my beautiful Taylor is sitting just inches away from me, but is miles away emotionally.

He pulls up to the front of the building. I grab the photo of the two of us that rests on the dashboard. Taylor looks straight ahead, but watches me from the corner of his eyes. "Shyla, this won't fix anything," he says. "I've learned to look ahead and not back. Looking back only stirs up problems."

He turns to meet my gaze and I nod before closing the door to the SUV. When I return, my mother is asleep on the couch, waiting for me like she did when I was a teenager. I grab a blanket and cover her. "Mom, I'm here. I'm going to bed. I don't want to to talk," I whisper. She tiredly opens her eyes to acknowledge me and insist on conversation. "Mom, don't worry. I am too tired to talk anymore. You should go to a bed," I say before she can utter a word. Of course, she ignores my suggestion and lies on the couch. Such a martyr she is.

Instinctually, I sneak to check the wine cooler and the wastebasket for empty bottles, and am relieved to see no evidence of a relapse.

The cleansing calm of a shower calls for me, so I sit in the tub with the shower on, letting the water cascade over my body. The medicine cabinet looks so inviting as it tempts me to collect one of its contents, the razor that has always been there for me, but I resist. I made a promise to Taylor that I wouldn't give in, but he made one to me too. He was supposed to be with me, to help me work through the pain, but when I really needed him, he shut me out. It's easier to shut it all off than to think about the lies, I get it. I just found out much of the story of my life was a fabrication, but I wasn't haunted the way he was. I was spared. Unlike Taylor, I didn't think I was abandoned or sacrificed by my mom. But he has held onto that belief, that image of a cold, uncaring mother for so long. To think of her as someone else, even a loving figure, would be to kill his image of her all over again.

The picture of the little bright-eyed boy who was so terrified of the world around him, beaten and abused by the people who were supposed to nurture him, remains imprinted in my mind's eye. What did Taylor do when he looked in the face of fear? He didn't think only of himself; he protected me. He says he doesn't care, that he's broken, but he does. He was a little boy, just six or seven years old, dragging a clueless toddler into a dark closet so that she wouldn't have to hear the screaming or see the abuse. He was brave. He was scared, but he was brave. And I don't need the blade to center me. Just thinking of the man I love more than anyone in the world as a helpless child, using what little power he had to protect me, overwhelms me with emotion. I won't dishonor his bravery by breaking my promise to him.

I sit in the shower until the water turns icy. Slowly, as if weighed down, I pull myself out and put on a plush robe. Sleep evades me; my racing thoughts will not rest. I am not ready to talk to my mother again so I tread lightly through the condo so as not to wake her. I understand why she did what she did, but I can't rid myself of the feelings of betrayal. I don't know what to do with this new knowledge. Like Taylor said, nothing has changed, but at the same time, everything has. The only thing I can do is work on my laptop. 1:43am. *Fuck me.* Between each task I look at my phone, hoping I'll get a call or a text from Taylor, but there's nothing. Taylor is the one I can share my pain with and he has left me alone, spinning out of orbit, into the vast darkness.

Shortly after, there is the faint sound of footsteps echoing from the stairwell that leads directly to one of the condo entrances. I glance at the clock again, holding my breath. *2:15am.* Harrison has been parked out front and would never let anyone come up to my apartment on his watch, but I no longer trust my world or the things that I once held to be true. I slowly wait at the door as the footsteps approach, peeping through the peephole. And while I have no way of knowing who it is, I can feel the air around me become alive with his energy. A pair of distressed dark brown boots under denim lands on the top step. Then the figure emerges. *It's him.*

I quietly slide the door open and his eyes widen when he sees me. Putting my finger up to my pursed lips, I slide out the door.

"I was just about to — How'd you know I was here?" He whispers, sliding his phone into his pocket.

"I could feel you coming," I say closing the door behind me so that we are alone at the top of the stairwell.

"Listen, I'm not here to see your mother. I'm here for you."

"I know. It's okay, she's asleep."

"I shouldn't have reacted the way that I did. It's just that ever since I met you, everything I knew about my world has slowly disintegrated. And it's amazing to feel what I feel because of you, but it is forcing everything to the surface in ways I could never imagine. Shyla, there is so much rage inside of me, in my core, and I have kept it all trapped deep for 25 years. And I have to guard everything because if I let anything out, the rage comes with it too, and it's dangerous. So I lash out, because I want to protect you from seeing what's really there. It's ugly, it's dark, and you may think you have seen it all, but you have only seen pieces of it. But, I don't know what to do because the things I have told myself to make sense of my world, to move ahead, to keep everything locked down deep inside of me...I don't know what the truth is any longer. I'm afraid I'll burst wide open."

"I understand. It doesn't seem real," I say looking down. "It feels like this is all happening to some other person. Maybe that's my brain protecting me from losing it."

"But I remember you," he whispers in a raspy voice into my ear as he leans over me. "I remember my little friend who I never spoke of because I thought I would never see her again. I thought she had died with the rest of them." And he buries his face into my neck, like a lost boy.

CHAPTER THIRTEEN

I let out a breath, not realizing I had been holding it since he leaned in. "I'm still here," I say. "I never left you." He begins to kiss my neck, at first softly, but the kisses then become more passionate, more aggressive. "My mother," I whisper. "She's in the living room."

"I don't care. I need you." *He still wants me. I am not my father. I am not his sins.*

Taylor unties the belt of my robe, allowing my naked body to peek through the opening. I rip the collar of his shirt open, some of the buttons pop like little firecrackers. His strong, muscled chest and abs peer through. I move down to his belt, unbuckling it as we kiss hard, almost so hard it hurts. He puts his large hands on my waist, making me feel so small, then slides them down to my ass as he picks me up. I wrap my legs around his hips as he lowers me onto the stairs that lead to the rooftop. My robe opens up, serving as a a spread for me to lay on. He kisses a trail down between my breasts, then stomach, onto the side of my pelvis. The chill in the air raises goosebumps all over my body.

Finally, he reaches his destination. As he purses his lips to gently suck on mine, I moan and he takes one of his hands and covers my mouth to soften the sound. I run my hands through his messy hair, pulling it hard and wrapping my thighs firmly around his neck. He rolls his tongue slowly and softly, making love to it. He stops short of making me come and then he rises, looking me directly in the eyes. His glare is powerful and it feels like he could steal my soul if he stares long enough. I am still scared he'll see Alan's eyes now that he knows, so much so that I am tempted to look away, but he doesn't even blink as he slides inside of me. His forehead presses against mine; we are nose to nose as he slowly thrusts his hips. The ridges of the staircase dig into my back with his weight on top of me, but the pain stirs me in the same way being tied and spanked would. Taylor bites my lower lip and tugs on it hard enough to make me jump, while still staring at me with *those eyes*. One of my hands grabs the metal banister and the other presses against the cold concrete wall as I brace his thrusts, making my best attempt at lengthening my moans so that they don't cut through the stairwell and into the living room where my mother is sleeping. Whenever I focus my eyes on Taylor between rolling them back in pleasure, he still stares deeply at me as if I would disappear if he looked away. He's telling me with his body, with his eyes, that he's not going anywhere, he won't forsake me because of my father's trespasses. And so I choose to embrace Taylor's attention, not to look away or close my eyes in the presence of his blue stare. My hand reaches to the back of his head, pressing our faces even more closely together as we pant in unison. I begin to flood with gratitude, sadness, anger. Everything overtakes me at once.

"Taylor, don't hate me." I beg. That is now my greatest fear. That over time, when he digests all of this, he will begin to see Alan when he sees me. It might start small: over dinner I smirk a certain way, and he gets sick to his stomach when he realizes he has seen that smirk before. Or I might get angry, and the fiery way I throw my hands up loses its cuteness and starts to look more sinister. Those moments become more frequent, and before he knows it, he can't see me anymore, he can only see a version of my father.

Taylor wraps his arms around me and picks me up, as if to respond with his body, to hold me more securely as he engulfs me, pressing me against the wall. I lose control of my volume again; I fear my mother might wake, but the risk of it all, stimulates me even more. He covers my mouth firmly with his hand, never breaking our gaze, answering me with his eyes. He's not letting me out of his sight. Finally, his eyes soften as he comes inside of me.

We lay on the landing, his head resting on my semi-exposed stomach as I twirl pieces of his hair in my fingers.

"I am so fucked. There's no point in going to sleep now," he laments.

"Do you want to come in?"

"No, I like it out here."

"What are we going to do?"

"I'm not sure there is anything to do."

"I don't want to push the issue, but my mother said there is a lot more to the story. There is a lot we don't know. We both need to find out about our history."

"Why don't you finish with your mother first? Honestly, I don't know if I want to know."

"I can't keep what I find out to myself."

"I understand, but that's different than some sort of crusade to — I don't know what the fuck — find out something that will make a difference. I know everything I need to know. Your mother said what she had to say to me a long time ago. And I am grateful to her, you know that, but that was decades ago. If I wanted to dig up the past, kick up dirt, I could have. I have the resources to do it, you know that. But my mother is dead and I still believe what I feel about her. Maybe some of the details have changed, but the ones that count haven't."

His mother. Lyla being alive could change everything. Again, I decide to push that revelation aside until I have more information. Just like he said, if she is still dead, it changes nothing.

"You were a beautiful child," I tell Taylor.

"Likewise. You were like a butterball turkey with a little bushel of hair." I yank a piece of his hair. "Ow!"

"Shhhh! So you're okay?" I ask.

"Are you? This revelation is really more about you than it is about me. You need to stop worrying about how it affects me."

"I don't know. I don't think it's sunk in yet."

"Yeah."

"I just can't believe that all these years have passed, and that we would lead entirely separate lives. I mean your dad didn't want anything to do with us, and yet we found each other anyway."

"What did you say about my father?"

"Oh, I didn't tell you. He didn't want my mother to ever get in touch with you."

"She said that?"

"Yes. I mean, it makes sense from his perspective. He thought she was one of them."

Taylor says nothing, but his facial expression changes, from relaxed to pensive. I wonder what's on his mind, but I know better than to try and pry it out of him. In that moment, the world is so still, it's almost too quiet. It's like we are flies trapped in a spider web, waiting for the threads to quiver. It can't be this simple. You don't get a bomb dropped on you like this and just go along your merry way. The web of lies, secrets, and betrayals in which we are entangled only grows larger and more complex, tying me closer to Taylor, but making it all the more difficult to untangle ourselves from the threats that may lie ahead.

"I should go back in."

"It's so peaceful out here. We should just hide out here together."

"I wish I could spend all day with you. I want to be close to you. But, I have to talk to my mother before getting to work. Speaking of which, work is going to suck so hard today. As you know, I cannot function without my beauty rest."

"Yeah, I don't think you're going to make it."

"I better start brewing the coffee now. I'm going to be staying here until my mother leaves."

"I figured."

As we stand up, Taylor grabs the robe belt from the floor, gently wraps it around my waist and ties it. "Well, text me if you find yourself snoozing on the job."

"That's almost a guarantee."

He gives me a gentle jab on the chin, and we both smile, but beneath it, I can see melancholy in his eyes. I watch him walk down the stairs as I prepare to face my mother again. Then he turns back.

"Shyla."

"Yes?"

"I'm not my mother, and you're not your father."

I nod, but I can't shake the feeling it wasn't me he was trying to convince.

✿ ✿ ✿

It's about five in the morning when I walk back into the apartment. The scent of coffee brewing awakes my mother.

"Good morning," I say as she rises from the couch.

"Good morning. Where did you go last night?"

"No where in particular. I just wanted to be alone."

"You went to see him, didn't you?"

I don't respond. In this case, it's me that should be asking the questions. She sits in silence for a while.

"Will you ever forgive me?"

191

"I don't know. I'm confused, mom. I understand why you did it, but it's still hard to come to terms with the fact that much of what I have known about myself—about you—is a lie."

"I always feared this day would come and you would never speak to me again."

"Mom, I'm not going to stop talking to you. That is, unless there is more you haven't told me."

"No, that's most of it. I mean, there are stories, these were years of my life, but as far as pertaining to you…"

"What about Taylor? You said there is so much he couldn't understand."

"Does he know? About me?"

"Yes. I told him."

"Does he…does he want to see me?" She asks so pathetically, it hurts my heart.

"I don't think he's ready. He's not that little boy anymore and he has done so much to try and move past this. I don't know if he wants to bring it all back up. He has always had a philosophy about moving forward." *That is one hell of a positive spin on it.*

"Shyla, it would mean the world for me to see him. To tell him about his mother."

"It's a very touchy subject for him."

"I can only imagine, but I have to tell him. He has to know. I owe it to her and to him."

"I promise I'll try, but he's very strong-headed."

"I have to ask you a question. I know you're very private, but I need to know this…"

"Okay."

"Are you in love with him?"

I turn away to pour coffee into my mug to buy some time. I never liked talking about my relationships with my mother. Call me immature, but it just felt…icky. I'm not prepared to share with her the depths of how strongly I feel about Taylor. I am very protective of our relationship, our secret universe. I have become so guarded about it that I haven't even really told Kristin, the person to whom I tell everything, how deep my feelings have become for Taylor.

"Yes."

Her eyes well up and I am not sure if it's from joy or dread. "I can't believe you two found each other."

"I'm still trying to process all of this," I say as I bring her a mug of coffee. "Did you meet Lyla in C.O.S?"

"Yes, I was a member before her."

"Then why did you come back to her hometown? You weren't from here, right?"

"Right. I was born and raised in California. I came here because I wanted to be close to her and foolishly I hoped she might show up here one day, for me and Taylor. She's gone though."

"Gone as in ran away, or dead?"

"Why do you ask?"

"Whether or not you meet Taylor, this needs to stay between us. This is very important."

"Yes, of course."

"Do you think it's possible Lyla could still be alive?"

"Are you asking because her body was never found?"

"Yes."

"Trust me, I hoped for that. But I knew if she was alive, that after a few years, once the dust settled, she would find me. I moved here because I thought if she were to surface, she would know where to find me and Taylor. It was our original plan after all, to move here and start new lives. I thought there was still a chance we would do that, it would just take her a little longer to come around from where ever she may have hiddden. When she didn't, I came to terms with the fact she's never coming back. She's dead. If she was alive, she would have come back to us. Every so often though, I do wonder, but it's just a childish fantasy," she looks wistfully into the distance.

"You think she was killed before the suicide?"

"I can only speculate, but I always thought that when you and I escaped, Alan figured out Lyla helped us and became enraged. Like I said, in is own twisted way, he loved you very much. He would have been very angry, and I wouldn't have put it past him to lose it." Hearing how much he loved me is of little comfort. To think Taylor's mother may have been murdered specifically because she helped me escape only adds to my vague sense of guilt for contributing to Taylor's suffering.

"But mom, it doesn't make sense that he would spare Taylor. You said yourself he was jealous of him."

"Maybe it was plain luck, or maybe he was sick enough to think the greatest torture of all would be to leave that child alone in this world without his mother." *If that was Alan's plan, it worked out perfectly.* "There is one thing, but again, I don't think it holds much weight."

"What is it?"

"In the shoebox, there are a few postcards." She grabs the box to search for them. "They were sent to my attorney at the time. All of us got plenty of mail, some from admirers and a lot of hate mail, but these were odd as they were from various cities throughout the US, but there was nothing written on them. After almost a year, they stopped."

"Who do you think it was?"

"I thought — I hoped — Lyla. We used to fantasize about traveling, but after the year was up and I no longer got any postcards, I figured it was a weird admirer. I don't see why she would have just stopped like that. Like I said, she wouldn't just leave us like that.

194

I thought about going to the last state to search, but where would I even start?"

She hands over the old, discolored postcards, held together by a rubberband. The only text is typewritten and addressed to Marie Portero. "Marie Portero?" It was the name Mr. MacAllister found in the old articles about the suicide.

"That's my real maiden name."

I roll my eyes. "Of course, Ball was completely made up, wasn't it?"

"Yes."

"Is Auntie Gigi really even your sister?"

"Of course, but she knew. I ran away from my family to join C.O.S and she welcomed me back. She agreed we should not tell you about all of this unless it was necessary."

"So your maiden name is not Kyle, your married name is not Ball." Just like that, my name feels artificial, without history or roots.

"So I am really Shyla Peters."

"You are whoever you want to be."

"This is so bizarre. Can I keep these?"

"It's all yours. The whole box" I scan them and find the last postcard was from Iowa about 24 years ago. This might be the break Mr. MacAllister needs.

"I have to get ready to go to work, mom."

"Sure. I'm heading out this afternoon. I figured you would want some time alone to work all this out. Whenever Taylor is ready to meet, I am too."

"I need time mom. This is going to take me a while," I say through a frown.

"I understand, but please remember we did what we thought was best at the time."

I know she wants me to hug her, to make her feel like she did the right thing, but I can't allow her to believe decades of lies can be forgiven in one night.

The office is empty when I arrive early in the morning, hoping to ride my second wind before the inevitable crash from lack of sleep. After unsuccessfully attempting to concentrate on my work, I text Taylor.

Shyla:
Got to work early, but I can't focus.

Mr. Sexypants:
I don't blame you.

Shyla:
My mom wants to meet you. She's pressuring me.

Mr. Sexypants:
No.

Shyla:
She says there are thing she wants to tell you, face to face.

Mr. Sexypants:
I told you, it's pointless. This is between you and her.

Shyla:
You were so young, you couldn't possibly have remembered everything. Memories change. Shit, I'm not the person who we thought I was.

Mr. Sexypants:
You're still you. I'm not going to discuss this over a text. When will I see you?

Shyla:
My mother is leaving this afternoon. I'll come over after work.

Over lunch, I meet MacAllister at a deli, and give him the postcards explaining to him that these were sent to a friend of Lyla's years ago and may possibly trace back to her. The lead reinvigorated the grizzled P.I., and he seemed eager to follow this new trail. I don't tell him that my mother is Marie, though he'll likely find out himself if he keeps digging around. I haven't properly wrapped my own mind around my newfound identity, let alone disclosed it to someone I barely know.

I drag ass at work all day, trying not to nod off at my desk, simmering with a plethora of feelings I am unable to vent. Again, I am forced to keep the news from Kristin until I can craft a way to tell her without spilling Taylor's part of the story. While I have gained so much from my relationship with Taylor, I feel as though I am slipping away from the world. His pull is so strong, that as I become closer and closer to him, I slowly drift away from everyone else around me. I am still very close to Kristin, but small things have changed. My relationship with her is more contrived as I have to navigate the bits of information I can divulge to her in a way I have never had to before. Like Taylor, I am carefully beginning to mold an exterior image of myself that is far different from the person I actually am.

I doze off in the back of the car as Harrison drives me home. I was never one who could pull an all-nighter and operate like a normal human being the next day. The back seat of a vehicle has never felt so comfortable. The car stops, but since Harrison doesn't mention we're back, I assume we are at a stop sign or light. When the back door opens, I startle.

"Shhh…" Taylor leans in, taking my arm and wrapping it around his neck. He carries me into the house as I nuzzle my face into the warm crook under his jaw. It brings to heart warm feelings of being carried to my bedroom as a child; those were much simpler days. Or so I thought.

When I wake up alone in the bedroom, it is pitch dark. I feel around for Taylor and find I am alone. I shake my head to rid myself of the drowsiness and blurred vision and see it's 10:34pm; my head is engulfed in that disoriented feeling one gets from a really hard nap. The house is dark except for a light on in the great room, where I find Taylor reading a book.

"I thought you'd sleep through the morning."

"Then I'd miss out on seeing you tonight," I say groggily.

"Well, here I am," he says, throwing his arms up.

Taylor wears a pair of thin rimmed glasses, and a white t-shirt over a pair of navy lounge pants. I find the mix of sophistication and casual to be especially appealing. "How did the rest of the time with your mother go?"

"I don't know. I didn't know what to tell her. It's like a I am feeling every emotion at once. Not just mad, or sad, or even forgiving. I don't know what to feel. What am I supposed to do now? Change my name?"

"It's just a name."

"But it's fake. Ball doesn't exist."

"Every family name started somewhere. So what did you think your dad's name was?"

"Desmond Ball."

"Desmond? Interesting."

"Yeah, I know. Desmond the crackhead. It sounds so fake now that I know it is."

"Wait — Desmond. Des. Desi…Ball. Was your mom a fan of I Love Lucy?"

198

"You don't think? No!"

"I think she sort of used I Love Lucy to rename you."

"Oh my god, she did!" We both laugh, finally adding some levity to the weight of things. "Speaking of names...my first name..." *Should I tell him?*

"Go on."

"Nevermind."

"You think I could figure out that she named your fake father after Lucille Ball and Desi Arnaz, but I can't put together the fact that you're named after my mother?" My mind wanders for a moment to our discussion in Costa Rica about children. *We will never have children, he will never allow Peter's legacy to live on.* "Come. I need to show you something."

He slides on a pair of shoes and instructs me to do the same. We take the elevator to the garage level, the same elevator where we had sex the night I found the journal. I scan the floor and find one of my buttons in the corner.

"Looks like Irma missed a spot."

"I told her to leave it there," he says with a wicked smirk.

"She must think you are so weird."

"She got over my bullshit a long time ago."

We exit at the garage, rows of fluorescent lights turn on sequentially when we step out. He leads me past all of his cars to a door with a keypad on it. After punching a few numbers, he opens the doors and flips on a light switch. In front of me is a two-lane shooting range. To my left is a cabinet containing several pistols and revolvers.

CHAPTER FOURTEEN

"It's time you learned how to protect yourself."

"Can't I take tae kwon do or something?"

"Come on, you're like 80 pounds soaking wet."

"I wish. Not even close to 80, but like five pounds less what I am now would be great."

"Shut up."

"Okay."

"Seriously, I don't want you depending on anyone else. If you ever find yourself in a bind, you're going to learn how to bust a cap in someone's ass."

"Bust a cap?"

"Oh yeah."

"Why now?"

Taylor thinks to himself for a moment. "Because I've failed once. And I am going to do everything in my power to make sure you have everything you need to be safe. They'll have to get through me and Harrison, but I want you to empower yourself."

"You didn't fail. There's nothing you could have done. Eric is gone. Plus, I'm really scared of guns."

"You won't be after I teach you. And I know Eric is gone, but apparently there is a lot we don't know."

"I don't know. You know how to shoot?"

"Yup. My father used to hunt and now I keep guns in the house for personal safety. With all of these new developments…more than ever, I don't trust anyone. I think the timing is right. I know you feel like things are out of control. I want you to feel in control; I think this will help."

He pulls out several handguns and boxes of bullets.

"You should become a secret agent. You race cars, you're a marksman. Do you know how to jump out of airplanes?"

"Anyone can jump. The question is: do you know how to land?" Taylor asks slyly. He takes me through how to load and empty the gun, how to flip the safety, and all of the general precautions. "Alright, this is a small caliber pistol, so you won't have to worry so much about recoil. I think this is the one I want you to keep in your condo."

"You want me to keep a gun in my condo?" I whisper as if anyone could hear us.

"Well, it wouldn't make sense for me to teach you without giving you one." He clips up a target sheet of a zombie, which is unusually tongue-in-cheek of Taylor, and presses a button that zips it away. "Here." He hands me goggles and earmuffs. "Now relax your shoulders and hold firm, but take a deep breath before you squeeze — don't pull — the trigger."

"I'm going to kill us."

"You'll be fine. Now I am going to stand over here," he says, backing away to the corner.

"Taylor!"

"I'm kidding!"

"Here I go." I exhale a long, drawn breath out and try to squeeze — not pull — the trigger. Honestly, I don't know the difference. A shot rings out and I hit the very bottom corner of the target. "Woohoo!"

"Woah there! Gun down during celebration dances. We're not the Taliban here."

"It looks like I have successfully shot that motherfucker in the thigh," I gloat.

"Okay, go at it. You want to aim for the center of mass — gives you the best chance of hitting your target."

I start to let loose, feeling more in control and powerful with each squeeze of the trigger. Taylor's right, this might be just what I needed to snap me out of the jumble of scattered thoughts brought on by the most recent news. My shots don't land perfectly, but they move closer to the center with each attempt. Occasionally, I go to the head for fun and even land one. Whenever I look over, I see Taylor leaning against the wall to my side with his arms crossed, a look of amusement on his face.

"Your turn. I wanna see you shoot this thing."

"You sure? You seem to be having fun."

"Yeah. I like to watch," I say flirtatiously.

"Put that one down there. I'm going to grab another one."

I lay down the gun and switch places with Taylor. He grabs a larger gun, slides a magazine in the handle and pushes it in forcefully with a loud click. Watching him so intently prep the weapon, his muscles contracting and relaxing as he moves, his taut ass under the navy lounge pants, his intense and masculine focus, makes me really horny. *Holy shit he looks so fucking hot right now.*

"Stand back Shy, the shells go flying around with this one." He raises his arms with the gun in hand, the lines of muscles in his arms and shoulders clearly defined, and pulls the trigger. This gun is much louder than the one I was shooting. He unloads his gun on the target, forming a small circle of bullet holes in the chest of the very unlucky zombie. When he puts the gun down, I can't resist; watching him hold the gun and just fucking own it like that makes me want to get on him right in the range. My desire surprises me, as I have

203

never found guns particularly interesting or appealing. Slowly I walk up to him from behind and wrap my arms around his hips, sliding them down his frontside onto his penis. I rub my hands over the soft fabric of his pants as it stiffens underneath my touch. He turns around.

"Does Ms. Scared of Guns want to fuck in here?"

"Something about that was really hot."

He picks me up and sits me in the other empty shooting lane, whipping off my shirt, massaging my breasts and sucking on my nipples. "Fuck, Taylor." I whip off his shirt to reveal his strong, lean torso. He pulls my hair back, so that my chin tilts up.

"You want to do something dangerous?" He asks, the flecks of green in his eyes seem to glow devilishly.

"Uh huh," I gulp, both terrified and exhilarated by the proposal.

"No questions then. You're gonna do what I say."

I nod and he walks out of my line of vision. I swear I hear him mess with the guns, making my heart race in anticipation. I haven't the slightest idea what he has planned for us and the idea that it involves a gun only confounds me more. He returns with a large revolver that we hadn't used. Its barrel is long and not too slender, but not too thick. The look on his face is dark and mischievous. He glares at me with his smoky stare, his nostrils flaring.

"Don't say a word," he commands. We're not in the darkroom, but he is that man right now. He is Master Holden. He slides the gun in his mouth, and I sit on edge, wanting to rip it out of his hands. The sight is terrifying, for a split second I think I could lose him. But what is even more terrifying is the look in his eyes: wild and unafraid. It's like he has a death wish. I obey and remain silent as he slowly guides the long barrel out of his mouth, a crooked smirk peeking through. He takes

204

the gun and holds it against my face, grazing the cold, wet barrel down my cheek, then across my chest to my left breast, circling my nipple, then down my stomach. My reaction is to suck in, try to keep away from it, but my anxiety only serves to entertain him. He slides it down my legs, stopping right between my thighs.

He presses his left hand on the front of my neck, pushing up against my chin forcefully so I lay back, my head hanging upside down off of the edge. He slides my pants off, then my panties.

"I saw you watching me. You're turned on by my bad side, aren't you? You like a bad boy, don't you?"

"I'm with you, aren't I?"

"You have no idea how bad I can get," he says, rubbing the gun between my legs.

"I think I have an idea."

He whips me back up. "No you don't. Suck on it," he says pressing the gun to my lips. I stare down the silver barrel of the gun, trusting that Taylor has removed the bullets, but that doesn't make me feel any safer.

"I can't."

Taylor cocks his eyebrow, and then bites his lip, containing his dissatisfaction. He dangles the gun by a finger in front of me, signaling he can wait here for as long as it takes me to obey.

I can say the safe word. I can say it. But I don't want to make him stop, I want him to make me do it. He makes me do things I would never have the balls to do otherwise.

He stares expectantly. He won't beg and he won't ask me again.

Hesitantly, I purse my lips around it; it's cold and firm. At any moment something could go terribly wrong. *What if he forgot to remove a bullet?* But it's that danger, that moment of facing something that could kill me that reminds me how badly I want to be alive: to fuck, to scream, to laugh, to cry, to feel butterflies in my stomach. Every cell inside of me brews with nervous energy; it's probably terror, but I think Taylor and I both have something inside of us, something broken that turns those heightened feelings of anger and pain and fear into unmitigated libido.

Once that initial fear of death subsides, it converts into sexual energy in the way an atom under the right circumstances can trigger the oblivion of an entire city.

And now, I understand that look in his eyes when the gun was in his mouth. It's that moment when you realize that the thing that makes others squirm is the thing that takes you to your height. It makes you come out of yourself and be free in a way you could never be otherwise. And somehow, it makes you feel powerful.

I gain confidence, I start to suck on it, not like some foreign piece of metal, but like a phallus. "Yeah, baby, suck it like a cock." The look in his darkened eyes tempts me suck on it harder as I maintain eye contact with him. "You're a bad girl too. Very fucking bad."

I pull the gun out of my mouth, smirking as I then push it down back between my legs. I barely cock my eyebrow, almost daring him, but inside, I am terrified. I have pushed things up another level. I am not sure if it's to test Taylor or myself. *Why the fuck are you tempting him?*

"If you don't think I'll do it, that only means I've been much too gentle with you." He pulls my hips closer to give me more room to lie back and then before I know it, he is sliding the cold, wet barrel inside of me. I gasp in a mixture of disbelief and excitement. I should tell him to stop, but I can't, because I don't want him to. He purses his lips around my clit as I moan in a mixture of ecstasy and horror. The thrill of death and sex, those opposing forces coming so close together in one moment make it hard to breathe.

206

"You are much fucking nastier than I could have ever hoped for," he says, sliding it in deep, "and that's a good thing."

He bites my inner thigh and I let out a yelp. He does it again, harder than the last time. "Taylor!" I pull on his hair. He slides out the gun, puts it down and pulls out his hard dick. Watching him hold it in his hand is one of my favorite sights, as he teases me with it, rubbing it on my labia and clit.

"Your pussy is one of my favorite spots in the world. Warm, soft, wet, creamy…I love feeling it clench around my cock, your tight little pussy." He takes both of his hands and rubs inward circles on my inner thighs as he bites his full lower lip. "I'm going to slide it in slow, I want to savor every last inch of me going inside, of hearing your cute little gasp as I enter you and make you mine all over again."

"I'm already yours."

"But every time I come inside of you, another part of you becomes mine," he whispers.

He keeps his promise, sliding so slowly just so he can tease me. I watch his thickness go in, millimeter by millimeter, it is a thing of beauty. He begins to move his hips rhythmically as I lie all the way back, my head hanging off the edge, upside down. His lips smack as he sucks on his tip of the barrel to moisten it for my clit. As he massages it, he pulls in and out of me. "Tell me you're mine. Tell me I own you." I brace the two panels to either side of me as I come telling Taylor exactly what he commanded me to. As I do so, he leans in, bracing my face with the gun still in his hand, and whispers in my ear. "It was loaded, baby."

And while I should be infuriated, I should smack him right across the face, I don't know what I am. I just feel a surge of something unfamiliar and strong rise inside of me. I tempted death and fucked its brains out. I am the daughter of Alan-fucking-Peters. I have the boy he couldn't kill inside of me. *We are invincible.* The element of surprise as I come only elevates the surrealism of the experience and my moans are interspersed with delirious laughter.

❊ ❊ ❊

Taylor sits at the breakfast bar as I make myself a snack.

"I can't believe we did that, Taylor. You're fucking nuts. It wasn't really loaded, was it? No, it wasn't." I coax myself aloud.

"You'll never know, will you? Telling you would take away the mystique. Plus, it doesn't matter anymore. Rest assured, all precautions were taken."

"Except, you know, removing the bullets." I want to be angry with him, but it's just not there. *I fucking liked it.*

He smirks and takes a sip of his water. "Whatever was in there, you surprised me," he says, punctuating the sentence with a finger point.

"How so?"

"I don't know. I expected you to freak out, but as usual, you surprised me."

"If you thought I would freak out, why would you do it?"

"Because I want you to push your limits. That's why they exist. That's where you find out who you really are. I know I can push them with you, because you and I, we have something that transcends."

"I don't think I'll ever figure you out," I say, biting into a pickle.

"Likewise, but that's what makes us so fucking good, isn't it?"

"Or so fucking bad." Taylor cocks his eyebrow at me. "Oh, I brought the shoebox. I haven't had a chance to look at my baby pics. It's a big deal for me. Part of the heaping delicious serving of bullshit my mother fed me was that the albums of my childhood were stolen. So I only had one baby photo, everything else from my childhood is from when I was four and older."

"I don't have infant pictures either."

"I guess we were in the same boat. Come look with me. Do you think you would remember how I looked?"

"We were so young. I just remember fragments. Many of which were not the greatest times."

"I have to say something to you because you need to know it."

"It's not about your mom trying to —"

"No. No, It's about me."

"Okay," Taylor says skeptically

"You're my hero."

"Oh, come on." He rolls his eyes.

"No seriously. You were just a boy, up against adults, and you thought of me. You protected me. What a brave little child you were. Really. I'll love you forever just for that."

Taylor looks down, sometimes my affection for him is like his glare is to me: too much to take without shrinking away. "Well, I don't know what to say."

"Oh my god, have I made Taylor Holden speechless?"

"I guess I knew you were special even then." I smile at him warmly and walk over to his side of the counter kissing his back, taking in a deep inhale of his scent.

The brown shoebox is old and frayed, the lid nearly useless as its sides have all bent away from the box. Taylor joins me, resting his arm on the back of the sofa and crossing his ankle over his knee. I show him a picture of my mother holding me. "Wow, she did look a lot like you, minus the whole flower child dress. You also have a way better rack."

"Are you checking out my mom's boobs? Gross! What is it with cults? They either dress like Little House on the Prairie or flower children?"

"I don't think they are known for their impeccable fashion sense." His light mood around this subject matter is a relief.

"Hey, I think this one is us too!" This picture is of me, shirtless in a diaper, a few straggly soft large brown curls springing from my head, my tiny feet in adult shoes, laughing a belly laugh. Taylor is wearing blue long johns and it looks like he is doing something to make me laugh, but the camera angle doesn't capture it. "I still can't believe this is us. I guess we had some good times, despite the situation."

Taylor shrugs. "I don't remember many times like that. I wish I could, but at that age, it's the loudest memories that stick."

I find another picture, of my mother and his mother, standing side by side, so much youth and beauty wasted. I'm not sure if Taylor wants to see it, so I move it to the back of the pile and continue sorting through the photos. I find a solo portrait of me, I would guess that I was two or three, in a red floral dress. "Here's another one of me," I say, passing it to Taylor.

"Look at baby Shyla," he says observing the picture. "Wait, there's something stuck to the back of this." The pictures are old and from the looks of it, have remained untouched in the box for years. Many have stuck together over time from moisture. He carefully peels the smaller photo away from the back of my baby photo and his face instantly transforms when he sees it. His hand trembles, his breathing becomes shallow, his eyes full of dread. The look of terror is raw; it's as though he sees a ghost, yet he remains transfixed on the image in a trance of sorts. Within seconds, his expressions become more intense: his trembling stronger, his breathing heavier, as if he will boil over if he continues at this rate.

"Taylor?"

He doesn't respond.

"Taylor?" I raise my voice.

He stops abruptly and looks up at me, his eyes much like when he awakes from a night terror.

"What is it?"

"Nothing…I have to make a call. For work."

"Taylor, I know it's not nothing."

"I'm fine, Shyla. Jesus."

"Alright," I say softly.

He stacks the two pictures back together, puts them on top of the pile and stands up to walk towards his office. "You should go to bed anyway, otherwise your sleep patterns are going to go crazy."

"Yeah, I guess, but I'm wide awake."

He glides down the hallway as I take him in, understanding that even asking him to look at innocent baby pictures allows for variables Taylor cannot control. He turns around. "Shy, I forgot to mention. I'd like you to come with me to visit my father this weekend. It's his birthday and he wanted me to come for a small dinner."

"Really?"

He nods. For some reason, despite proclamations of his feelings for me, I never expected to meet his father. Not because his feelings for me are not real, but because he has a tendency to compartmentalize so many different parts of his life, and I thought that his father and I might never overlap.

"But…are you going to tell him who I am? He's going to hate me."

"I don't see the point in hiding it. I plan on keeping you around, you know. He is a reasonable person and he also knows I make my own decisions. To hate you for where you came from would mean he would have to hate his own son."

"Of course."

When I hear the door to his office close, I reach for the pictures he set down. The one on top is him and me, of course, but the one he reacted to is tucked underneath. Hesitantly, I pull it out from the stack, and I understand his visceral reaction.

It is a candid picture of Taylor, maybe five or six year old, fiddling through a children's book on the floor. Sitting in a wooden chair hovering over him, watching him, is Alan Peters, intensely glaring at the little boy, his usual deceivingly friendly eyes holding something sinister.

CHAPTER FIFTEEN

We rise early on Saturday morning for the three and a half hour drive to Randall Holden's estate. Taylor insists we stay there the entire weekend as the property is vast and the area a beautiful place for outdoor activities. The fall chill is beginning to set in and there is a slight mist in the air, so Taylor wears a navy anorak with worn-in jeans and brown boots. I opt for a army-green canvas jacket with a thick cable knit grey scarf, and a pair of jeans tucked into navy Le Chameau rain boots. We look straight out of a fashion magazine fall editorial spread.

"Taylor, I have to tell you, I am kind of nervous." Taylor did tell his father, who was shocked as the rest of us. He claims he never knew what became of my mother, or that she had ended up moving to the same state as them. Taylor swears his father holds no ill feelings towards me or my mother. "Nothing to worry about, he's okay. Nan is okay too. They're really boring actually."

"Haha! Well I guess I have that to look forward to. It's just all the baggage that comes with me before I have even met him, it makes me a little tense."

"There's no pressure. Just be yourself. You're not here to impress anyone, I just don't want to leave you alone when I come visit my father. I love your company. Plus, it's beautiful and quiet up there."

Taylor takes our cognac-colored leather overnight bags, loads them into the back of the SUV, and we begin our journey. The view is haunting, a heavy fog settles into the surrounding barren trees, not a glimmer of sunlight breaking through the overcast sky.

"So you haven't spoken to your mother yet?" Taylor asks.

"No. She's called twice, but, I don't know. I don't know what to say to her. Am I supposed to just go back to the way things were? If not, am I supposed to dwell on it? I mean, how many things can I ask her before it's enough, ya know?"

"I do. All I know is asking questions only opens up more questions. I don't think once you open up Pandora's box it ever ends until you decide to shut it completely."

"Is that why you prefer not to know more?"

"Like I have told you before, I know everything I need to know. Anything else would be extraneous. I know what happened to me. I was there."

"It's just…I am struggling with who my father was. My mother says he adored me, and I have trouble reconciling that with the person everyone says he was. Maybe there was another side to him." Taylor remains silent. I saw his reaction to Alan's photo. This man has been dead for 25 years and his image alone still makes Taylor tremble. "Can I ask you something?"

Taylor nods.

"Can you tell me what he was like? I'm sorry to ask you, but I need to know. Even if it's bad." Taylor swallows hard, his Adam's apple rising and falling like a cresting wave. "Nevermind. Forget it. That was a really stupid question. It's not fair of me to ask that. It's just that I had this image of a pathetic drug addict my whole life and now…"

"You have the image of a megalomaniacal sadistic psychopath?"

His question is sharp like a dagger. *How can he love me when he hates my father so strongly?* "I know it, intellectually, but it's so abstract. I know he was terrible, but only in a very distant way, like a story on the news. I guess I can look him up, I am sure there are articles and stuff."

"I know you've already looked up C.O.S. You're way too curious not to have once I told you about my childhood."

"Yes, but not specifically into him. Most of the stuff I found spoke about what happened in the general sense. I know he was the ringleader, but still I can't conjure up an image of him."

Taylor nods, but says nothing. We sit in silence for about fifteen minutes. I lean my head against the window into the foggy mist, counting the trees as they pass.

"When I was a child in C.O.S," Taylor starts out of thin air, "in the middle of the night, sometimes he would punish me for things I did earlier in the day." I sit up and turn to face him. "So if I did something disobedient, or sometimes I wouldn't even know what I did to piss him off, I guess I just existed, instead of punishing me on the spot, he would wait. That way, I would be on edge all day, a form of mental warfare, I suppose." My stomach tightens, and I regret asking him about Alan Peters. Taylor's hands clench the steering wheel. "He would give me this look; I knew that look that signaled to me I would get it later. So when I went to bed I would try really hard not to sleep so I could hear his footsteps when he was coming, not that I had anywhere to hide. But it was like he had this uncanny ability to wait until I couldn't stay awake any longer. I used to slide a chair in front of the door so I could hear him open it, but when he figured that out, he took the chair away." I attempt to hide the look of horror on my face.

215

"Then when I was finally asleep, in peace, so exhausted from fighting and fear, he would come into the bedroom and cover my mouth and carry me outside where no one could hear me. Sometimes he would wake me up by choking me so I couldn't cry out. Then he would use his belt, or a switch, or his fists, and he would beat me. He would finally tell me what the beating was for. Maybe I looked at him in a certain way, or my mother looked at me in a certain way, or I spilled a cup of milk, or I told him to stop when he was choking my mother, or accidentally bumped into you when we were playing. There was no rhyme or reason, I could never tell what would set him off. And so, everyday I lived in terror, afraid to be kind, or to laugh, or to hug someone, or to defend myself, because any of those things could get me dragged out in the middle of the night to a vicious beating. Those nightmares I have, sometimes I am that kid again and he's coming to get me in my sleep. Other times, it's me as an adult who finds him and I choke him to death in his bedroom, but when he finally dies and I get a better look at his face, it's me lying there, not him. Sometimes it's other things." I catch myself holding my breath, clutching the sides of my seat. I understand why he doesn't talk about it; I don't know if it could help, the damage is too deep. "If he had never committed suicide, I would have killed him myself eventually. So, that's the kind of person your father was."

I sink into my seat, ashamed. Ashamed I had the nerve to ask him that question so selfishly, that I could be so thoughtless. I've seen the night terrors, I've seen his anxiety about being touched, his intimacy issues, and yet, I asked him to relive his most painful memories to satisfy a curiosity about my father. When he screamed "no!" in his sleep, when he swung wildly, or tried to choke me, he always said he thought I was someone else. Now I know who that person is: my father. And in a very warped way, he *was* choking a piece of him, through his only living descendant. If he wanted to destroy the memory of Alan Peters, all he would have had to do was finish the job when he started choking me that night.

Whenever I feel a moment of self-pity, I must remember: *I was spared. Taylor was sacrificed.*

There will be no kind words, no assurances of Alan Peters being a *nice guy, just misunderstood*. No, it will always be stories of abuse, of control, megalomania, murder, manipulation, and obsession. Even his adoration of me was just another manifestation of his narcissism. I so desperately craved the father I couldn't remember that I almost felt special about how he loved me over everyone else, but it wasn't me that he loved, he looked at me and saw not an individual, but an extension of himself. I was proof that he was not impotent or half a man; he could produce, he could create. He could be immortal. And now I cannot decide if I am angry at my mother for lying to me all of these years, or for finally telling me the truth.

❉ ❉ ❉

We pull through the gate of Mr. Holden's estate and drive down a long path past small guest houses and tall trees, finally pulling up to his sprawling red brick mansion. It looks old and established, like it belongs in these woods just as much as the aged oak trees that surround it. It stands upon the backdrop of a large lake, which is completely engulfed in low-lying fog.

We pull right up to the house. I become stricken with that swirly feeling in my gut when entering completely new and intimidating surroundings. "Come on, he's probably inside." Taylor pulls open the unlocked front door, letting me in first, and then he wipes his feet on the doormat and I follow suit. The sound of frantic footsteps and heaving comes closer as a huge fawn

Mastiff comes barreling towards us and jumps up placing both of his huge paws on my shoulders, flailing his tongue at my face as I lean back to avoid the bath.

"Robert, down!" Taylor commands.

"The dog's name is Robert?" I laugh.

"Yeah," he rolls his eyes. "Sorry I forgot to warn you. He's 150 pounds, I'm glad he didn't knock you over. He's really a huge baby. Come here Bobby." Taylor kneels on one knee and rubs Robert behind the ear. It's the most tender I have seen him with anyone (or thing) besides me.

Then footsteps approach and finally a man turns into the entryway.

He is tall, with an abundance of salt and pepper hair. His face is weathered like a smoker's, but I can tell he was once very handsome as he still has that strong jawline and crooked smile his sons inherited. He walks with a slight limp and a cane, Taylor told me he has a painful autoimmune disease that has made it difficult for him to walk, which is why he retired and passed H.I. to his son. Taylor blames it on his chain smoking and stress-riddled life.

"Son!" He says, his face glows with love in a way that I know Taylor is unable to return to him.

"Hi Randall. Happy Birthday." There will be no hug, no pat on the back, not even a handshake, but his father already knows this. Mr. Holden looks over to me. I smile so hard I think I almost dislocate my jaw. *Shyla, calm down, don't try so fucking hard.* "This is Shyla, the woman I told you about." *I love that he called me a woman.*

"Nice to meet you."

"It's so great to finally meet you, Mr. Holden. Happy birthday."

"They aren't so happy when you're as broken as I am," he says jokingly, but with a sprinkle of truth.

"Come on in. Taylor can show you around, this is his house too. Call me Randall, by the way."

He limps in and we follow him to the kitchen. "Drinks?"

"I got it, dad." Taylor goes to the fridge and grabs us bottled waters. I am so touched to hear him say "dad." Maybe because this is his way of showing affection.

"I decided to push everything up to make it a Linner. You don't mind, do you?"

We both inform him we are famished.

"Where's Nan?" Taylor asks taking a gulp from his bottle.

"She went riding, she should be back in time to join us. Why don't you two get settled and I'll meet you in the dining room?"

As Taylor carries our bags down the second floor hallway, I mouth to him. "How did I do?"

Taylor disapprovingly shakes his head. "You're fine. Just relax."

"He seems very reserved. I should probably not drop any f-bombs."

"Really? He was being warm. He's kind of a badass. He built H.I. from nothing. Raised two difficult sons. I think you being a pretty little woman brings out the softer side of him."

"Well I'm glad I could do that, but then I would hate to piss him off."

"You're like Holden kryptonite. You'll be fine."

"He loves you a lot. I could see his eyes light up when you walked in."

Taylor shrugs, innocently, like he can't help how lovable he is. We enter a large bedroom decorated to match the colonial style of the house, with dark greens and maroons; the aroma of pinecones wafts in the air. Taylor settles the bags on the floor.

219

"I'm sorry about what I asked. In the car." I have to bring it up, I know he's not holding it against me, but I feel sick about it.

"Forget about it. Let's go eat before I dine on one of these potpourri bowls."

We head into the dining room where we there is an unbelievable spread. It's like a high-end restaurant buffet, and in the center is a beautiful white cake, adorned with glossed strawberries. *Small dinner my ass.*

"Have a seat," Randall says from the head of the table. "I hope you are as hungry as you claim."

Just then, a woman with short whitish-blond hair in riding gear walks in. She is ghostly pale, with some of the clearest blue eyes I have ever seen, almost freakishly so. It occurs to me that this is the mother of the man who raped me. I have to share a meal with this woman, not that any of it's her fault, it's just so bizarre. I wonder if she knows where her son is, if he has reached out to her since leaving town, but I think it's more likely she is just another lonely Holden.

"Hello Taylor, how are you?" She says with the warmness of a stale coffee.

"Well, Nan, and you?"

"Just had a wonderful ride on Strider." She turns her gaze to me with her icy blue eyes. "Hello."

"Yes, Nan this is Shyla. Shyla, this is Nan."

She smiles politely and shakes my hand. " Yes, I'm Randall's wife. You all get started, I need to shower. I don't want to sit at the table like this. There's enough food for a week out here."

We sit at our place settings and Taylor and Randall start to dig in, so I follow their lead. Taylor loads his plate with one of everything it seems.

"So Shyla, what do you do?"

"I am an assistant creative director at an advertising firm." I hope Taylor will move the conversation along, but he is too focused on his food. "Your home is beautiful."

"Thank you."

"How long have you lived here?"

"Oh, about 25 years, since Taylor was about seven. Before that we didn't live in this house."

"It's okay, she knows." Taylor says between bites.

Randall is taken aback. "Oh, of course you do. I am not used to speaking about that so openly. Well, then you know I didn't have him until he was seven and this was the home we bought shortly after, to have a fresh start as a family."

"I would have loved to grow up in house like this." Taylor gives me a playful eye roll. That's right, this house was probably a war zone between him and his brother.

"You grew up in the city?"

"Yes. Just my mother and me."

"How is she doing, your mother?"

This is awkward. "She's well. She doesn't live here anymore. She took a job out of state."

Taylor finally speaks up. "Shyla and her mother both struggled to get out of poverty. It seems like after I was found, they had to start all over on their own."

Randall's face becomes solemn. I want to believe that comment wasn't a dig, but Taylor is far too smart to say something like that and not realize its implications. As grateful as he is to his father, I believe he is upset at how my mother was told to go away without recompense. When she discovered Taylor, our roles reversed and he became the adored one, and I the fatherless inconvenience.

"I'm sorry to hear that. It is admirable what you and your mother have been able to overcome," Randall says stoically. He is hard to read. Not as hard as Taylor, but still difficult nonetheless.

I try to steer the conversation in a lighter direction. "The fog is so heavy today."

"Yes, the forecast says it will clear up tomorrow. Perhaps Taylor can take you out on one of the boats and show you around."

"That would be great."

"We'll have a lot of fun tomorrow," Taylor assures me.

Eventually Nan walks in, her hair freshly slicked back and wet, wearing a white oxford shirt over a pair of cropped wine-colored slacks. She grabs a far smaller plate than mine and just a few appetizers. I eye my plate and then Taylor's plate, which are nearly equally full of food. *Great, they are going to think I am an impoverished food hoarder.*

"How was your drive up?" She asks.

"It was fine, no traffic, but a lot of fog," Taylor says.

"It didn't settle here until the afternoon. You seem to have brought it with you." Taylor lets out a half-hearted smirk. "Your brother is up to no good again. Looks like he's found some trouble. The police called here with questions."

Well this is a little heavy for a family birthday brunch with a new guest.

Taylor sits upright, his chair makes a loud rubbing sound against the floor that cuts into the silence of the dining room. "Yes, did they tell you what he did?"

Randall remains silent.

"I told them we did not want to speak to the police regarding matters of Eric, that we hadn't seen him in years and they could speak to our lawyers if they had any other questions." Her indifference is shocking, but I believe she is fatigued by a lifetime of her son's erratic behavior. Either that, or it hurts to know what he is up to. The topic of discussion makes me want to slither under the table.

"I guess dad didn't tell you he was following Shyla recently." *Shut up Taylor!*

"Well for Christ's sake! No he didn't. I am sorry Shyla. These two boys could never get along." *Well that is the understatement of the millennium.* "I didn't even know he might have been in the area until the police called. As soon as they started questioning, I shut them down. You try your best to do the right thing, but they are who they are. Randall knows better than to bring up Eric's bad news I suppose. It's not like Eric doesn't know where to find me if he was interested in seeing his mother again. I will always be here, but I have given up on trying to track him down. I have had way too many sleepless nights over him." Her aloofness baffles me. I'm not sure if Taylor understands that it's not just him she is aloof with, but that it is likely her general disposition. She kind of reminds me of a cyborg. My mother, who often worked with drug addicts who ran away from home would deal with parents who would endlessly comb the world over for their kids. Although, I understand why she would want to avoid the pain of hearing about her greatest failure.

"It's fine. Everything's okay now," I chime. *Yes, your son is now a fugitive rapist. Everything is a-okay!*

"He didn't do anything to you did he? Is that why the police were asking about him?"

"No. I haven't seen him in a good while," I say, turning to Taylor for some assistance in ending this topic of conversation.

"I think I'm going to take Shyla for a walk around the property. You're welcome to come, dad."

"No, this weather makes me achy. You two go ahead."

We grab our jackets and emerge out of the front door. Taylor walks towards the lake briskly and I follow behind him.

"That was really weird," I say.

"Which part?"

"I don't know, I guess all of it. Nan bringing up Eric like that for one. Oh and thanks for mentioning that Eric was stalking me, that helped a lot."

"I like to remind them both that it's better he's gone."

"I didn't realize they would call your parents. Does your dad know about the investigation? That he attacked me?"

"He said the police mentioned he was a suspect in an assault case. The cops can't disclose your identity due to the nature of the crime. I made sure with the detective that even though it was a family matter, you did not want them knowing you were the victim."

"I didn't even think of that possibility. That they might find that out. I really don't want them to know that. It would be so weird and uncomfortable."

"I can't promise it won't ever come out. If they find him and we have to go to trial…"

"God. I just hope he stays away."

"Even if it did come about, you have nothing to be ashamed of. Eric is in the wrong. We are doing what we have to do to right his wrong. Lucky for us, Nan is really in denial about Eric. She's really pissed at him for leaving. She's not the type to blindly defend her son as you can tell."

"I hope you don't mind me saying this, but she's very icy. I mean, almost robotic."

"Yeah, I told you, she's a little frigid towards me. It goes both ways though."

"I think she's a little frigid in general, Taylor. She seems pretty indifferent about her own son."

"Well she thinks Eric just up and left one day and never came back. So she's really bitter about that. She doesn't know about the agreement. Eric didn't want her to know about the accusations against him of trying to have me killed and my father didn't want to deal with her blaming him for the whole mess. So she thinks he left to start over, away from all of us. He was always a handful, so it made sense."

"Oh my god, so all of you just let her think her son just up and left?"

"Yes. It worked for all sides."

"Probably not for her though."

"It's better she doesn't know what her son is capable of. You heard her, she doesn't even want to know."

"I suppose. It's just weird how she is so open about it, yet so avoidant at the same time."

"Welcome to the Holden family. Thick skin required as there is no pussy-footing. You're the first woman I've brought home, so I think they realize you are a special person. They also both know about your newly discovered past, so I think they know you 'get it.'"

"Well there's one benefit. Thirty-two years old… They must've hounded you all the time about making some grandkids since Eric is out of the picture."

"No, they know me and they came to terms with it all a long time ago. They just thought I'd be a perpetual bachelor, jumping from one casual relationship to another." *I didn't know sex slaves were casual.* "My father was pretty shocked to find out about you."

"I guess I cracked the code."

"I could still end up a bachelor," he says playfully.

"You better watch your mouth," I say in jest. While he was joking, the thought stings a bit. "Hey, was it me, or were you sticking it to your dad with that comment about me and my mom being on our own?"

"It wasn't you."

"What was that all about?"

"I don't think he treated you fairly. He was wealthy. The least he could have done was set you and your mother up. He told me he was in shock and didn't think of it. When the dust settled, he claims he didn't know how to find her, but I don't buy that. That was just an excuse. It seems no one wants to be reminded of their mistakes, so it's easier to just pretend they didn't exist."

"It is what it is. We all have fucked up at some point."

"It's just, I look at all of the things I had, and I know you went without for so long."

"It's okay. It builds character."

"So do sports and charity work. It's no excuse. You should have been helped. Your mother saved my life. He should have helped her."

"My mother wanted to do things her way. I'm not going to blame your father for what happened to me and you shouldn't either."

"I hold people responsible for what they could have done better. First, he impregnates a sixteen year old girl, then he turns his back on the woman who saved me. It makes me question his integrity. What else he has hidden from me? He protected my piece of shit brother who tried to have me killed. He didn't even warn me Eric was in town. For too long I have cut him slack because he did what he was supposed to do as my father."

Tell him. Tell him his mother's body was never found. "But you said you didn't want to know more."

"That's different."

"I'm sorry, but I have to call you on some of your bullshit."

"Excuse me?"

"My mother wants to clear stuff up and you don't want to hear it."

226

"There are facts, and there are opinions. Your mother wants to convince me that my mother loved me. Well fuck that. What she put me through wasn't love, and nothing your mother can say can change my opinion. Love is shown, not spoken. Unless Lyla can crawl out of a grave and prove herself, the case is closed." I don't say anything, just continue to walk alongside Taylor. "Listen, I know you are trying to help. I do. But just because your mother decided to open up to you, it doesn't make me obligated to have to talk to her about it. I want to move forward with you, not sit around reminiscing about our extraordinarily shitty pasts. You could tell me my mother was a guardian angel, you could tell me that she had good intentions, but it won't make the nightmares stop, it won't make me a nicer person, it won't make me hate people less, or want to hug my family. I am who I am. There is something you need to understand about me. Who I am with you, is not who I am with everyone else. It's important you remember that, or you will be disappointed."

"I'm sorry. I won't ask again."

"You know I have no problem asking for what I want so there's no need to insist upon something. If I want to do something, I'll tell you."

We hike through the woods to a high point where Taylor used to go as a child.

"When I wanted to be alone, which was often, this is where I came." In the vista the tops of trees peek out from a dense mist. Green, gold, and orange mountains along the horizon look too perfect to be real. We sit on a large rock. "It's still here," he says pointing to an etching of his name in the stone in jagged letters. "It's getting dark, we should head back. I hope you worked up an appetite because they really do expect us to eat all that."

We return back to the house and eat another meal. A woman floats around the house who was not present before. Apparently she is Randall's caretaker, Marnie. She tells us that Randall is resting in his study. Nan left the house to run errands. Once we are finished, Taylor says he has surprise plans for me later. Just as he is about to explain, his cell phone rings.

"Shit, it's Nan. She has a flat. Stay here, I am going to go get her quick."

"You sure you don't want me to come?"

"No, it's starting to rain. You'd just be sitting in the car. It shouldn't be long. Make yourself at home. There's a TV in our room or in the living room."

The front door slams and the beams of light from the SUV filter through the front window curtains as he pulls away. I settle on the living room couch and flip through the television channels, looking for something to watch. The house is so still that I forget that Randall is still somewhere in it. I find some detective show and settle in, after a while I nod off, only to be awoken by Marnie.

"Miss Shyla?" I shoot up, a little embarrassed that I was caught snoozing on the couch. "Sorry honey. Randall wants to see you in his study."

CHAPTER SIXTEEN

The ornate wooden door to Randall's study is ajar. Hesitantly, I push it open just enough to get a view of him tending to a crackling fireplace. After he puts the poker back in its place, he flexes and extends the fingers of his right hand, wincing in pain.

"Mr. Holden?"

"Randall is fine, Shyla. Come have a seat."

I cautiously sit across from him in a large buckskin wingback chair in front of the fireplace. Seconds pass, but the silence between us feels like it will never end until he finally speaks.

"What's he like?"

"I, uh, Taylor?"

"Yes."

"I'm not sure how to answer that. What do you mean?" I ask.

Randall looks down, as if trying to find the right words. "You know, I've made a lot of mistakes as a father, but I've tried. I tried so hard with those boys..." His voice trails off, but I say nothing. "Eric was so emotional, so sensitive. I could never get him to think with his head," he clenches his fists in frustration. "And then Taylor...when I finally got him, he just, I couldn't break through. He was always so sad. It was always in his eyes."

I gently nod. I am all too familiar with the sadness he speaks of.

"I was wrong for what happened with Taylor's mother, we should have never — I should have never —

been with her. But I'd do it all over again: the shame, Nan hating me when she found out, even losing Eric, for that boy. I've lost one son; he comes and he goes for months, years even, at a time. All I have left is Taylor, and I am so proud of him, but at the same time, it's like I don't even know him."

"I understand Taylor can be…aloof, but whenever he speaks of you, he does so very fondly." Randall's openness is so unlike Taylor and I wonder if this is who he is, or if it's desperation from years of loneliness.

Watching Randall's eyes just barely glimmer at my words chokes me up. This is what it is like to love Taylor and not get it back, this is the effect that Taylor has on everyone else. He absorbs love much like a black hole, never reflecting it back, just sucking the light away from its source.

"He talks about me?"

"Yes. He told me he is very grateful for the life you provided him. He knows you tried your best." Randall smiles faintly.

"I just need to make sure you have his best interests at heart. I know he seems strong, but really he is fragile. And I can tell he feels very strongly about you."

"Your son—Taylor—is…protective. Charismatic. Funny. Sarcastic. He's a great cook too. He's stubborn as hell, and he can be very direct, sometimes forgetting about people's feelings. You're right, there is a part of him that is tremendously fragile, but at the same time he is so strong, so capable."

"Funny, huh?"

"Yeah, at least I think so."

"Does he allow you to touch him?"

The intimacy of our conversation is premature, yet it feels completely natural. We both are isolated by our love for Taylor and finally there is someone we can speak to who understands. And while I have only been in this state for months, Randall has been alone in this love for decades.

"Yes."

Randall's moistened eyes reflect the flames burning in the fireplace like small mirrors.

"I thought he might never find that," he says warmly.

I smile. "I have to admit I was nervous coming here. I thought you might not like me, because of my history."

Randall snaps back into the present. "I can't say I was thrilled when he told me, but Taylor is a grown man and he is capable of making his own decisions. I didn't know what to expect, but when you came through the door, I felt at ease. You're just a young lady, and like Taylor, you didn't get to choose your circumstances. Nonetheless, you have to understand that I've spent my entire life trying to move him away from C.O.S. I hope I don't offend you by saying this: my first instinct was to think that somehow you sought him, because of your common circumstances and his wealth."

"I guess it's natural to think that. I can't prove to you otherwise, but I had no idea about my father until days ago. I work. I make my own money. Taylor is rich and I can't make that go away, but he came after me. He courted me."

Randall seems satisfied with the answer, or at least he pretends to be. "So Taylor tells me your mother just told you after all these years?"

"Yes, my mother wanted to shield me too. I'm not even sure it has really sunken in."

"It's a painful past. I am sure she had your best intentions in mind." *Isn't there a saying about good intentions and where they end up?*

"Is that why you haven't told Taylor his mother's body was never found?"

231

Randall's eyes open wide and he sits back. "You are bold; I can see why Taylor has taken such a liking to you." Then his voice raises with a touch of alarm. "Does he know?"

"No, I haven't told him because I am not sure it's worth it."

"Well, then you know why I haven't."

"Do you believe she's dead?"

"She's been gone for decades. It doesn't even matter anymore. How did you know? *Your mother.*"

"Yes."

"Taylor knows he can ask me anything. He never wanted to know about Lyla. Despite what she brought him into, I don't hate her. She was young and confused. I harbor some of the blame for that."

"But if you told him his mother was dead, then how would he know what to ask?"

"She is presumed dead. Legally. That is not a lie. I never said where her body was. Taylor assumed that and it wouldn't take much digging around or asking to know otherwise."

"I guess it's my turn to hope I don't offend, but I believe that is lying by omission."

"Point taken, but I did what I had to do to move that boy forward. Imagining his dead mother might be alive somewhere does not allow for that."

"He told me you put a picture of her on his mirror."

"Yes. I wanted him to know that it was okay to think about her, that I wouldn't be offended or upset. Like you said, he is stubborn. He never wanted to talk; for the first year he was here he didn't say a word. And then he seemed to find his way on his own and I was so scared if I pushed I might silence him again." *His way. BDSM, isolation, night terrors. That's Taylor's way.*

"He has done a lot with H.I. He has become such a success despite the circumstances."

"Yes, he has." There are few moments of contemplative silence before Randall speaks again. "Forgive me for being so personal, but, you have probably figured out we Holdens don't beat around the bush. You love him don't you?"

"Um...yes. I do." I only hesitate because I wonder if this is something that Taylor wants me to share with his father, but I cannot lie. The conversation thus far has been too intimate to do so without Randall knowing.

"And he you?"

"I think you should ask—"

"Both you and I know Taylor won't tell me. Not those words."

I nod.

He pauses, absorbing my words, nodding ever so slightly to himself. "Well then, tread carefully. The kind of love you have is only written about in books. It is born from suffering. It is a painful love that often comes at the expense of a great tragedy. All sense evaporates within its heat. And nothing that intense lasts forever."

"I'm sorry?"

"He's always been sad, but you've brought him happiness. There is no doubt about that. We both know however, that type of happiness is fleeting, it exists only for that person. Eventually, one needs to find it inside of oneself."

"I'm not sure I understand what you're getting at?"

"It's just sage advice. Nothing more. As I said earlier, you and Taylor will do what you please. I just wanted you to know. I could never get through to Taylor, but maybe I can get through to you."

"Get what through? That we shouldn't be together?"

"That you should seriously consider if two people who share such a past can ever escape it, especially if those two people continue to stay in each other's lives."

"With all due respect Randall, you're wrong."

"How so?"

"We have a chance to be happy, to stay happy. You don't understand what we have and just because we spoke here, and I told you some things, doesn't mean you do. In fact, it is our pasts that make us relate to each other in a way no one else can. There are no other people for us, we were meant to find each other."

"That's precisely my point. No one understands, it's you two against the world, isn't it? I sincerely hope you can stay happy, but so often what is born from tragedy, will end in tragedy."

"Just because our parents screwed up, doesn't mean Taylor and I are destined for heartbreak. Your son is an amazing man, and he deserves to be happy and to be loved."

"I couldn't agree with you more and I hope you will convince him of that."

Just then, there is a tap on the door. Taylor walks in with a puzzled look on his face.

"Taylor, I was just getting to know Shyla over here. She is great company."

"Yes she is," he says suspiciously. "Nan is downstairs. We got a spare on her car, but she'll need to get the tire patched tomorrow."

"Thank you for helping her."

"Of course, you're welcome."

"Well, I think I will head to bed," Randall says, rising from his seat. "Shyla, it was wonderful getting to know you."

I smile and nod. "Happy birthday."

"Happy birthday," Taylor says.

Randall nods assuredly at us both as he exits the study.

Taylor turns to me. "What was that all about?"

"I'm not sure. He just wanted to get to know me I guess."

"Was he nosing around? You look upset."

"A little, but I think he's lonely. It seems like he wants to make sure you're okay. He just seems concerned about you, that I might hurt you somehow."

"Unbelievable. I apologize you had to go through that. He needs to relax. This is all Eric's fault. He thinks I am all he has left, blah, blah, blah. Somehow that entitles him to badger you. I'll tell him to leave you alone."

"No, don't do that. I think he just wishes he knew more about you."

"He thinks he does. Sorry about that, I should've known he would try to pry."

"He was very open. It was weird, I guess because it took so long for me to get to know you and he's an open book."

"I suppose, but he's smart too. He only discloses what he feels he must."

"He asked me if I loved you."

"Really? Fucking Randall." He shakes his head.

"It's okay."

"No it's not. It's incredibly intrusive. What did you tell him?"

"What was I supposed to say? I told him the truth."

"That you hate me?" He says jokingly.

"Oh shut it."

"And what did he say?"

I wonder if I should tell him about the warnings his father gave me, but I don't want to start a tiff between them. Taylor and I have a special relationship, and in a way that conversation with his father felt like an anonymous support group for Taylor lovers. To reveal too much would be to betray that kinship. I soften the message.

"He just wanted me to be careful with your heart. I think he's nervous about our pasts catching up to us somehow."

"Ugh. You'd think I was a 16 year old girl going to prom, the way he speaks about me. Just ignore him, he's being dramatic." *I guess I know where Eric gets his flair for drama.* "Does he think dead cult members are going to come out from the grave and find us?"

"He told me he had reservations about my past, that at first his hunch was I was after your money, but that he understands my position now."

"Ugh, you two did cover a lot. You two probably talked about more stuff than my father and I cover in a year."

"He's very open; direct."

"Yup. I have full faith in your ability to hold your own, but like I told you, he's a force."

"Except when it comes to you."

"Meaning?"

"Well, just that you're you, you know? Impenetrable. It seems as though he feels he's walked on eggshells with you because he is afraid to lose you again."

Taylor nods his head. "So, I want to take you somewhere tonight. Somewhere special," he whispers.

"Where?"

"It's a surprise. Come, I have something for you." He leads me to the bedroom and asks me to have a seat. On the dresser is a bottle of champagne chilling in an ice bucket. He pours us both a glass and sits next to me.

"So…what's next?"

"Have a couple of glasses. I need you to be relaxed."

"You're trying to get me drunk?"

"No. Just a little loose."

"Okay…" I say suspiciously. Eager to get on with the night, I down the glass. "Gimme another," I demand.

236

"Let the record show you are drinking at this pace on your own free will," Taylor says as he fills my flute. "I'll be right back."

Taylor digs into one of his larger bags and pulls out a box. "I want you to wear this tonight. It's required attire."

I curiously cock my head as I walk over to the box resting on the bed. With my available hand, I lift off the lid. Inside is a strapless leather bustier, a feather masquerade mask, tall boots, a garter, and some other accessories I can't yet make out.

"What's all this?" I ask in disbelief.

"It has to do with the surprise."

"Taylor, we are at your dad's house!"

"He's already asleep, so is Nan. Plus, I made sure you packed your trench, didn't I?"

"You did…I honestly have no idea what this is all about."

"I know, that's the fun part."

"I don't know…"

"What did you tell me? The other night in the gun range?"

"Harder?"

"Well, the other thing."

"That I'm yours?"

"Yes."

"I can't have you fighting me on everything. I've trusted you by opening up to you, bringing you home, now you have to reciprocate. Don't you trust me?"

"Of course, but…"

"It's a simple yes or no."

"Yes."

"I promise you will not forget this night."

"That's what I'm afraid of," I say as I pour myself another glass and chug it. After placing the empty glass on the dresser, I know now is the time to take the leap.

"I'll be right back," I tell Taylor as I carry the box and its contents into the en suite bathroom. The first thing I pull out of the box is the bustier, which is thick and structured. After examining it for a bit, I realize I will likely need his help tightening the corset, so I place it back in the box and put on the other items. A black crotchless pair of panties goes on first, followed by a pair of fishnet thigh-highs attached to a garter. There is also a tight leather mini skirt, and when I say mini, I think it came from the cow's ankle or something. It zips up like a glove. Finally, I zip up the boots. Besides the mask and bustier, there is one thing left to add to the wardrobe: a choker. At first I thought it might be a decorative cuff, but it is far too big for my wrists. It buckles like a belt, and on the front side is a metal ring, I can only think of one purpose for this attachment. It worries and excites me all at once.

I stare at myself in the mirror, admiring my topless figure clad in shiny leather. Makeup and hair must be done to match the severity of the heavy materials and metal. Out of my makeup bag comes a blood-red lipstick and blush (much like the color of the darkroom) and some smokey eyeshadow. I finish off the look, with thick black eyeliner and heavy mascara. Finally, I slick my hair back into a side-parted, low ponytail. *Who is this dark, dangerous woman staring back at me in the mirror?*

Once I feel brave enough to ask Taylor to strap me into the top, I take a deep sigh and slowly open the bathroom door. He's looking through his luggage before he turns and sees me standing there, holding the corset over my chest. He's seen my breasts more times that I can count, but tonight feels new.

His eyes brows arch. "Wow."

"I was wondering if you could help me put my top on…" His father said I was bold. He doesn't know that his son turns me into a meek little girl.

"Of course." He blows air on his hands and rubs them together before softly sliding my ponytail over my shoulder. After I secure the top on my torso, he begins the tighten the cross-section of straps, starting from the very bottom and working his way up. We don't say a word, the only sound in the room is of our breath, inhaling and exhaling in unison. I trust Taylor, but that doesn't make the unknown any less nerve wracking. "Is that tight enough?" He asks.

"Yes. I think so, I've never worn one of these before. My oxygen consumption is limited to the baseline amount I need to survive, so I think that's about right." I turn to face him.

"You look incredible," he says, kissing me on the neck. Goosebumps raise on my arms and my nipples harden. One look down below shows me I'm not the only one with an erect body part.

"I'll be right back," he says softly, disappearing into the bathroom. I grab the bottle and pour the remainder of the champagne into my glass. I think the only thing keeping me sane is the liquid courage Taylor has so cleverly provided. Ten or so minutes later, he emerges from the restroom, wearing a fitted black suit, with a crisp white shirt, the first few buttons undone, his hair slicked back. He hasn't shaven in a couple of days, revealing the perfect amount of stubble against his still-tanned skin. He looks simply perfect, but I was expecting more of a Village People look to match my attire.

"You look surprisingly normal considering the outfit you chose for me."

"I wouldn't look as good in that as you do," he says, generously revealing that crooked grin of his.

"What's with the mask?" I ask.

"It's optional, but I think you'll want to wear it. I'll have one too," he says patting his chest pocket. I'm not a complete idiot, I have an idea of where we are headed, but it's only an idea in the vaguest sense.

"Are you sure your dad is asleep?"

"I promise you he is. It's way past his bedtime."

As Taylor leads me outside the door, I try to make as little noise as possible, but it's nearly impossible with the five-inch platform boots I am wearing.

"We're taking one of my dad's cars," he says before leading me to the garage. This one is modest compared to Taylor's, holding just five cars. He opens the passenger door to a black Rolls Royce and guides me in.

"It feels like we're stealing his car," I whisper.

"That's because we are," he says as he pulls out.

"You have like fifty cars and you steal your dad's?"

"It's always more satisfying," he says with a wink.

"So are you going to give me any hints?"

Taylor squints as he debates to himself whether or not to tell me anything. "Where we're going, it's not too far from my father's so I thought this would be the perfect time to introduce you. I haven't visited since I met you."

"Why's that?"

"I think you'll understand when we arrive." He turns up the volume on a song he plays through his iPhone.

"That song is so familiar. You played it in the darkroom once, really loud. I couldn't hear anything but that song. What's it called?"

"The Ruiner."

Taylor pulls into a long driveway, driving for a few seconds until we approach a large wrought-iron gate. He rolls down the window and presses the button on the intercom.

"1021 Red," he says.

There is a five-second lag, and then the gate slowly opens. *What the hell was that?*

"My stomach is in knots. I'm so nervous."

"Don't be," he says, stroking my head. We pull up to a large brick mansion with a circular driveway. "Masks," he says, pulling out a black eye covering, his eyes contrasting sharply to its darkness. Mine is black as well, but more bird-like in shape, like a raven.

A young man steps to the passenger side of the car, and helps me out. Taylor tosses him the keys and he drives out of sight.

"So are you going to tell me now?" I whisper, holding his hand so tight, I might break it.

"Just relax, let the night take us where it will. I just want to show you some things." In other words, no.

As we walk towards the front door, it opens in our presence. A rather large man in a black suit is behind the door. Behind us, the door shuts almost instantly followed by the sound of locks securing.

The house is old, but lavish and well maintained. The bannisters are intricately carved, dark-colored tapestries adorn the walls. Expensive-looking sculptures encased in glass sit atop wooden platforms, built-in cabinets display ornately decorated china.

"Red, you handsome devil. It's been too long!" A woman who appears to look amazing for her forties greets us. She is not wearing a mask. Her hair is fire-red, pin-straight and long. She too is wearing all black: a low cut latex tank, matching black pants, and platform ankle boots.

"Yes, circumstances have changed a bit."

She looks over to me. "And who's this pretty little thing? Is she yours?"

"Yes."

"Mmmm…"she licks her lips, looking at me like a piece of freshly grilled steak.

"This one won't be shared." *Shared?*

241

"I think she's nervous, Red," the woman says to Taylor. "Is this her first time in a place like this?"

I want to say something, but it's as if I am invisible. Taylor nods.

"Well, if you two need some company, let me know," she winks. *Back off bitch.* "Philipe, get these two some drinks." Seconds later, a young man, in a leather vest, full mask, and teeny-tiny shorts brings a tray with drinks. I grab them for the both of us.

"He's mine," the woman says to me with a smirk.

"I'm going to give her a tour," Taylor says.

"Yes, it's a good night. Some very interesting members are here."

Taylor guides me up the left of the two matching staircases to the second level. When no one is within earshot I whisper to him: "Is this some sort of sex club?"

"Yes. A high-end one, only the very wealthy and thoroughly vetted can join."

"Oh my god." I cringe. I don't know what to do with myself.

"We don't have to do anything. I just wanted to show you around, and show you off." He grabs my ass and I jump. "Just remember, no matter what you see, that everyone here wants to be here."

"Okay," I gulp. "I just feel so out of place."

"Look at you. You fit right in."

"Who's the woman?"

"That's Lane. She's the owner."

"She is interesting."

"I've known her for years. She does a great job with this club."

"I guess. Have you —?"

Taylor looks away, hiding a smirk. "Shy, this *is* a BDSM club and she is not only the president, she's also a member."

I can't help but smile at the comment, but deep inside I feel the heat rising. This woman just paraded around like she owned the place (yes, I know she does) and then talks over me like I'm just some two-bit sub. *I'm not just some sub bitch, I am his love. You were just two flaps of meat he could stick it in and slap around.*

"Well, I don't like her," I whisper.

"Shhh…it's not about her," he says. Just then, a man completely covered from head to toe in black walks by holding a leash. A pretty, long-legged blonde with a ball gag in her mouth is on the other end. She tries to eye Taylor, but her Master gives her a good tug when he spots this, and she stumbles to catch up.

"Is she going to get in trouble for that?"

"It's up to him. Come on, we can't just stand here forever. You're going to stop asking questions and I'll tell you what to do."

As I follow Taylor, the sounds of moaning, flesh slapping against flesh, and whipping permeate the dark corridor. I am submerged in anxiety, which only makes me more bound to Taylor because he is the only familiar thing right now. Finally, he stops at a door and opens it. My hand begins to tingle, and I realize this is because of how hard I am clenching his.

A fireplace provides the only light in this room, and in front of it is woman with short spiky hair, her breasts exposed a top a corset, her bottom completely bare. She is being penetrated by a man from behind who is holding her leash while she sucks off another guy.

Her hands are tied behind her back.

CHAPTER SEVENTEEN

There are others standing against a wall, forming a gallery of sorts. They all wear masks, each one different, some covering more facial features than others. All are wearing dark clothing, some, like Taylor, are wearing street wear, but others are wearing the velvet, leather and latex I expect to see in an establishment such as this one. The woman at the center of the show is in complete surrender, the two men owning her body. I look at the dark figures around me, immersed in the live show before them. *Who are these people?* For Lane to have a mansion of this size and a staff, she must have many high-end clients. Are they hiding in plain sight like Taylor? The men in front of me could be soccer dads, politicians, or high-priced attorneys. I am officially occupying a secret underworld very few even know about.

I avert my eyes from the spectacle in front of me, it feels so intrusive, watching this woman at her most vulnerable. *Do these men even care about her or she just an object to them?* I find myself judging the people in the room, but then the cold hard truth slaps me: *Taylor is one of these men.* I imagine Lane in the center, sucking Taylor off, and I slowly boil. I may be his, but he is mine as well. I clear the thought out of my head before it can escalate any further, again trying to focus on the woman's eyes to see if she is enjoying this. How can I truly determine if she is enjoying herself when pain and degradation are her turn-ons?

I pity her, but at the same time there is a thrill inside of me. At her most vulnerable, she is the center of desire for these men. They all want her, they all share a connection, in a way. Even though she is submitting, her sexuality is powerful. *Taylor is one of these men.* I look over to him, his eyes are narrow and focused. He is turned on. *Why is it that he brought me here? Does he want me to become just like her?* It's not something I could do. I can't submit to a man other than Taylor. If this is what pleases him the most, I am not sure I can provide that.

That bitch Lane probably did everything he ever wanted and would do it at this moment if he asked. Images of him inside of her aggressively flash in my mind and now I cannot get rid of them. My hands begin to shake, I am the angriest I have ever been at Taylor and yet I can't quite articulate why. It's not that he brought me here, it's that he's shared these intimate moments that I don't think I am capable of with other women. I have been jealous before from ideas of what he has done, but here it is in front of me. The life he had, the 35 women he has likely brought here and shared or fucked is something I can't compete with.

His hand begins to creep up the back of my skirt and before it can lead to anything, I storm out of the room, slamming the door on Taylor as I run. "Shy? Shy, what's going on?" He says trailing behind me down the dimly lit hallway.

I don't answer, I just run faster in these godforsaken boots past closed old wooden doors, the sounds of kinky sex filling my ears. The smell of it fills my nose. He grabs my arm. "Let go!" I shout. *I am a very shitty submissive.* A couple of people in the vicinity look at us, and he hesitantly slides his hand off of my arm. As I run through the foyer to exit, I pass Lane.

"What's wrong lil' girl?" She asks.

"Fuck off," I say, pushing my way past the doorman and stepping outside into the damp autumn air.

Taylor walks behind me, but keeps his distance. Out of my periphery I see him gesture to Lane to indicate he has this under control, which makes me fume even more. After taking a few steps away down the driveway I realize I have no jacket, no car, no where to go, but I am too stubborn to stop, so I just walk along the property. When we are out of sight, Taylor utters the first words since he grabbed my arm.

"Shyla, what the hell is going on? What are you so pissed about?"

I spin around. "How could you bring me here? Around these women you fucked? That Lane bitch, the way she looked at me...I almost slapped her."

"You're jealous? That's what this is about?"

"I'm not like Lane, or *Em*," I say mockingly.

"That was all a long time ago, Shyla and I am glad you're not like them."

"You shared all these things with them. I'm willing to do it all, because it's special to me. You're the only person I would ever do this with, but to you, I'm just number 36."

"You think you're not special to me?"

"Do you want to share me? Do you want me to be like that girl we watched? Is that what this is about?"

"No. I told you I want you all to myself."

"Then why am I here?"

"Do you want to leave? That's all you had to say."

"No!"

"Then what is it Shyla? What the fuck do you want from me? You can't keep saying you want something and then throwing it back at me because of your shame or insecurity. None of this works if you don't trust me or yourself."

"But, I can't stop thinking about it. You did those things with Lane. I don't want to share you, but it's too late for that. I already have."

"Shyla it's just fucking! It's only been you. It's only you!" Taylor lets out in exasperation. I stand there in silence. "You feel like you're somehow less than these women or because they came before you that makes you less important to me? You need to stop with the insecure bullshit. I took you here because I trust you. There was no pressure to do anything. You keep saying you'll do whatever I want, but you fucking fight me every step of the way! You wanted this godammit," Taylor paces, running his hand through his hair, his jacket parting open. "You told me you wanted to do this! I said we could be vanilla and now you try to make me feel like shit about it? Fuck you for that! You want it, you know you do, but you won't be satisfied until you can put it all on my head. This is all about being terrified of who you really are."

My lip begins to quiver. I want it; I am scared how much I want it. When I saw that woman, I was terrified that I could become her. If Taylor wanted me to go to someone else, I say I wouldn't, but if nothing else would make him happy, I know I would give in eventually. I can't show him he has that much power over me. I want to be everything to Taylor and the thought of it frightens me. The jealousy of the subs is real, but it's only because I want to be better at it than those women before me.

"You're right," I say softly.

Taylor opens his mouth to shout again, but then catches himself when he realizes I agree with him. He looks confounded for a second, but then he recomposes.

"Well, then we're gonna fucking do it my way," he says, hooking his finger around the O-ring on my collar, dragging me back to the entrance of the house. I open my mouth to say something. "Shut up," he says firmly. And for once, I obey.

He pulls me up the stairs and again, the doorman lets us in. "Lane!" Taylor calls out like he owns the place. I can't catch my breath; my heart pounds powerfully. Lane runs out to the mezzanine atop the two adjoining staircases, a look of confusion on her face erased when she sees he has me by the collar. She wanted a piece of us tonight and now I am afraid she just might get what she wished for. He cocks his head, directing her to follow us as he leads me to wooden double doors. Taylor busts them open with the type of confidence that leads me to believe he was either certain no one was on the other side or he just didn't give a shit.

"Lane, close the fucking door and sit over there," his firmness, his complete and total ownership of the moment gives me a thrill. Especially watching him completely dominate that red-headed bitch. She follows his directions.

"Oooh, are we going to have some fun?" she asks.

"Shut the fuck up. You're going to sit over there and you are going to fucking do what I say."

She cowers, her body language changing in an instant. *She must be a switcher, I read about those.* Taylor still has me by the collar, and he pushes me down to the bed with it. I fall back, watching his frustration and rage translate into something else. He rips off his jacket and thrusts it across the room, then he unbuttons his shirt angrily as he scowls at me.

"Lane, crawl over here slowly." He doesn't even look in her direction and he points to a spot beside him on the floor, he glares into my eyes as if daring me to defy him. Instead, I am hypnotized, in complete awe of him and his unfettered dominance. Lane slips down from the upholstered wooden chair, getting on all fours. She slowly slinks over towards us, her long fiery mane grazing the floor, arriving to the foot of the bed, just where my right leg dangles. "Lick her boot slowly," he says, not breaking his gaze with me, his abs peaking through the unbuttoned shirt. My breath pauses for a second. I believe this is a little gift from him for Lane making me feel inferior and it only solidifies how much I want him at this moment. Lane, looks up at us, doe-eyed, and she grabs the heel of my boot, extending her tongue, slowly gliding it over the patent leather of the foot of the shoe, running it up the entire length. As she reaches the top, Taylor interjects. "Don't touch her skin," he says raising a finger but still not looking at her. "Shy, you see that woman there? She is nothing to me, nothing." I look over to her for a second, suddenly feeling guilty for putting her in this position, but then I realize she might like the putdown. "Look at me. She was only a convenient place for me to stick my dick. Now she's going to watch, she's going to learn her place. Lane, get on the bed. Play with her hair." She crawls on the bed, slowly unraveling my ponytail, so that my hair fans out onto the comforter beneath us. She strokes my hair gently, a far cry from the confident and boisterous woman who greeted me not an hour ago.

Taylor pushes my skirt up and I tense. I've never had anyone watch like this before, and I don't know what to do with myself. "Relax," he commands, with the first hint of softness in his voice since I stormed out. As much as I loathe to admit it, Lane's gentle caress helps put me at ease. He firmly rubs my inner thighs as I try to prevent myself from hyperventilating; the tight corset makes me hyperaware of my breathing. Taylor finally pulls off his open shirt and unbuckles himself, whipping his belt out in one motion like an angry father about to spank his child. I hold my breath thinking he might use it. Instead he keeps it taut in his hands for a few seconds, relishing the effect the moment of uncertainty has on me, then throws it to the floor. He rigorously pulls out his erection as his pants drop. "No one makes me as hard as you do," he says, holding his firmness in his hand.

I catch myself biting my lip and then he does it too. Lane pulls all my hair away from my face, but will not do anything further unless Taylor commands her to do so. Finally, he tells her to undo my top. Hook by hook, she meticulously undoes my bustier; I let out a large exhale as my breasts become exposed. "You nervous?" He asks.

I nod.

He leans on top of me, whispering into the ear opposite the one Lane is laying next to. "It's always been you. Do you understand? Before I even knew you, it was you. No one else. You aren't number 36, you're number one. You're my first." He slides his fingers into my mouth and I suck on them, grabbing his thumb and pinky as I suck on his forefinger and middle finger. He softly pulls his hand away and slides his wet fingers inside of me, but he doesn't even need to, I am so ready for him to enter me. Everything below is so hypersensitive, just aching for his touch, begging for him to make me explode. He completely spreads the corset, so that my entire upper body is bare now, but I feel sheltered in his presence. I trust him with my body.

Lane's fingers delicately massage my scalp, calming my breathing as Taylor finally plunges into me. I wrap my booted legs around him as I wail with pleasure. I try to embrace him, but he grabs my wrists and pins them overhead, elevating his upper body so that he can take in the scenery. "I need you to just surrender to me. Just fucking surrender," he commands in a breathy voice as he thrusts into me. "You can't keep fighting this. I can see how bad you want this. You won't lose yourself, I promise."

But there is that last part of me, the last hand I haven't showed. If I don't fight him anymore, all doubt will be removed. I am a goner.

"I…I just can't," I whisper.

"Just fucking surrender to me. Let me take it all."

I stare at him in silence, unable to let go of that last piece of my old self. He presses my face with both hands and leans in close. "Just fucking surrender to me already," he says powerfully as he goes deep inside of me.

"Yes," I whisper. "Yes." He smoothly gyrates his hips like a snake, maintaining constant friction.

"Can I touch you?" I ask, my breath shallow.

"Yes," he says.

Even though Lane is still stroking my hair, it's like she's not even in the room. "Do you see where Lane is and where you are?"

I nod.

"You are the one. You. You're the center of my universe."

I nod as he dives into my neck, sucking, kissing, biting, his rock hard erection, stimulating everything inside of me. I dig my nails into his muscled back as I call out his name over and over.

Taylor lies next to me, shadow from the dim light casting various shapes on the curvature of his muscles. "We're done here," he says to Lane, who is still twirling my hair. She nods, rising from the bed, then makes brief but deliberate eye contact with me as I lie there, still exposed. There is a humility in her eyes I did not see before, and I find myself having an unexpected affinity for her after this shared experience. She exits without saying a word.

"So what now?" I ask.

"Do you understand now?"

"I think I do."

"It wasn't so bad, was it?"

"No. Actually, I can't believe I am about to say this."

"What?"

"I don't hate her so much anymore."

"That's why I like being a Dom, people are much more enjoyable when they do what you tell them to."

"But you can't control everyone."

"Maybe not, but I'm not interested in everyone. Though I'd beg to differ that you can't control most people."

"So you think you can control me?"

"No. You and I, we do what we want." He knows he doesn't have to control me, I'd willingly follow him off of a cliff.

"But isn't that what this is all about? Me surrendering?" The word comes out of my mouth as though it weighs 1000 pounds.

"It's still your choice. You always have a choice. I was just helping you allow yourself to make it. But damn you make it hard. It's like breaking in a mare. I've never wanted someone so badly who has made it so difficult for me to give her what she wants."

"I can't believe I just did that…I say, rolling onto my stomach and covering my face with my hands. I just met her."

"That's the thing, you didn't have to do anything. I'll take care of you. I know what you want. I can sense your limits, I can tell when you want something."

"How so?"

"I don't know, instinct I guess. Your kisses taste sweeter, your scent, the way you move, the pitch of your voice when you moan. You don't know you want it, but your body tells me you do."

"You and your psychic sex panther ways."

Taylor rolls his eyes. "I just want you to see, this is not about a competition. Even if it was, you've won by light years. It's my responsibility to take you to those places you can't go yourself. Sometimes it's scary, but those risks carry the greatest rewards. Lane was never a threat in any way and now you know that from experience, not just words."

"Sorry, I just get so jealous. I want you all to myself."

"You have me all to yourself."

"I know, but even before we met, it's like I want to go back into time and claim you."

"You've had me since I was four years old, Shy." *My beautiful little guardian.*

"Will we come back here?"

"I think you'd like that."

"I'm still scared. What will be next?"

"Scared is good, it's what makes us feel so deeply. I don't know what's next, I know when I'm in the moment. No other man will have you though. I'm not interested in sharing you."

"Does that go both ways?"

"I only want you."

"What's the benefit of coming to a club then?"

"Oh there are other ways to use people. Lane barely touched you, and it had a great effect."

"You made me feel like a queen today."

"Like I said, it's my responsibility to make you feel good."

"You make me feel so bad."

"Oh, but you are."

❀❀❀

The ride home is quiet, but comfortably so. Exhausted from the emotionally loaded day, I want to crawl into bed with Taylor, feel his warm skin enveloping mine. It's just past 3am when we return the car to the garage and tip toe back into the house. Feeling like two teenagers who stole daddy's car, we creep through the home, hoping not to get caught. As I try to stifle my giggles, I poke Taylor to try and make him laugh. Of course he's not ticklish, so he wraps his arms around me, playfully swinging me in a circle. As we make the full turn, Randall is standing at the end of the dark hallway in his robe and pajamas watching us with a smirk.

"Hi," Taylor says stiffly. "Sorry, did we wake you?"

"No, I was having a tough time sleeping tonight. You two just getting in?"

"Yes," Taylor responds.

Please don't notice my hooker boots.

"Looks like you were having some fun." He finally got a glimpse of the Taylor he was so curious about.

"Yes, it was a long night. We're tired. We're heading to go to bed." I stand there in silence, feeling so busted even though we never needed permission to go out in the first place, being adults and all.

"Well, goodnight or good morning I suppose."

"Goodnight," both Taylor and I say in unison.

"Oh Taylor," Randall says as we are about to enter the bedroom.

"Yeah?"

"Did you enjoy the Rolls?"

Taylor grins, the glimmer of youth illuminates his face. "Yeah, dad. She's all in one piece; I promise." *Dad. He knows how to play people so well.*

We slide into the bedroom and once the door is closed, we let out muffled laughs.

"Wait, did you really not tell your dad you were taking it?" I whisper. I thought Taylor was sort of joking about that or that his father wouldn't care.

"Shyla, I wasn't bullshitting you. He never lets anyone touch his Rolls, even me."

I shove him. "You always drag me into your shenanigans. Now he thinks I am a terrible influence on you," I whisper loudly.

"But you are. I wanted to impress the pretty girl who I was taking out tonight," he says, throwing me over his shoulder. I let out a yelp. "Shhhh! Randall's gonna ground me," Taylor says throwing me on the bed. "I am so beat."

"Me too."

We both yank off our clothes, and entwine with each other, becoming a crumpled, sleeping pile of limbs on the large wooden canopy bed.

CHAPTER EIGHTEEN

The ride back from the Holden estate is sunnier and warmer than the ride up.

"I have plans for you," Taylor says.

"Such as?"

"Oh, you'll see in time."

"Why does that make me nervous?"

"Because you know I'm disturbed."

"Well, at least you're self-aware."

"I may have many issues, lacking self awareness was never one of them. I know myself very well."

"I always thought I did, but apparently, I don't know anything about myself."

"You are very self-assured, I just think you are far more complex than you give yourself credit for."

I ponder the thought for a second, and he's right. Accepting the job offer, leaving Rick for Taylor, my tendency towards masochism, helping Taylor frame Eric, I guess I am rather complex. And to think I always found myself to be rather dull.

"Maybe complexity is not such a good thing," I say.

"It's the best thing."

My cell phone rings, I pull it out of my jacket pocket and sneak a peek, it's MacAllister. *Shit.*

I ignore the call.

"Who was it?"

"Wrong number."

"It said Mr. MacAllister. Do you usually preemptively store stranger's phone numbers on your phone?" *Why the fuck would I save his name on my phone? I suck at top secret investigations.*

"Then why did you ask?"

"Why did you lie?"

"It would be easier to just explain that than who it was."

"We have plenty of time to talk on this drive. We'll be sitting here for a while."

Normally, I am pretty good at crafting a quick story, but he has me frazzled, and nothing I can think of seems to make sense other than the truth. So I go with the truth, sort of.

"It's Kristin's cousin. He must be looking for her."

"You refer to her cousin as 'Mister?'"

"He's much older."

Taylor frowns pensively as he looks at the road ahead. I think I may have pulled it off.

"It's just that, if it was just her cousin, then why would you lie about who he is?"

"I don't know. I just did, okay?" Going on the defensive has always worked for me in the past.

"Shyla," Taylor says calmly. "You're not going to actually try to lie to me here? I am a professional bullshitter and you, well, I know you. I can easily find out who he really is. I would prefer you just tell me."

He has me cornered, but I can't reveal the information about his mother like this. I have to do that willingly, he needs to know it was my choice to reveal that. I elect the next option; it will no doubt make him angry, but at least I can avoid opening up the wounds of his childhood. It's about time I tell him about the texts anyway.

"Taylor, I don't want you to be mad at me when I tell you this. Please."

"Oh fuck. What is it?"

"Please promise you won't."

"I don't make promises I can't keep. Fucking tell me."

I take a deep sigh. "A while back, actually that night when we played corny songs and danced...the night you choked me in your sleep." Taylor's diverts his eyes remorsefully. "I got a text from an unknown number, calling me a whore. I didn't tell you at first because I thought it was a wrong number and we were having fun and your mood changes so easily. Then it started happening more frequently, feeling more personal. Finally, I texted the person back and he or she confirmed that they were directing the messages at me. You were so stressed and so I hired Kristin's cousin, who is a P.I., to see where they were coming from. By then, all this drama had started, and I didn't want you to overreact, and then I held onto the information so long, that I didn't want you to get mad at me because I didn't tell you in the first place...I don't know why I didn't tell you. I guess you were so mad at Eric, and at the time I wasn't convinced he was as bad as you said he was, and I thought that you might get more angry and do something stupid."

"Who were the texts from?"

"Mr. MacAllister said they were sent from disposable phones, that he couldn't find the identity of the person so easily. By the time I found that out, it was too late. Eric had already did what he did. So, I never told you because I know you'd be pissed that I didn't tell you about the messages earlier."

Taylor sits in silence.

"Say something," I beg.

He looks straight ahead. "You fucking lied to me. You put me, but more importantly yourself at jeopardy trying to somehow protect Eric from me?"

"I'm sorry, that wasn't my intent. I was trying to protect you from doing something that might get you in trouble. You were already so angry with him. It just got all twisted after a while and everything happened so fast."

"And I sit here always wondering if there was something that I could have done to protect you, all the while you hid the fact that someone was threatening you while we were trying to figure out why the fuck Eric was here?"

"I'm sorry. There's nothing you could have done. It wouldn't have mattered if you knew about the texts."

"Don't tell me there's nothing I could have done! You have no fucking idea what I am capable of."

"That's what I was afraid of."

"You need to get something straight Shy -- I don't need to be watched out for, or taken care of. I make the fucking rules. I take care of the problems. Your job is not to spare my feelings, or protect me from myself."

"I care about you, I was just trying to help."

"Well you can't help. You don't understand what people like me and Eric are capable of."

"You and Eric are not the same type of people. But I know exactly what you mean, which is why I didn't want to stoke the flames."

"Well the flames are blazing now. Your hypocrisy is confounding."

"What?"

"All you ever want me to do is open up to you, but you selectively keep little nuggets of info to yourself when you unilaterally decide it's best. It's bullshit, it's hypocritical. I expect more from you than that."

"I'm sorry."

"No you're not. If I didn't just make you, you would never have told me, would you?"

"That's not true."

"How am I supposed to take your word for it?"

"I just wanted to give it some time."

"It's been high time."

"I fucked up. I'm sorry. I should have told you. You're right."

Taylor pulls over the car abruptly onto the dirt shoulder of the road and stares me down intensely. "I am Taylor fucking Holden. You do not coddle me. You tell me how it is at all times, good or bad. I take care of things. I do not need any fucking body to protect me. I am the person people should fear."

His brow is furrowed, his glare frigid. It may appear as a threat directed to me, but I know it's not. It's an assurance. Taylor wins. Taylor always takes care of business. If I am to be on his team, I am his responsibility, and it means I tell him everything.

I nod.

"No more lies," he commands.

"Okay."

The rest of the drive is silent. Just because I apologized does not mean he's not still fuming. He's right, I cannot keep the truth from him, while I maintain some sort of double standard for myself. I must tell him about his mother, but first, I have to find out what MacAllister called about. I must have every last bit of available knowledge before confronting him.

We make a stop for gas and I go into the ladies' restroom with the cell phone.

"Shyla?"

"Yes, sorry, I have to be quick. I am on a road trip. Any news?"

"You're not going to believe this, but I think I found Lyla Bordeau."

"What? She's alive?"

"The postcard was a huge break. I flew out to the town where it was postmarked which is actually in a different state from the postcard itself, in Montana. It's very small, just a few hundred people. I started going through county records for women who would be her age living in town. I narrowed it down to a few dozen. Swung by a couple of their houses, even spoke to a couple of them. As I was about halfway through the list, I walked right past her on the street. I knew it was her instantly. She has aged remarkably well."

"Oh my god. Does she know about you?"

"It's a small town, people knew I was snooping around, but I told everyone I was looking for my adopted sister. So the attention was diverted regarding what I was really looking for. Anyway, I followed her back to her house. Did a little digging, she has a couple of adult children, had a husband who passed away. She seems to have completely moved on. I am going to email you the file. Her alias is Elizabeth Murrow."

"Have you spoken to her?"

"No. I didn't want to tip her off. She might disappear again."

I thank MacAllister for his work, and he promises to keep mum about the situation despite the fact that her "death" is a cold case.

"Ready?" Taylor asks flatly as I approach the SUV.

He walks over to the driver's side as I slide into the passenger seat. I do my best to conceal the complete desperation I feel inside. He was livid about finding out about the texting situation. How will he react to this? I must tell him; there are no longer any excuses, but I am completely unprepared for how he might respond.

I hold my phone tight until a chime alerts me a new email is in my inbox. Taylor won't even look at me, so this time, I don't worry about him seeing my screen. Sitting at the top of the inbox is a new email from Mr. MacAllister with the subject: Bordeau File. My finger itches for me to open it, but that is too risky of a proposition with Taylor sitting beside me. I calmly slide the phone back into my pocket doing my best to maintain a blank facial expression. Normally Taylor would notice something is off, but something already is off with us because of our argument, so it acts as a shield for the real emotional roller coaster stirring beneath.

My mother. This news will affect her immensely as well. On one hand I am sure she will be thrilled to know her friend is alive, yet at the same time, there may be a great sense of betrayal. Mom was so certain Lyla would come back to them, she even started a life in a new place to be easier to find. Instead, Lyla started a whole new life, made new friends, formed a new family. Who is Lyla Bordeau? Who is this woman who has left so many damaged lives in her wake?

Then there's Randall and his warning. Maybe I am trouble, maybe Taylor and I together are even more trouble. Ever since I met Taylor, I have had a terrible habit of stirring up shit around me. Maybe it wasn't destiny that lead me to Taylor, at least not in the sunny romantic movie type of way, but an ominous fate. The kind where two lovers are fated for inevitable tragedy despite all the things people have done to prevent such a future. But it doesn't matter, because despite the warnings, despite the trouble, the danger, all I want is to be with him. I feel alive when I am with him. Even if it hurts, I want to be with Taylor.

I have only known Randall for a few days, but I feel a connection with him. He is another member of the "Taylor Holden has rocked my world club," of which I am the president. Unfortunately for Randall, that's not enough. I don't give a shit about Randall's reservations, I don't care if bringing Lyla into the picture fucks with Randall's world, or the life he believes he built for Taylor. That man impregnated a 16-year old girl, and we all reap what we sow, even if it is 32 years later.

When we arrive to the house, Taylor makes a beeline to the bedroom. He has a four-day business trip tomorrow and has to repack for the trip. I must tell him tonight; I can't sit with this information for the next four days. Besides, I am already in a shit storm, so I might as well get it all out while it's raging.

"Taylor?" I say, leaning against the doorway to his bedroom. He is already unpacking his bags.

"Shyla, I don't want to talk about it any more. You're sorry, I know. I have to get ready for this trip."

"I, uh."

He looks over at me, rolls his eyes, and sighs. The only advantage I have coming into this is that he seems to have an inability to stay angry at me for long. "Don't look at me like that."

Quietly, I sit on the bed and watch him pack for a few moments, trying to build the nerve to speak up again. "Taylor." I attempt to sound forceful, but this time, my voice chokes up, my eyes well. At first, he doesn't look up, being so focused on the task in front of him, but then he pauses and looks up at me quizzically.

"Shyla? What is it?"

"What am I about to tell you is because I want to. Because I love you, not because you're mad at me or because of what happened earlier today. I swear it."

Finally, Taylor stops everything he's doing and walks over to me, his tall shadow eclipsing the light from the lamp on the nightstand.

"What's wrong? You can tell me."

"There's one other thing I haven't told you about MacAllister and why I hired him," I say, reaching for his hand as I take a deep breath before revealing my final secret.

CHAPTER NINETEEN

I look into Taylor's eyes for a moment, taking in one last second of peace before things may change forever. I am about to change everything he thought he knew about his life. If there is anyone who knows what it feels like to have the sad truths you knew about your past to be a lie, it's me.

"Can you sit?" I ask.

"No. Just go ahead and say it," he says sternly. His hand remains limp in my soft grasp.

"I don't know where to start. When, when you told me about C.O.S, I started looking into things. You know I get curious. You said it yourself. And I found out there were others like you. I didn't know at the time that I was one of those people. But I got curious, because I don't know, I thought maybe we could find out more and maybe if we had more knowledge, we could use that to help you."

I pause for some sort of reassurance and to collect my thoughts, but Taylor remains completely silent. His only movement is that of his chest rising and falling with each breath.

"So when I called MacAllister about the texts, I asked him to look into C.O.S some more. I never told him your name, or that you were involved in it. In fact, you probably know your identity was kept private."

Still, not an utterance.

"Well, he called back and told me that your mother's body was never found at the scene. I found this out on the same day Eric broke into the condo. I didn't expect to have all this knowledge and I didn't know what to do with it. But I didn't want to tell you because, she might still be dead, and it was pointless to bring anything up unless we could find evidence she might be alive. She is presumed legally dead, but it didn't sit right with me or MacAllister."

Taylor looks up and away for a second pulls in his lips as if holding something inside of him. He returns his stare at me, remaining eerily stoic.

"And with the Eric stuff happening, I didn't want to compound it further unless I knew for sure. So I paid him to look into her, but we hit a dead end. Everyone from C.O.S who might have known something, believe she was murdered by Alan Peters." *My father.* "But MacAllister and I didn't believe it. If Alan was evil as we all know he was, why would he let you live? It didn't add up. But we were stuck, until my mother told me the truth about me. She thought Lyla was dead too, but she had some empty postcards that were sent to her and we thought that maybe, just maybe it was a clue. It was a longshot."

Finally, Taylor's stoic facial expression breaks, his eyes weigh heavy, his jaw tightens, his breathing becomes louder, as if he knows in his soul what I am about to say next.

"Taylor, we found her. MacAllister is sure of it. Your mother is alive," I say as I rise to stand in front of him. He doesn't respond, and for a moment I wonder if he understands what I just said. "Taylor, *she's alive.*"

His jaw tightens further. He looks down at my hand, and pulls it out of my grasp.

"Please say something Taylor."

"My father. When you two spoke, did you talk about this?"

"Listen, I can't speak for him, but I did confront him. I asked if he knew her body was never found and he said he knew. He figured she was still dead, and if she wasn't she may as well be, so he never told you. At the time I didn't know she was alive. I'm not sure he would have wanted me to tell you, but I think you have a right to know."

Taylor stands still, I imagine trying to process everything. So many things no longer make sense now that she is alive.

"I know where she lives."

"What has she been doing all these years?"

"She started a new life. She got married, but she's a widow now. She had another child. I believe she works at a hardware store…"

The change I see in Taylor's facial expression is so sharp, it frightens me.

"What gave you the right?"

"Wha…What?"

"Who gave you the right to investigate my past, my life, talk to my father without ever telling me?"

"I didn't know it would go this far. Your father asked to speak to me."

"Of course, you just hired a P.I. hoping for nothing."

"I didn't know what to expect, but I just had a feeling in my gut there was more. Apparently my hunch was right, there was so much we didn't know."

"You went behind my back. This has been going on behind my back? For months! How many secret phone calls? How many lies, Shyla?"

"I didn't want to tell you until I was sure."

"Stop trying to protect me! Fucking stop it!"

"I know, that's why I am trying to get this all out at once. No more secrets, I swear."

"What do you want from me, huh? You want me to hop on a plane and reunite with this woman? You think that somehow everything will magically be better? If you don't want me how I am, if you think I'm broken or something, then maybe you shouldn't be here."

"No. I don't know what I wanted you to do, but I thought you had the right to know. And I want you to feel better for you, not for me."

"Shyla, if I wanted to know every little detail, I could have found out a long time ago. This is my fucking life. My life! You ran an investigation behind my back, without my consent, about me and my past."

"It's my life too now! I'm with you now, and I was with you then. Our mothers were best friends, your mother and you put yourselves on the line so I could get out. I want to know about her too. I have a right too, this is my past too."

"She's *my* fucking mother!" His voice booms, punctuating the argument, as he stabs his finger into his chest. I stand there silently, allowing him to stew. I know how he feels, his head must be spinning, trying to trace back his entire life and think of every time he was told a lie relating to her, every instance where someone could have told him the truth, but refrained. Or maybe he's rueing the day he met me, when his life was lonely, but much simpler.

He presses his fist against his mouth, his eyes bouncing with hundreds of thoughts. "I'm going to the condo tonight. I need to be alone."

"No, no, no. I'm sorry Taylor. I swear to god, there are no more secrets. This is everything. I had to tell you. It's the truth. Just because it changes everything, doesn't mean it's not the truth."

"I'm leaving. I'll be back in four days."

"Taylor please. If there is anyone who knows what you are going through, it's me."

"You don't know shit about what I'm going through."

I know what pains him more than anything. It's not that she's alive, or that I did all this behind his back, at least that's not the crux of it. He could have continued to live with the image of her as a cold-hearted cult follower, or even a child deserter, but no, she left him there among the dead bodies and moved on. She had another family, raised another child. As much as he speaks of moving on, he never really has. It's not that she was dead to him that hurts so much, it was that he was dead to her. He thinks I don't understand that feeling, but I do. I have lived with it all my life: the image of a father I grew up with, who was so much more real to me that the one I just learned of, abandoned me too. He left me to be with his drugs.

I could say all this to him, but I know his mind is far too crowded to listen to me right now. He needs his space, just like I needed mine when I ran out of the condo after my mother broke the news.

"I'm going to go now. I'll have Harrison come back and bring my bags in the morning."

"I can do it."

"No, he's got it."

I don't push the matter. He grabs his wallet and keys, heading the the bedroom door.

"I'm sorry I hurt you," I say to him as he passes through the threshold.

"Don't worry. You're not the first woman to do that to me. I'll be fine."

His comment almost stops my heart, it hurts so bad I can barely breathe.

"I love you so much," I barely utter as leaves my sight. I'm not sure he hears me.

※ ※ ※

I wake up to the sound of someone fumbling in the bedroom. The worst possible scenarios pass through my mind. It can't be Eric, he's somewhere hidden in a jungle, but who knows anymore? I reach over to the nightstand for anything I can use as a weapon.

"Who's there?" I ask in a shaky voice.

The closet light turns on.

"Shyla. I'm sorry. I didn't want to wake you." It's Harrison, thank god. I forgot Taylor sent him to pack his bags.

"Oh no, it's fine. I should have slept in another room." But I wanted to sleep in the bed we share, so I could smell his scent on his pillow and pretend he was still here with me.

It's 6am, so I stay up. I observe Harrison grabbing items from the closet for a few minutes before I speak up.

"Let me do it."

"It's fine, I've done it for him before."

"Please, allow me. I know what he likes to wear when he travels." *I need to do this.*

"Okay," he nods gently.

Wistfully, I grab the remaining items he will need for his trip. I pack them lovingly, hoping somehow he'll feel it when he opens the bags. I stare at the open luggage for a while, it feels incomplete and I can't close it until I figure out what is missing. Then it hits me.

I rifle through my jewelry box, looking for the small card that he gave me in St. Petersburg. I place it on top of his clothes and finally, I am able to zip up the bag and send it off to my distressed love, hoping somehow my he will feel me with each garment he pulls out of the bag. As I drag the luggage out of the closet, I pass my jewelry box again. Peering out is the black velvet bag holding the necklace I have yet to return to Emily's family. I don't know why I haven't, but I think it's because I had plans for it. It should be returned ceremoniously, not delivered by a FedEx carrier.

Harrison reenters the room when he hears me fumbling with the luggage and relieves me of it. "Can you tell him that I wish him a safe trip?"

"Of course," Harrison smiles.

I grab the satchel out of the jewelry box. I may have shattered someone's world last night, but today, I am going to make someone whole again.

CHAPTER TWENTY

"This is Chad at Rubix Marketing. I am unable to take your call. Leave a message."

"Hey Chad, it's Shyla. I forgot to tell you, Bella from Bella's Intimates wanted me to meet her at her store today. She has some new projects she wants to discuss, so I'll be coming in after lunch. Let me know if you need anything."

I throw on a pair of jeans, red rain boots as the weather looks questionable, a chunky sweater and my army green anorak. My hair is slicked back into a neat ponytail, and I put on some natural makeup tones to disguise my puffy eyes. A quick google search on my phone yields the address of Emily's parents' home. It's about two hours north, so I estimate I can make it there about 9am, spend a little bit of time chatting if they are home, and make it back by twelve-ish.

A sense of responsibility consumes me. I must return this safely into the hands of Emily's parents. She is part of the unfortunate club of those who have loved Taylor and never received the same in return. It is maddening enough to love him and be loved back by him, and so I can only imagine how bewildering it must be to love this man only to find out he will never feel the same way about you. That every kind gesture, every moment of seeming tenderness was for himself. That you were just a tool for him to work out his own pain and desires. That you could be replaced in an instant. I don't think I could survive if I found out he felt that way about me. Unlike Emily, I have hope that he will return to me, but she knew she would never see the world through the same lens again, she would never be able to walk through the earth on a Taylor Holden high. Taylor can convince himself that she moved on, that her death had nothing to do with him, but he doesn't understand the power he has over those who love him. I do.

Harrison drives Taylor to the airport, making it the perfect time to deliver the necklace without anyone being the wiser. I hop into Ladybug and embark on my lonely voyage as a proxy for Taylor's redemption.

As I arrive into the small quaint row of houses on the town's main street, a misty rain begins to settle in. Through the windshield wipers, I look for street signs to lead me to the Brown residence. Finally, after a few turns, I pass a modest white house with a small porch. A weathered hunter green rocking chair sits to the right of the front screen door. I park on the side of the street, as to not intrude on the driveway, which is occupied by a Subaru station wagon. This indicates to me someone must be home. I sit in the car as the squeaky song of the windshield wipers plays rhythmically as I pull the necklace out of the velvet pouch and admire it for one last time. I give myself a quick once over in the visor mirror, wiping some smudged makeup from my eyes and take a deep calming breath before stepping out of the car and onto the Brown's front lawn.

My stomach twirls. I hate knocking on stranger's doors, but this isn't about me. I ring the door bell, but after no response, I am not sure it works. I open the unlocked screen door and just as I lift my fist to knock, the red wooden door opens. On the other side is a woman who appears to be in her 50s. She is very thin, her weathered face bordered by a salt and pepper bob. Her face is bare and she is dressed simply, in a pair of jeans and a plaid button down shirt.

274

"May I help you?" She asks with suspicious politeness.

"Hi, I uh, I'm an old friend of Emily's. I was hoping I could speak to you for a moment. I have something of hers I would like to give to you."

Just as I complete my sentence, my phone rings, but it would be too rude of me to look, so I ignore it.

Her face becomes solemn, but warm as she tilts her head. "Yes, of course," she says holding a faint smile as she steps to the side and welcomes me in.

"I hope I am not keeping you. I thought I should come personally, and I didn't have a phone number."

"Oh no, I am just going about my morning routine. I was planning on going to the garden store, but this weather means I won't be able to do much anyway. Would you like some coffee or tea?"

"Tea please."

"Come join me in the kitchen."

I sit at an old wooden table as she places a tea kettle on a white gas stove. I stare at the flames, reflecting upon them for a moment before revealing the memento.

"How did you know Emily?"

"We worked together at Holden Industries."

"Oh, she loved it there. But then she met Evan and wanted to start a family back here," she smiles. "I didn't know much about her friends in the city. In fact, I didn't know any of them. No one from Holden Industries that I know of came to her funeral. Were you at her funeral? I don't recall."

"No. I'm sorry. I didn't know about her passing until after the funeral. I think that was the case for many of us at H.I."

"I'm sorry, it was such a shock when it happened."

"No, please don't be. As you said, you didn't even know of me. We were work friends, we lost touch after she left."

"You said you had something for me?" The tea kettle screams. "Chamomile or peppermint?"

"Peppermint please."

She pours the steaming water into two old teacups, rimmed in gold, with curvy handles, adorned with dull pink and purple flowers and green leaves. She steeps the tea bags in each cup and slowly places mine in front of me at the table.

She sits across from me, waiting for me to complete my original thought, tails of steam lazily dancing up to her face.

"So, I worked at H.I. until recently and well, I came upon something, that after some investigating I believe belongs to your daughter." I pull out the pouch from my pocket, untie the rope and open the mouth of the bag, pouring the necklace onto the table.

Her eyes well up. "I can't believe you found this. How? I dreamed I could bury her with this. She told me she had lost it before moving back and she was so devastated. We both were, it was her grandmother's, who gave it to me, and then I gave it to her. She was very close to her oma who passed a few years ago."

"I know it was important to her, so I didn't want to mail it. I wanted to make sure it arrived safely."

"Where did you find it?"

"It was caught behind a drawer in a filing cabinet of all places."

She clutches it in her hand and presses her fist against her chest, a look of strained joy on her face. "Thank you," she says in a breath. "Thank you."

"You're welcome," I say. *Finally, something I didn't completely fuck up.*

"Would you like to see some photos of her? There are some on the mantle with her wearing this necklace."

"Of course."

"You know it's so nice to talk to someone who knew her. Sometimes when someone dies so young, it's hard to keep their memory alive. She had no children, no husband. Just me and her father."

"Didn't she have a fiancé?"

"Evan? Oh, Evan," she says with pity. "He took her death the hardest I think. I've never seen anyone collapse the way he did when they found her body in the river. He searched like a mad man for her and he kept apologizing that he had let us down by letting her leave the house that night. He was a mess, so much so that I was more focused on helping him grieve than myself those first few weeks. Then we found out she was pregnant and it got even worse. After her funeral, he skipped town. I think this whole place reminded him of her too much and the life they would never have," she says, cupping her tea in her hands.

"Oh my goodness. I had no idea that she was pregnant."

"Of course, you mentioned you lost touch after she left her job. I didn't mean to spring that on you. Well, we are a small town and me and her father know everyone. The coroner did us a favor and kept the pregnancy out of the papers."

"I'm sorry, we have been talking here all this time, and I never asked you for your name."

"Sure honey, it's Evelyn. People call me Ev."

"I'm Shyla."

"Come, let me show you some photos."

She guides me further into the house, to a sitting room with old fashioned bluish-gray settees and oak tables with Queen Anne legs. On the wall furthest from us is a large white fireplace, the mantle crowded with far too many photos. I walk over cautiously.

"You can pick them up. I know there are a lot, but I like to pass by every day and think of her."

"Of course," I say.

The photos are arranged in chronological order from left to right. Some bald baby photos, a giggly toddler, a toothless third grader, a cheerleader in a red and white getup with a high side ponytail, proud parents beside their only daughter holding up her college degree. Then there is a picture of her holding a big smile for the camera, a hand wrapped around her shoulder. I follow the hand to its arm, which leads to the tall young man beside her and I can't help but take a few steps back, stumbling into the table behind me and nearly knocking down a lamp.

"Is something wrong?" Ev asks.

"Uh no. I'm sorry. Who…who is that?" I ask, already knowing the answer, but hoping that I am somehow miraculously wrong.

"Oh, that's right, you never met him. That's Evan, bless his soul."

I stare at the photo in disbelief, silently praying my eyes are deceiving me, but I know. I know that dirty blond hair, those freckles, those pale eyes, that crooked smile, those lips that stole a kiss from me. *It's Eric, oh my fucking god, it's Eric.*

I do my best to hide my shock and disbelief. All my mental resources are focused on doing this, leaving very little to piece together what it all means. He wanted me to find this, he wanted me to look into Emily Brown. I look at the clock above the fireplace to pretend to read the time.

"Oh no. I have to run, I have to get back to the city for work. I am so sorry, I wish I could stay longer."

"Okay Shyla. Thank you so much for this. You have no idea how much this means to me."

I nod with the biggest smile I can muster, which is hardly existent. As I approach the door, I give her one final goodbye and she embraces me, not just a friendly embrace, but one filled with gratitude and it makes me feel like a fraud. Once I get to the driveway, I stumble across the street to Ladybug, frantically digging for my phone to call Taylor. The call goes straight to voicemail. *Shit.*

"Taylor, it's me. Listen, I know you're upset, but I just found out something huge. Eric is Evan Sumner... Evan Sumner was Em's fiancé. Eric was engaged to Em. This is crazy," I say in a shaky voice. I pull out onto the rain soaked road, the droplets hit the windshield like mini battering rams. "So, I don't know what this means, but something feels off. Something is not as it seems. Call me as soon as you get a chance." I recall that I had received an earlier call and see it is in fact from Taylor. The rain, flurry of emotions, and handling of the phone makes my driving erratic, so I pull over on the isolated two lane road onto the dirt shoulder for a moment to collect myself.

I retrieve the voicemail. "Hey Shyla, it's me. I just want to hear your voice. I found the card you packed...I don't know. I don't know what to do with all this, and I know you were trying to help, but my god you are such a pain in my ass. But that's what I love about you. You are so fucking hard to handle, and it drives me fucking nuts. So, when I get back —"

A loud rap makes me jump from my seat. Through the raindrops cascading down my window I see the black barrel of a gun just inches from my face. I think about slamming on the gas, but by the time I reach for the gear shift, that gun will have blown my face away.

The barrel taps against the windshield again. "Unlock your doors, Shyla. Hands up on the steering wheel." the voice says calmly. I cautiously abide.

Seconds later, a rain-soaked Eric slides into the passenger seat of my car. "Start driving."

All the while, Taylor's voicemail murmurs in the background.

CHAPTER TWENTY-ONE

"You really are a handful. Now I know why Taylor is so into you, you're hard to predict." Eric says to me as I shakily pull out onto the road. "I can't believe you made me."

"Please don't shoot me," I beg, looking straight ahead.

Eric looks down at his gun and puts it back into his waistband. "Don't worry, I have no intentions of hurting you. I need to talk to you and now that you know, I need to see Taylor. The only way that happens is through you. I'm sorry it has to go down like this."

"Where are you taking me?"

"Just drive around for a bit. I'll direct you after we make this call to my beloved brother."

"What do you want?"

My phone lights up and vibrates on the floor of the car. It's Taylor.

"Perfect. I was just about to call him." He reaches for the phone on the floor. "Hey brother…Woah, woah…slow down." I imagine Taylor reciting some sort of speech a la Liam Neeson in Taken. "I think I should be the one asking questions. Apparently I beat the shit out of Shyla? Thanks to you two lovebirds for that." Eric eyes me as he says this. "Listen Taylor. I am gonna be brief so listen up. If you want to see Shyla unharmed, you are going to meet me at the coordinates I am about to send you. I'll send the time too. Don't be a minute late. Oh and it's an open field for miles. If I see anyone else, she's dead. You know my background and you know she'll be gone in a second if I sense anything. Don't bother tracking the number either, you know it'll be pointless…Sure, here you go."

Eric puts the phone up to my ear. Taylor's voice is on the other line. His voice is calm, as if he is trying to assure me with his tone "Shy, are you there?"

"Yes. I'm okay. Taylor I don't tru-"

Eric yanks the phone away from my face. "I'll see you soon, *brother*," he uses that last word as if it were a dagger.

Eric hangs up the phone and starts writing a text. He waits for the little swoosh sound and then throws the phone out of the window. "Shyla, that was posturing. I won't kill you. I just need to see Taylor."

"You're going to hurt him."

"What happens between my brother and me is our business. He and I have some things to discuss."

"No. Please don't hurt him," I cry.

"I'm sorry Shyla, but this is not up for discussion. Unfortunately, you got dragged into his shit and I am sorry for that. Really, I am. You are a victim of his too."

I think of my Taylor, the boy who guarded me in the closet so many years ago being riddled with bullets and I can't let it happen. It's my turn to shield him. I do the only thing I know I can do at the moment. I brace both hands on the steering wheel and turn the car sharply to the left.

"No!" Eric screams, grabbing the steering wheel, making the car swerve sharply to the right. He and I battle over the steering wheel, the car zig zagging on the road haphazardly. Finally, he yanks Ladybug so hard in his direction that the car hydroplanes, spinning 180 degrees, its rear slamming into a tree. "Dammit Shyla!" Eric exclaims. He pulls his gun out of his waistband and points it at me. "Why are you making me do this? Get back on the road. Dammit!"

"I thought you said you wouldn't hurt me."

"I really, really don't want to. Please don't make me hate myself even more." Unfortunately, the damage to the car is only to the rear bumper and the car continues to operate just fine. "I want this to be amicable between us. Don't fucking do that again. If you cooperate you will be back with Taylor tomorrow. I swear this to you. I don't want to restrain you right now. Are you going to fight with me, or just make this as easy as possible for both of us? Please make note of how restrained I am being right now considering you almost killed us both."

I gulp nervously, there is no way I can overpower a man of his size even if he didn't have a gun. Taylor has asked—demanded—that I trust him. *He takes care of things.* I can imagine him watching this scene unfold, furious with me for taking such a risk and so for once, I am going to let Taylor take care of us his way.

"Okay," I say. "I'll go along."

We drive a few miles south., Eventually he guides me to make a turn, and then another, and we end up at a small motel on a quiet side road. I scan the parking lot for someone, anyone to give the *help me* eye, but the lot is empty on this dreary, wet fall morning. Eric leads me to a room and makes me sit on the bed. Though I am not religious and I never pray, I silently hope to god that he truly has no intentions for me in this room.

"Look," he says, pulling the magazine out of the gun and sliding back the chamber to show me the gun is no longer loaded. "I just want to talk to you. You have to understand why I came back, okay?"

"What does it matter what I think?"

"Because it does. Because I am not a cold-blooded psychopath like Taylor may want you to believe. And because I like you. I think you're a good person, and for some reason my brother attracts really good women.

And I don't know, I just can't let him keep getting away with everything."

"Taking me hostage is not really scoring you any points with me," I say boldly. I do believe he doesn't want to hurt me. It may be a false sense of security, but Eric has always seemed familiar to me.

"Well, framing me for torture and rape isn't helping you out either." *Touché motherfucker.*

"Except there is some truth to those claims." *Shit, stop being so fucking ballsy.*

"No, no there aren't. But I'm willing to chalk all this up to the fact that shit has gotten really out of control. I hope you'll give me the same benefit of the doubt."

I nod begrudgingly.

"But first, I'm hungry as hell. Following you today worked up my appetite. You have to be hungry too." *Well I was, until all hell broke loose.*

"I'm fine."

"You'll be hungry once your nerves settle. Come on, follow me." He walks to the bathroom. I stare at him, immobilized with distrust. "Listen, I can't leave you lallygagging in here while I get food. Cooperation; remember?"

I hesitantly walk over to the bathroom, he pulls out a pair of handcuffs and cuffs me to the the plumbing underneath the sink. Then he pulls out duct tape from his bag, and tapes my feet together, then my hands. "I'm not gonna cover your mouth, but if I come back and you're screaming, well then, I'll have to do it for the rest of our time together. Besides, we are in a shit hole in the middle of nowhere. No one will hear you. I paid off the illegal maid to stay away from this room."

"I won't scream, okay?"

"Any special requests?" *You're fucking kidding me.* I just stare back at him.

"Suit yourself."

He closes the bathroom door behind him. I count to 10-Mississippi before trying to pull on the cuffs and break the pipe, but it won't budge. I scan the bathroom for anything that could be used as a tool, but all there is is soap and a shower curtain. It only takes me a few minutes to realize I will be staying here, and going along with at least the early parts of Eric's plan. Sweat pours down my brow, I try to wipe it, but without free hands it is nearly impossible. It stings my eyes so I take a few deep breaths to center myself and cool down. For now, I believe that Eric does not want to harm me, but I know he has a different fate mapped out for Taylor. My heart floods with worry at what he might do. Taylor has been impenetrable, he has had no weakness until meeting me. I thought I gave him strength. Now I may be the death of him.

About 15 minutes later, there is the sound of someone entering the motel room: paper bags fumbling, chairs being moved, and then the television being turned on.

"Hello?" I call out in an inquisitive tone, but not loud enough for Eric to think I am calling for help.

Eric opens the bathroom door. "Sorry, I was just setting up the space." How strange that a captor would apologize so much to his captive. He pulls the tape off of my ankles which were luckily covered in pants. My wrists aren't so lucky. "Shit, this is going to hurt," he says. "Alright, one…two…three!" He yanks off the tape and I hiss at the burning pain, my wrists instantly turning red. He gently rubs them to distract the pain, then he uncuffs me. I walk out to the bedroom, where he has made a makeshift eating area for us with a small table and two mismatched chairs. He has me sit in the chair furthest from the door making it impossible for me to access the exit without getting through him first.

"I got you a cheeseburger, fries and some diet coke. There's not a lot of variety out in these parts. I hope that's okay."

"It's fine. Thank you." *Did I just thank him? Wait, that's good. I should make him feel like he can trust me.*

We pull our food out of our respective bags and in this moment, it feels a lot like the first time we met at the bar, just two people sitting together over food and drink. I unenthusiastically bite into a fry. He grabs a few at once and then bites into them at the same time. "Mmmm. These fries are really good," he says smiling at me. He's right, maybe it's the hunger, but they are fan-fucking-tastic. "Listen, I know you hate me right now, but can we at least agree that these fries are delicious?"

"Yeah," I say, looking at him out of the corner of my eyes, trying not to shovel the entire box down my mouth.

"So, I guess you now know that I'm Evan."

I nod.

"Listen, let's get it all out there Shyla. I don't have shit to hide now. I'm a fugitive from the law," he says laughing in apparent disbelief.

"Let's," I say dully.

"Why don't you ask me what you want to know?"

I get in one more scrumptious fry before I start. "Did you really leave the country?"

"Yes. I left right after I saw you, under my real name. I had a pre-arranged flight to leave the country before I came to see you. At that point I had no idea you and Taylor would frame me for rape and assault. I thought at most you might call the police for breaking and entering. Leaving the country gave me some time to lay low, allow the trail on me to go a little cold and Taylor to get comfortable. It gave me the time and space to figure out my options. In my line of work I have special contacts, fake identities, yadda yadda. I came back into the country under Evan Sumner. FBI and the police have no idea I am in the U.S."

"Your line of work…the detective said you didn't have a security firm."

"Well, Eric Holden doesn't. Evan Sumner did. I sold the company months ago."

"How long have you been following us?"

"Since you returned from vacation. I wasn't sure what to do. I still wanted to get to Taylor more than ever, but if I ambushed you together, even when you were alone, that would be too messy. I'd have to get one of you alone. I preferred not to bring you into this, but Taylor is always secured, whether it be at H.I. or having his 'driver' around. So I knew if I could get you alone, well, I could cripple him, get him to come over to me easy. When I saw you leaving the house alone today, I had to follow you. Then I realized where you were headed, and holy shit, I knew you were going to make me. So I had to make very quick plans to intercept you on your way back. I couldn't afford you going back to the police with this info."

"Shit."

"What?"

"I've done it again. Every time I do something behind Taylor's back, I get us neck deep into shit."

Eric smiles. "That's why he's so into you. He likes to tame, and you challenge him. But don't be so hard on yourself, it's Taylor who gets people into shit."

"He doesn't put it so nicely," I say.

"Why were you going to visit Ev anyway?"

"I found Em's necklace and I wanted to return it."

"The necklace? The one her grandmother gave her?"

"Yup, that one."

"Dammit, Shyla. That's why I like you. It's shit like that. Perfect mix of nice girl and total obstinate pain in the ass."

"Yup, and look what it got me," I say gesturing to the decaying room around me.

"Shyla." Eric looks into my eyes with his glassy blue eyes. He has Nan's eyes, just like Taylor has Lyla's. "You're gonna be fine. I promise."

I nod. *I won't be fine if you hurt Taylor.*

"And thank you for returning the necklace, Em was so heartbroken about losing it. Where did you find it?"

"At H.I. She never lost it at Taylor's like she thought. So are you going to tell me what's really going on here? Why you came back to town in the first place?"

Eric sighs, raking his golden-brown locks with his fingers, then scratching his neck. "Yeah. It's hard for me Shyla. It's still really hard."

"I know all about confronting tough subjects."

"So you know, Taylor and I never got along. And you and I need to talk about that too after we finish talking about Em. Then I was asked to leave."

"Oh yes, because you tried to have him killed."

Eric rolls his eyes. "Taylor's not right Shyla. You may not see it, but he's not."

"And that justifies killing him?"

"You couldn't possibly understand what it was like growing up with him. He was like a child of the corn. And then my dad, choosing him over me, it was a slap in the face because ever since he came into the picture that's all my father ever did."

"But that's not Taylor's fault."

"Taylor is no saint."

"I know, but he's no monster either."

"Shyla, he is capable of becoming a monster when it suits him, I promise. Anyway, we're getting off track

288

here. After being gone for so long, I decided enough was enough. I wanted to see if somehow he and I could coexist again. I missed my parents, my mother thinks I just abandoned the family." For a moment, I feel for him: Nan's cold indifference towards her drifter son. "So I came back a little over a year ago, to H.I. As I was walking into the lobby, I saw a pretty girl, she looked so sad, talking to someone just out of my view. Eventually, he stepped out from behind a pillar and I saw it was Taylor. I hid, I could tell by watching that if his mood was already sour, and if he saw me, there would be no chance at reconciliation. They were having a discussion, well it looked like he was telling her something. She kept nodding, and then he just walked away from her, when she was in mid-sentence. As though her words were worthless, as if she was just made of thin air. God, she looked so sad when he turned his back on her. Em stood there frozen, in disbelief. Her hands were stuck in the middle of a gesture. I think it finally registered who she was dealing with at that moment. She slowly dropped her hands and started to calmly walk towards the exit, but then she started to run, just sobbing. And I couldn't help myself, to see how he made this girl cry like that. I wanted to know who Taylor had become, and she seemed to be the perfect person to give me insight. I followed her out onto the sidewalk, and I approached her. I asked her what was wrong. She was hesitant at first, but we went to a park and talked."

"She didn't know you were Taylor's brother?"

"No, never. I had been using Evan as an alias for a couple of years before that, running my businesses under that name. I wanted nothing to do with the Holden name for a while. It was easy to keep that identity up. Eric Holden didn't exist in the world of Evan Sumner and vice versa."

"And then?"

"And then, she and I became close quickly. I couldn't be with her and be a Holden, so I decided to forget about coming back home. She confirmed that nothing about Taylor had changed, it just morphed. His need to control, his ownership of those around him. Once he found the slightest imperfection in a person, he disposed of them like garbage. And the things he made her do…" Eric drifts away for a moment. "Our relationship was a whirlwind. We moved up by her parents, and I thought, fuck it, I don't need Taylor or my parents, I could start over. In the end, they chose Taylor over me. At least my father did. But Taylor, fucking Taylor, he ruined everything, as he always does. He stole her from me long before I even met her."

"She never got over him," I say. *I know Em, I know how impossible it would be for you to get over Taylor.*

"Oh it was far worse than that. Sure, she never got over him, but she also never got over the person she became for him. She was a small town girl, her eyes were big over the hot-shot Taylor Holden, and he took her and used her in ways most people can't ever imagine, and then when he was finished with her, discarded her like a rotten piece of meat." *Oh how the same story sounds so different coming from another person's mouth.*

"Well, did he force her?"

"No. But, he manipulated her. And Shyla, I am fucking warning you, you need to watch out for yourself. I have been trying to warn you, he is not who you think he is."

"Eric, with all due respect, I am so sorry for what happened to Emily, but Taylor has always been very clear about his lifestyle and he has been with me from the beginning. You don't understand our relationship. You couldn't possibly understand the history we share."

"You know, Em thought she saw something in him too, but when it was over, he sucked the innocence right out of her."

"But he left her."

"Well, yes."

"So she would have stayed with him. It was the fact that he left her that made her so upset."

"Wow, he really has you. It's the fact that once he was done with her, she was nothing to him. It's like he has no soul."

"Well, you don't know the Taylor I know."

"Oh, sure. He's just a bundle of warmth and joy."

"No, he's Taylor. Someone who has suffered things you and I can only imagine, and despite it all has been able to become an amazing human being."

"Wow. *Amazing?* That's one way to put it. Do you know what he did to Em? Maybe he does this stuff with you, maybe not. I have to admit, you seem to be special to him. You still have that spark in your eyes, like he hasn't sucked out all of your dignity yet. When people are an inconvenience to Taylor, he discards them, but not with you."

I stare intently.

"He dehumanized Em. Sure, she worked in his office, but every night when they came home, she stripped down to her naked body and he put a collar on her, he literally walked her around like a pet."

I hold in a wince. Taylor has told me about his subs in the general sense, but hearing the details from Eric, he says it with such a distaste, as if he has sour milk in his mouth.

"She couldn't look at him or talk to him unless he permitted her to do so. He fed her, bathed her, kept her locked up in his little dungeon room whenever he didn't need her."

"But he never imprisoned her. She could leave at any time." I hear my voice outside of myself, as if I am listening to some stranger defend Taylor.

"And then," Eric pauses for a moment, his pale, freckled face flushes with rage. "He would give her away, like a trading card. Watch as other men had her, defiled her, did things to her that would make her shiver months later. Sometimes he would just give her away for a whole weekend. When she asked him why, he would just say 'because it pleases me.'"

I bite the inside of my lip.

"He doesn't do that with you, does he?"

I don't answer.

"No, he wants you all to himself. If I were another man, I would do things to you to get back at him, but I'm not." *How noble of you, Eric.*

"You already have."

"No. Listen to me: no."

I roll my eyes.

"I don't know what he's told you about me. Yes, I may have crossed the line with him years ago, but I have paid for that. That's the only thing I've really done wrong. Taylor hates me because I challenge him. I call him on his bullshit. He could never handle that."

I bite my tongue. There's no point in arguing with his claims of innocence.

"You know what else he would do to Em? He would fuck other women, he knew she didn't like that, but he would make her watch. Just to make her jealous. He would make her do things just to exert his control over her, like make her shoplift from convenience stores. Just so he could feel the thrill of telling her what to do."

"But she could leave whenever she wanted." I recite the line like a drone.

"Listen, I didn't care, that's how much I loved her. I just wanted to move on. And we were happy for a while, we were, but then the cracks started to show…she started to drink. At first it was here and there, but then I started finding hidden bottles around the house. She slept the days away. Cried when she was awake. Told me I couldn't love her, that she was used up and worthless. No matter what I said, she wouldn't believe it." *I wonder if she wanted him to tell her she was, so she could feel the way Taylor once made her feel.* "I got her to go rehab, and we were back on track, we started planning for a family, but one night, she left her email account open, and god I wish I hadn't looked…"

"What?"

His emotions begin to pour out of him. The pain seems to be as raw as the day he first saw those messages. "She was sending Taylor messages everyday. Begging him to take her back. That she would do anything to be his again. That she would be his slave all over again if he would just take her back and I fucking lost it. There was so much detail, and she sent him pictures. He wouldn't reply and so each email got more desperate, more pathetic and lowly. The things she promised she would do to get him back…We got into an argument, she left the house, and well, I guess you know what happened."

By this time tears are streaming down Eric's cheeks, his face flushed from remorse and sadness. And dammit, I don't want to, but I feel so badly for him, for the love who would never love him back, at least not like she loved Taylor; and for the child he would never see. Em was to Eric as Taylor was to Em. Like a mist, he could see her and yet he couldn't get a hold of her. Against all common sense, I walk over to his side of the table and I rub his shoulder. Because it will make him trust me, and because it's the right thing to do. He grabs my hand, leaning his cheek on it. His quiet cry progresses to sobs, the warm, thick tears falling onto my hand.

293

"Shyla, I lost everything that day. He destroyed her. She could never stop being his slave, she couldn't get out of his grasp," he says between sobs. "She was going to have our child. I didn't know, I'm not even sure she knew yet. I would have never let her storm out like that." But I know, I know that it wouldn't have mattered. He would have had a shell of Em. I know what it's like to be with a person who loves you with all of their heart, but who makes you feel numb. For all the vileness, for all the depravity he sees in Taylor, Taylor has a way of making us feel alive; born anew. But I can't say these words to him: that Em never really loved him back, that he was convenient: he was the guy she was supposed to love, and so she went along with the picture book romance, all the while, her essence was slowly dying. It's a bitch, knowing that the right person for you is the most dangerous. When Taylor wouldn't have her. it was like a death sentence to her soul.

To watch this large hunk of a man crumple in front of me, full of so much devastation, overwhelms me, and I begin to cry with him. "I'm sorry this happened to you. I am so sorry," I say and he wraps his arms around me and cries into my waist. I don't know what to do other than to accept his embrace and stroke his hair. "Shyla, I didn't rape you. I'm not that kind of guy," he says. My brain spins with so many conflicting thoughts and emotions that I don't know what to do other than live in this moment. Part of it is self preservation, but some of it is pure empathy for this destroyed man in front of me.

CHAPTER TWENTY-TWO

Once Eric composes himself, I drift onto the bed adjacent to his seat at the table. Our knees nearly touch, we are so close.

"Eric, I feel for you. I really do, but Em was her own person and she made all the decisions that led her to where she ended up."

"We are going to disagree fundamentally here. If it wasn't for him, she'd be here. He fucked her head up. You can't manipulate people like that and get away with it."

"If it wasn't for him, you would have never met her."

"Well it would still have been for the better."

"So that's why you came back, when I met you?"

"Yeah, after she died I wanted Taylor to pay. He has stolen everything from me Shyla. H.I. should have been mine, and then Em. My career and my love. My child. What does a man have left but vengeance? So, I went to do some recon, and I found out he recently hired a new assistant."

"That's why you scoped me out at the bar?"

"Yeah, I had no idea you would look like you do. Then again, I should have known with my brother. Of course, shortly after talking to you, when you said you were looking for a new job, I figured you were done at H.I. But shit, Shyla, I liked you a lot. I thought we had chemistry. It had been a long time since I just talked to someone, I used to be that kind of guy, but after Em died, I closed up."

I nod. *Eric has always been so emotional, Randall said.*

"Then you told me he was your boyfriend and I thought, not another one. Not another girl he'll just chew up and spit out before he moves on to the next one. And it threw my plans for a loop."

"What do you mean?"

"I wanted to warn you and I wanted to fuck with his head; I got emotional instead of methodical. I couldn't use you to get back at him by harming you because I didn't want to hurt you. Not after I met you."

"So instead you did the next best thing. Had sex with me and sent Taylor the dvd."

"No. I didn't. Whoever did that to you, it wasn't me, and I wouldn't put it past Taylor to use you to set me up."

"No, that's bullshit. It makes no sense."

"Well look what's transpired since. I'm a fugitive now. Short of killing me, he almost found a way to eliminate me. Shyla, Taylor is a genius of the worst kind. He is always several steps ahead."

"No. No, I refuse to believe that. You weren't there when he found out. You didn't see his face."

"Taylor walks around in a mask every day. You think he can't put on a show when need be?"

"That's ridiculous."

Eric pauses and steers the tone of the conversation in a different direction. "You know, saving you, it gave me a new purpose. It was like somehow I could make up for what happened to Em if I could save you from Taylor."

"I am sorry about Emily, but I'm not her. You don't need to save me. We're happy. You coming back is the only thing that has fucked with everything."

"Well, I can't just forget about all of this for you Shyla. At this point I realize I can't convince you that Taylor is disturbed. I need to settle things with him anyway. He has to know what he did and take responsibility for it. And at least for tonight, he will get to know the feeling of what it is like to lose someone he loves, if he's even capable of loving. Ultimately, he has to pay."

"I won't let that happen."

"You don't have a choice."

"So what are you going to do? Shoot him?"

"That's one question I won't answer."

"Please Eric, don't hurt him. I can't live with the guilt of him getting hurt because of me."

"It would be because of him."

"I am begging you."

"Shyla, this is not up for discussion. The stars have aligned to bring us all together, and I won't let Taylor get away with killing Em."

"He didn't kill her. She killed herself."

"Don't talk about Em like you knew her." Eric says firmly. His easy nature makes me forget I still am a hostage, but at that moment I am quickly reminded.

"So here we are then," I say, subdued.

"Here we are. Shyla. You're going to be fine."

"If you hurt him, I will never be fine. Never."

We sit for a few moments in contemplative silence. "Can you humor me for a moment?"

"I'm not going anywhere, Eric. Please allow me to humor you."

"Remember what I said in your bedroom? If things were different. If we really were two strangers who met in a bar, do you think you and I would at least have had a little something?"

"You mean if I didn't believe that you stalked me and tricked me into sex?" *I can't believe I am joking about this*. Eric rolls his eyes. "Well…you know you're good looking. Those fucking Holden genes. A blessing and a curse." *Ingratiate him Shyla*.

Eric smirks.

"So is that a yes?"

"Sure. I guess in another galaxy, a parallel universe, we could have, ya know…"

"I knew it wasn't just me."

"Don't go getting any ideas. That was a massive hypothetical."

"You kissed me back."

"No I did not. You scared the shit out of me and I let you kiss me because I thought I was going to die."

"Sorry about that. I would never hurt you. I had no intentions of hurting you that day. You have to excuse me, I was a little frantic, your sweet boyfriend had my ass whopped pretty severely and I was a little out of sorts."

"Well can you blame him?"

"That was a farewell ass-whoop for being back in town, a little farewell gift before being dropped off at the airport. It's a Taylor Holden hug."

"But his hunch was right, that you were here to hurt him in some way."

Eric shrugs. "Back to the kiss," he says with boyish charm.

"You are something else."

"I know," he winks. *He looks so much like Taylor when he does that and it freaks me out.*

I suck my teeth.

"What if it's my last night on Earth? What if I were to die tomorrow?" He asks.

"Don't say that." *Why do I give a shit?*

"What if it is?"

"I don't know."

"If you knew you would never see me again and Taylor would never know. Would you kiss me again?"

"I never kissed you. You kissed me." I remember the dream I had with him in a world with no consequences and the sex was so fucking good.

"Tomato, to-mah-to."

I shake my head disapprovingly. "Sorry Eric, I'm in love with Taylor."

"Your loss," he says standing up with a casual confidence both Holdens seem to have mastered. "Listen, I am going to shower, you're welcome to join me. I don't want to tie you up, but I am going to leave the door open to keep my eye on you. I have no problem chasing after you naked and I will catch you. Let's keep the cooperation going, okay? This is for Taylor's benefit too." Just to make sure I have no chance of getting far, he slides the table in front of the door.

Eric starts walking over to the bathroom, leaving his cell phone on the table. This could be my chance to call Taylor and let him know I am okay. "One more thing," Eric says spinning on his heels as he swoops back to grab his phone and his gun. *Well, shit.*

He pulls off his shirt overhead and throws it on the bed. After that, he pulls his belt buckle loose and whips the belt from his jeans. I try to divert my eyes in this tiny hotel room, but it's nearly impossible not to see his shirtless body. He grins, getting a kick out of this just like a Holden would.

Next, he drops his pants, and his tall athletic physique is standing in front of me in a pair of white boxer briefs. Apparently, he too packs the Holden heat. I should feel threatened that Eric may try something, but his tone is playful. So much like the Eric I thought I knew before the rape. He's trying to tease me, not force himself upon me.

"Aren't you supposed to be kinky?" He asks. "And you're getting shy over some nudity?

"Oh come on." I say. "I'm a free spirit and all, but what do you want me to do? Ogle you?"

"Doesn't bother me one bit," he says flirtatiously.

I give in, convincing myself it would be much less awkward to acknowledge him than to keep looking at the water-damaged ceilings of this dump.

"I'm looking at you. See? Big whoop!"

He smiles the Holden smile.

Alright, I'm going in. "Enjoy the show," he says as he whips his briefs off.

"Oh my god," I say, covering my mouth.

"I am so unimpressed. I had no idea you'd be such a prude," he says, walking off into the bathroom, his pale, taut butt cheeks reverberating with each step.

Eric turns the shower on, steam quickly enveloping the bathroom and spreading out into the bedroom. "You're steaming the place up," I complain.

"Thank you," he says.

"Oh shut it."

He whips the curtains off to the side, leaving them open to keep an eye on me. Then he steps into the shower. The steamy water cascades over the curvature of his body. *These fucking Holdens and their perfect bodies.* He makes a thick lather from the hotel room soap and rubs it all over his body, including his package, taking extra time there as if to taunt me, circling his hand around his dick and cleaning it as if he was jerking off. Afterward, he steps back under the shower head, the stream of water rinsing the suds off of his wet, firm body. He steps out completely naked, his towel over his shoulder, back out into the common area.

"You're getting the carpet wet." *That's probably the cleanest thing that has happened to this carpet in 30 years.*

"I have to keep a close eye on you. You're welcome to shower too, but same rules about the door apply to you," he says as he dries himself off.

"No thanks, I'll just stink up the place."

"Whatever," he shrugs.

As he dresses, I sit in silence, wondering if cooperation is the right tactic. What if I go along, and he just uses me to lure Taylor and kill him? I know Taylor wants me to rely on him, let him take care of things, but in the current circumstances, I am not sure Taylor's rules apply. What can I really do at this point? If I run, he'll catch me. I haven't heard a peep from anyone one else in this motel; we are in the middle of nowhere. He separated his gun and bullets, so even if I got a hold of one, I'd have to get a hold of the other, which would be miraculous. Cooperation is my only choice for now and I pray that Taylor has something up his sleeve.

"You know, people are going to start looking for me. I was supposed to come to work today."

"I'm sure Taylor handled everything. He knows it's important that no one knows about this." His last sentence sends a bolt of fear through my body that almost makes me jump. How could he let me walk away tomorrow? I made him. How can he be sure I won't tell the police everything I know? The smart thing for him to do would be to kill me and Taylor, then he could go on and do whatever the hell he wants.

"What will you do after tomorrow? After this is all over?"

"I don't make plans that far ahead. I focus on the mission at hand." Taylor is methodical, Eric is emotional. I am not yet sure which one is more dangerous.

"Eric, I am begging you, please don't hurt Taylor. You will ruin me if you do."

Eric agitates the thin, worn towel against his wet hair, pretending not to hear me. He walks it over to the bathroom and neatly puts it on its rack. If there was any place where towels on the floor would be acceptable, it would be in this hellhole.

"You tired?"

"More like wired," I say.

"We should go to bed soon, at least try. Early wake up tomorrow."

"What time?"

"I'll wake you."

"As if I could sleep."

Eric shrugs, his mood more solemn than earlier, but not alarmingly so. There is only one bed and I hope that he remains as much of a gentleman as he has been this entire time. The mattress is thin, the springs permanently compressed, so far from its heyday as a thick, plush mattress. There are no headboards to tie me to. I watch Eric examine the area with his eyes, trying to figure out the setup.

"Okay, I am going to cuff you to me. If you sneeze, if you so much as try to scratch your ass, I will feel it."

"No," I say, knowing it is pointless.

"I could tape you up, but that wouldn't be very comfortable for you."

I accept my fate.

He grabs the clicker for the shitty, circa 1990 television which has about 13 channels and points to my spot on the bed, furthest from the door. I reluctantly slide over, never letting my scowl leave him as I do so. He plops next to me, wincing after discovering how flat the mattress is, and throws one cuff on my right wrist. The sound of metal clinking informs me that I am resigned to be his prisoner for the night. Then he does the same on his left. He takes the empty gun from his waistband and puts it in the nightstand drawer, he waves the handcuff keys in front of me and shoves them down the front of his boxer briefs. *He would.*

302

"Even if I was drugged, I wouldn't sleep through a girl putting her hands down my pants," he jests.

After cycling through the 13 channels about three times, he settles on a riveting episode of Maury. "You are NOT the father!" Maury Povich says as a boney young man with roughly 13 teeth starts doing a improvisational dance on stage, his 400 pound former lover hobbling away in tears as the camera jaggedly follows her.

"Quality programming keeps the mind sharp," Eric says. As darkness settles upon us, I am not as much at ease as I was with Eric during the daytime. Something about the night, the mask of darkness, permits things to happen that would never be even entertained during the light of day. For a moment, the thought flutters through my mind. Do I seduce him? I subtly watch him: the glow of the television casts a bluish hue on his shirtless body. His lips curve into an amused smile as he watches more paternity test results, his glacial blue eyes are nearly transparent. Do I give him another opportunity at my body? The key is in his underwear, but then what? Without a loaded gun, I won't even make it to the door.

I am Taylor's. He would never forgive me if I took matters into my own hands like this. *Trust in Taylor,* I recite in my thoughts. *He makes the rules. He takes care of things.*

I wish I could say I did something bold, something daring. That I mounted Eric and rubbed his cock and made him so hard that he forgot all about the keys. That after I fucked him and he released himself inside of me, he fell into a deep slumber and I silently removed the key I hid under my tongue, unlocked the cuffs, and loaded the gun. Or maybe I spotted a weapon earlier in the bathroom (and used pure tenacity to retrieve it despite being taped up) then held it to his neck, promising I would slash his jugular if he didn't release me from the handcuffs. But no, all I did was sit there, praying that Taylor had a master plan in his endless labyrinth of a mind.

CHAPTER TWENTY-THREE

Time passes as it always will, a minute is always a minute, an hour is always an hour. But it so often feels like it spites us, those last moments with a loved one passing too quickly; excruciating pain that lasts for minutes can seem like hours. And so, I lie in bed in this pitch dark room with nothing to stare at, wondering if this night will never end because I so fiercely want to see Taylor again. And if—when—we do see each other, will that moment whizz by leaving me on my knees, breathless, trying piece together the scenes that flashed before me? Or will it be slow, each minutia being stamped into my consciousness for as long as I live?

Sleepyhead can't sleep. I can't tell if Eric is asleep, but his breathing doesn't have that shallow, rhythmic sound of a person whose body and consciousness have disconnected. I am not sure how long I lie there with my knees pointed to the ceiling. But then I know Eric is awake too, because he says something.

"You're keeping me awake. I can feel your restlessness."

"Well, I am so sorry about that," I say sarcastically.

He is silent for maybe ten seconds. Then he sighs, resigned to a sleepless night with me. "Tell me something about yourself Shyla."

"I am sure you know plenty."

"Not as much as you might think."

"I don't know. What do you want to know?"

"Hmmm…what about your favorite childhood memory?" *He had to go there.* My farce of a childhood is still a sore spot.

"I don't know…I don't remember much. I was an only child, just me and my mom. I guess the simple things. Friday pizza night was nice. We'd get a frozen pizza if times were good and watch one of those made for TV movies when they were still on network TV. What about you?"

Eric waits a few beats. "What has Taylor told you? About our childhood?"

Why bother mincing words? "That you were jealous almost as soon as he arrived. That you hated him, became very disruptive. Drugs, boarding school. Typical rich boy acting out stuff."

Eric laughs to himself. "I was disruptive?" He laughs again. In this darkness, it's like his voice just floats in the air, unattached to a physical being. "Shyla, do you understand how disturbed he was when he showed up? It was almost like he was feral, but he wasn't. He was very careful about what he showed our parents. He was quiet, helpless Taylor, the traumatized boy who never said a word and couldn't be touched when my parents were around. When it was just us, he was still quiet, but like fucking Damien from The Omen. He would fucking bite when I tried to play with him! Sometimes, if I looked at him for too long, he would attack me. My father said *I* was being aggressive, that I was provoking him. He couldn't be touched, or spoken to, or even looked at, and yet everything revolved around this boy. I became invisible."

"Taylor knows he was difficult, but he was a little boy and he was traumatized. He was damaged."

The bed springs squeak as he shifts. "That was just when he first arrived. As we got older, he got even better at his dual personalities. Taylor, the perfect student, who was fragile as glass. *Don't touch him, don't upset him, don't look at him. Eric, you're always trying to rile him up,*" he says in a cartoonish mocking voice. "Taylor became hyper-competitive, making sure that he was the favorite son. He would steal class notes to sabotage me for tests, hide my shit so I would run late for school and practice. I couldn't prove it, but I knew it was him. He fucking planted drugs in my bedroom! That got me sent away to military school."

"I don't believe this."

"Of course not, no one ever believes hysterical Eric. *Emotional Eric.*"

"I think your parents would have caught on."

"He drove me to the point where I did become rebellious. I sought out a bad crowd because no one in my own home had my back. And then it made me 'unreliable.'"

"So you never did drugs?"

"I did…but what they found in my room was planted, he knew that they would test me and I would turn up positive. I never brought drugs home. We had a cleaning lady who would find it within a day or two. And then, there was Becky." He has that sour look on his face again, I can't see him, but I can hear it. "I liked this girl, she was my first big crush, love really. My parents were out at a gala one night and I came home. The house was completely dark, except for some noise coming out of Taylor's bedroom. Taylor's bedroom door was halfway open, and Becky was in there, sucking his dick. He had her hair in his hands, shoving her face back and forth. When he saw me, he smirked at me. Just smirked that *I got her* smirk. It took her what seemed like forever to realize I was standing there in shock. She was mortified. He told her I was at the gala, that it would be just the two of them, so she didn't expect for me to come home. She ran out of the house in tears. He didn't even follow her; he wanted me to find them, show me that he had won, yet again. He used her to get at me."

I thought Taylor told me he didn't do anything until college.

"Tell me Shyla. Does that sound like an innocent victim to you?"

I don't answer. *I am a prisoner. I am a prisoner.* Taylor has warned me Eric is manipulative, that he will try to turn me against him. I am sick of telling Eric he is a liar, and the worst part is I am starting to believe there may be some level of truth to his claims. But I don't really know Eric, and Taylor I have known since I was born. He protected me, he was fed to the dogs so I could escape. He is my hero.

"He won't let you ever leave him; you understand that right? He disposes of people, but he is not the kind of person who gets disposed of. He will never let you go, you have become a prized possession."

I never wanted to leave Taylor, but the seed Eric just planted, the idea that Taylor would never *allow* me to leave him, grows into a pit in my stomach.

"That's not true. He's let me walk out. We have arguments just like any other couple."

I feel him sit up and I react by sitting up as well. "Shyla, of course he won't tie you down. He lets you walk out because he know's you'll come back. That's not what I am talking about. He will make you think you made the decision. He will manipulate your world so that you feel you need him. People are like chess pieces to him." *He wants me to want it.*

"You don't understand us."

"He'll be allowed to change, but you won't. That's how it works. If he tires of you, you'd be gone in an instant, but if you got fed up, he wouldn't let you go. I promise. Taylor gets what he wants, always."

I won't believe Eric. Taylor *loves* me. I am *different*. I am not Becky, or Em, or Lane or any of those weak bitches in his journal.

I am the exception.

❋ ❋ ❋

Sleepyhead falls asleep. Taylor would laugh at the fact that I can't even pull an all-nighter during a hostage situation.

"Shyla. Shyla, time to get up," Eric gently nudges me and only then do I hear his phone alarm going off. I'm a little embarrassed that I fell asleep, it doesn't make me appear as angry as I should be.

"I'm up. I'm up. I say groggily. What time is it?"

"4:30 am."

"Ugh." I pull myself up sharply, only to be whipped back down. I forgot I was still cuffed to Eric.

"Hold on," he reaches into his boxer briefs and pulls out the key. "There's mouthwash in the bathroom if you want to freshen up. Door stays open."

I nod, rubbing my barely open eyes. After washing up, I am more alert, but that only serves to make me think about the day ahead. The unknown. The ominous.

Eric stuffs his possessions into an olive green canvas backpack. He grabs his pistol, reloading the magazine. *Oh no.*

"Alright, let's go. We're almost done, please don't give me a hard time."

I nod. *Please Taylor, have a plan.*

There is one other car in the parking lot, a beat up and rusty diarrhea-colored Ford Pickup. It's empty. I glance up at the windows of the motel, not a shade drawn, not a face peering out of a window. Even if I did run, there would be no where to go. He would catch me before I ever made it to the front desk on the other side of the building. This time he makes me slide into the passenger seat of Ladybug, cuffing my hands behind my back.

"Sorry, but after that shit you pulled last time…"

"I get it," I say shortly.

We drive for about 40 minutes, twists and turns and backroads. Only one car passes us in the opposite direction during the entire drive. I look over, hoping to make eye contact, *please remember me*, but the man keeps his focus straight ahead. It seems Eric is purposely taking me to the mystery spot in a roundabout fashion; I try to remember how to get to the location, but get turned around 10 minutes in.

Finally, we drive down a long stretch into the woods until we come to a gate, the kind that marks a boundary, but is not attached to a fence or wall, so that you can walk right around it.

"Alright, we have a bit of a walk ahead of us," Eric says, emerging from the driver side of banged-up Ladybug, turning her off, but leaving the keys in the ignition. I try to interpret what that means, but that's too far ahead in the future right now. He comes around to the passenger side and uncuffs me. We march around the gate, which says boldly: NO TRESPASSING. *Oh god, he is going to off me Sopranos-style.*

"Are we going to get shot?" I ask as we trespass.

"No, this is acres and acres of unused land. Some rich asshole's lot. Don't worry." I follow him along an unkempt trail, stepping over fallen branches and large stones. He moves so briskly that I break a sweat trying to keep up with him. The weather has cleared up from yesterday and the sun is beaming through the foliage. Occasionally, I look up and see the clearest blue sky between the red and orange leaves. We hike for about 15 minutes and then emerge from the tight hug of the forest into a clearing. It is so abrupt, like a smack of flat green land right across the face. Eric glances down at his watch. I know nothing about the time or the

310

coordinates of the meetup; Eric was happy to discuss anything but that during my "stay" with him.

The clearing is huge, the wilderness on the other side of it so far away, it looks like a dark green shag carpet. We walk, and walk until we are at the center, then Eric stops.

"We're here."

"Where's Taylor?"

"We're a little early, he should be here in ten minutes or so."

Five minutes pass when I see him, well I assume it's him: dark hair and a smooth, assured stride. As he gets closer, I can make out what he's wearing, a heather blue t-shirt and light jeans. His pace is no faster than it would be if he were taking an afternoon stroll and it seems as though he'll never arrive. Then he's close enough for me to see his face. His look is firm; focused but relaxed.

I think it's because he is finally here, because I know something must happen right now, that fear, actually not fear, more like terror: that terror that had been laying dormant inside of me slowly floods my body. Much like a river rising in a storm, it spreads from my core to my toes, my fingertips. It submerges me, expanding to my ears, my eyes, my lungs. Like being underwater, everything is diluted, blurred, my movement labors. All of my senses are filtered through this terror.

Taylor stops about 15 feet away from us. "What do you want Eric?" He asks firmly. He glances at me, giving me a knowing look. I know he can see the dread in my eyes, but it doesn't break him.

"I want you to know the pain you've caused me," Eric says. I am in front of him, he clenches the hind waist of my pants tightly. His voice quivers, not with fear, but with rage.

"Fair enough. So what do you want to do?"

"I want you to pay for what happened to Em."

"You were in love with her?"

"She was going to have my fucking child and you fucked her up so badly that she drove off of a fucking bridge!" Eric screams hysterically. *Oh this is bad.*

"Eric, I am sorry. I had no idea, but she made her own decisions." *Taylor is not sorry, not in the way Eric wants him to be.*

"Bullshit! You mean when you gave her to other men like a trading toy? When you walked her around like a fucking bitch! When you disposed of her like an old rag?" And I feel the metal barrel of a gun bump into my head. *Don't collapse, Shyla.* "She was a good person Taylor, and you took her away, just like you did Becky!"

"Eric, Becky was so long ago. That was just sibling rivalry." Taylor continues to remain calm, in fact, I might be more frightened by Taylor's demeanor than Eric's.

"It's not just Becky, it's everything! You took everything. Left me with the scraps. I was your brother you son of a bitch! You had me disappeared and I am not just talking about when we were battling over H.I., from the moment you came into my life, you wanted me to vanish."

"You wanted me gone too. You're just upset that I won." I want to scream at Taylor for saying something so reckless.

"Well, now I'm gonna win!" Eric says, shoving the gun onto my temple. I think I wail or something, because Taylor's focus breaks for a moment. Eric whispers into my ear. *I'm not going to hurt you.*

"Easy Eric. You know she has nothing to do with this. She's just as innocent as Em."

"No, fuck this. Shyla is important to you, isn't she?" Taylor remains silent. "We can call it even right now." I clench my fists, trying to contain the horror. It's so strong that I wish for death at the moment to make the all-consuming fear end.

"Eric, what do you want from me?"

"I want you."

"No!" I scream, falling to my knees.

"Shyla, look at me, it's going to be fine. Look at me." I look at Taylor's eyes, but I can't, I won't give him permission to trade himself for me. I'll never see him again. "It's going to be okay Shyla. Remember when we first met?"

He's not talking about the coffee shop, he's talking far beyond that. I nod, even though I don't. "It's what I do for you. It's always been my purpose."

"No, no, no," I wail. Eric pulls me back up onto my feet.

"How do I know you won't hurt her? She knows your identity."

"Taylor, if you trade with her, we'll both watch her walk away. By the time she gets to anyone, we'll be gone without a trace. I left the keys in her car for her to go." Taylor nods. "You know I didn't rape Shyla. You know that." Taylor doesn't move an inch, he doesn't even blink. I think he doesn't want to irritate him any further by disagreeing.

"Please Eric. Let's just go our separate ways," I beg, trying to appeal to the side of Eric that cried into my stomach last night.

"Shyla, someone has to pay. My fiancé and child and birthright are gone and it's all because of him. I have nothing but vengeance left. He is evil. I have to do this for them. They can't have died for nothing."

"Let's do it," Taylor says.

"No. No. I won't let you," I scream, almost throwing a tantrum.

"Shut up, Shy," he orders. He gives me that look, that knowing look. *Don't fuck with this Shyla. I make the rules. I am the person people fear.* I go quiet, like he is my snake charmer, lulling me to submit from 15 feet away. I close my mouth and try to contain the panic, but my short, choppy breaths fill my ears. "Let her go, and when she is out of sight, I'll walk over." He raises his hands in the air.

Eric hesitates, as if it was too easy. I feel the same way. *Taylor, don't go with Eric. Don't leave me.* "Okay, okay…" I feel him nodding behind me. "Alright, Shyla. Go." But I can't move. I know if I step away, Taylor is dead. There is no other outcome. "Go!" Again, I don't. I look at Taylor and he nods just slightly, to tell me it's okay, but it's not. "Dammit Shyla," Eric says. Then he says *fuck it.* Not to me, not loud enough for Taylor, but to himself. *Fuck it.* I know that means something finite, it's a resolution, but before I can turn, scream, slap him, or do anything, he whispers in my ear. *I'm sorry Shyla.*

I open my mouth, just to scream no particular word, but I hope my scream will shift the course of events. That it'll bring Taylor and me back home, me watching him from the breakfast bar all smiles as he makes me French toast. But the scream never emerges, because I am shoved so hard that I am lifted off of my feet and as my eyes see the dewey, green grass come closer and closer, I hear it: *Pop pop pop pop.*

I am lost forever.

CHAPTER TWENTY-FOUR

Remember what I wondered when I couldn't go to sleep next to Eric in the hotel room, about whether time would move choppy and fast or in slow motion? The answer is both. As I was falling to the ground and I heard the gunshots, it was like one of those nightmares where you fall endlessly. I needed to reach the ground, so I could turn and see what was happening behind me. I knew the answer, but I had to see if I would have a chance to say goodbye. I had no doubt it wasn't me, I believed Eric when he said he wouldn't hurt me. Eric wasn't sorry that he was going to shoot me, he was sorry that he was about to devastate my world in the way that Em had devastated his when she drove off the bridge. Slowly, so slowly I fall to the ground and then BOOM.

Everything speeds up again.

I roll over and Taylor is standing over Eric, his gun pointed over Eric's lifeless body. *Pop*. Eric looks at me, a trail of blood trickling out of his mouth. "No!" I scream sensing Taylor is about to shoot again. Taylor looks at me, watching me as I crawl over to Eric. There is still light in his eyes, he is still alive. His eyes are pale like his mother's but they are not cold like hers. And then, the light is gone, his pupils, visible from feet away against the clarity of his eyes shrink to a pinpoint. *Oh my god. Oh my god. Oh my god. Taylor killed him.*

I come to my knees and stay there in shock, my mouth open, but unable to make a sound or produce any tears. Watching someone die kills you for a moment as well. I motion to touch him instinctively, this tragic man dying alone in a lonely field.

"Don't touch him," Taylor blocks me.

He pulls me up on my feet. "Taylor…" I say, burying my face into his chest. "He's dead. He's dead. Oh my god."

"Shyla."

"He's dead. He's dead."

"Shyla."

"Eric…oh my god."

"Shyla!" Taylor shakes me so hard my neck whips back. It works.

"What did you do? You killed him! You killed your brother!"

"Just because we have the same father does not mean he is my brother."

A wave of nausea hits me, but I hold it in. Taylor's voice is distant again. "Shyla, listen to me. You're in shock. You need to listen carefully. I am going to walk you to Harrison and he is going to take you home. You are going to wait there for me and speak to no one, not a soul, not even Harrison. Not a fucking word."

"Bu…but. The police. We are going to go to jail."

"Shyla. You need to be strong here. No one knows Eric is in the country. This is Evan Sumner. Evan sold his business and packed his bags a year ago and no one has seen him since. No one is looking for Evan and Eric will be on the run forever. You are in shock, but you are going to be fine. We are going to be fine." His eyes have no warmth, he is only giving me orders. This is no time for a grand reunion. "Wait a second, I have to make a quick call." He grabs a flip phone which is definitely some sort of throw away. "Yes. Done. Disposal." *When people are an inconvenience to Taylor, he discards them.* Eric's voice haunts me.

"Taylor, you had this planned all along?"

316

"Shyla, I made a promise that if I ever saw him again, if he ever laid a hand on you again, it would be the last time."

"What happened? I didn't see."

"He pushed you and he raised his gun to shoot you. I had a gun, hidden, in the back of my waistband." *I can't believe it. No, not Eric. I believed him.*

"But what if he didn't do that? Were you going to go with him?"

"I was going to do whatever it took, but I was going to come back to you."

Then I start to drift again, my body and mind unable to stay focused for long amidst dizzying series of the events. The man I shared french fries with yesterday died right in front of my eyes. My boyfriend, his brother, the killer. "We have to go. You need to get back to the house, and wait for me. I have to take care of business."

"No, I don't want to leave you again."

"Shyla, it's over. You are safe now for good."

He walks me to the other side of the field from where he emerged, then guides me through a path to get back to Harrison. They share a few words privately and then we drive off. No kisses, no warm hugs. He has to take care of *business.*

❊ ❊ ❊

There is a crumb on the kitchen counter. I stare at it wondering how it got there. *Is that a toast crumb? Maybe crackers? Taylor wouldn't have crackers for breakfast. Maybe he does when I'm not around the way I heat up frozen veggie burgers when he's not around.* Eventually, I plan to move from this spot, take a shower or something, but I don't want to make any real decisions right now. I want to get to the bottom of how this fucking crumb got here.

Taylor said to go home and wait and so that is what I am doing.

Between crumb contemplations, I run the scene over and over again wondering how we could have done something else, but the truth is someone had to die. All three of us were not walking out of that field as a result of some grand compromise. Eric said all he had left was vengeance; he had no family, no fiancé, no child. He was a fugitive. Maybe this was really a suicide by Taylor. I'll never know because I was too busy falling infinitely into the grass when it happened. I shouldn't feel badly. *Should I?* This man terrorized me and raped me. *Right?* He was just trying to turn me against Taylor with his denials and stories. He kidnapped me for fuck's sake. But he made me laugh, and he was the nicest kidnapper ever. Seeing the life escape his eyes, I will have nightmares about those icy blues forever. Call me crazy, but killing just doesn't sit as well with me as it seems to do with Taylor.

I stink. I want a shower so bad, but I won't move from this spot, it's too safe.

The front door opens and slams shut. I stand at attention, ready to see a remorseful Taylor, overwhelmed by what he has done, the adrenaline worn off from his earlier encounter. But his footsteps are fast, they are not dragging like that of a downtrodden man.

"Shyla! Shy—" He comes upon me at the kitchen. "Come here," he's manic, in an almost jovial way. "We have to get you out of these clothes and dispose of them," he says, unbuttoning my shirt frantically. "You have no idea Shyla. When he answered the phone." he kisses me for the first time since Eric kidnapped me. All over my face, my neck. He pulls off my shirt. *I stink.* "I missed your smell," as if on cue.

"Taylor, what's going on? Where's Eric?"

"He's gone," he says, picking me up by my behind and sitting me on the counter. "We're free." *Oh my god, he's... happy.*

"Gone? Taylor..." *You killed your brother, your parents will never have the chance to see him again, and all you can say is we're free?*

He pulls off my stained and worn jeans. "Shyla, when he told me he had you, when I saw you standing there with the gun to your head, the life we would never have together, the *children* we would never have, it all hit me so hard." He is saying all the right things, the things I would want to hear and I lap it up like a sweet nectar, the juices dripping down my cheeks and onto my collarbone. "I'm going to take some time off, and we're going to travel the world. We are going to make a life together," he says in one breath. He pulls off his shirt and I wrap my legs around his bare waist. He carries me to the bedroom, then to the shower in the master bath. It rains over us, and I can feel the filth of today run off of my body. I stare emptily at the swirls of dirty water disappearing into the drain.

"Shyla, when you told me about Lyla, I thought if that was the last time we saw each other I would regret it for the rest of my life." He kisses a trail down my stomach, and then rolls his tongue inside of my labia. I roll my eyes up in pleasure, but it feels so wrong, morally. *Taylor, your brother is dead. You took a life today, and you're turned on?*

He pauses and stands in front of me, his wet lips kissing mine. "Shyla, you did the right thing. We did the right thing. Eric was going to be a dark cloud over us forever even if we all somehow survived. He lost his way a long time ago." He pulls me close to him, and he's really fucking hard. *He's so bad, he's such bad fucking news.* "It's you and me Shyla. It's always been. He pushes me up against the cold shower tile, kissing my neck and we

319

both let out a gasp as he enters me. "I did this because I love you. It's more than love though, it's something else because I don't think this is what people talk about when they talk about love. I want to give you everything. I will do anything for you." The image of a beautiful dark-haired baby having the childhood we never did flashes in my mind's eye.

"I know what you mean," I say as he smoothly thrusts in and out of me.

He is infected.

*For updates on new releases,
including the third installment of the
Strapped Series, please visit:
NinaGJones.com*

*Follow me:
Facebook.com/StrappedNovel
Twitter.com/NinaGJones*

*If you enjoyed this book, I would
greatly appreciate a review on Amazon
or Goodreads.*

.

Printed in Poland
by Amazon Fulfillment
Poland Sp. z o.o., Wrocław

32859357R00183